# MONEY CREEK

# What Reviewers Say About Anne Laughlin's Work

## A Date to Die

[A]n entertaining mystery with a bit of sweet romance in the background. It's got all the ingredients for an enjoyable read: mystery, plot twists and romance."—*Lez Review Books Blog*

## The Acquittal—*Lambda Literary Award Finalist*

"Laughlin's other mysteries—*Veritas, Sometimes Quickly, Runaway*—have been stand-alones, but one hopes (I hope) that *The Acquittal* is the beginning of a Josie Harper series. Josie is a terrific character, written with verve and depth. She's immensely likable and the issues she's dealing with are presented forthrightly and sensitively without bogging down the mystery plot. With *The Acquittal*, Laughlin has added another strong mystery to her retinue as well as a fabulous new character I hope we see more of."
—*Lambda Literary Review*

## Runaway—*Lambda Literary Award Finalist*

"Anne Laughlin is one of those authors that I just enjoy reading."
—*C-Spot Reviews*

"[*Runaway*] is an easy read, with the story zig-zagging between Maddy and Jan. The second half of the book, working towards the final events in Idaho, keeps the pages turning. …Some of the word selection and observations are sublime."—*Lesbian Review*

## Veritas

"*Veritas* is a fun, well-paced and intriguing mystery with all the components readers of classic and competent cozies seeks. (It) is perfect reading for a cold winter night in front of the fire."—*Lambda Literary Review*

"*Veritas* by Anne Laughlin is, simply put, a good read. As an avid reader of romance and mystery novels, this book touched many chords within me. The characters are well drawn, even the supporting players. The story works both as a romance and a mystery. I found the intrigue interesting and thought provoking."—*Kissed by Venus*

"...*Veritas* is a quick read, but a fulfilling story. Laughlin's prose is natural and engaging whether she's writing about the politics of academia, Beth and Sally's multilayered romance, or the intricacies of a murder mystery. Named a Lambda Literary Foundation Emerging Writer in 2008, *Veritas* proves Laughlin worthy of the honor."—*AfterEllen.com*

"Anne Laughlin has given her readers a great first novel. Set in a small Midwestern town on a college campus, Laughlin skillfully draws the characters of both the town and the college, without using stereotypes. *Veritas* is a great, page turner of a first novel." —*Just About Write*

**Visit us at www.boldstrokesbooks.com**

# By the Author

Veritas

Runaway

Sometimes Quickly

The Acquittal

A Date to Die

Money Creek

# MONEY CREEK

*by*
Anne Laughlin

2020

# MONEY CREEK

ISBN 13: 978-1-63555-795-4

THIS TRADE PAPERBACK ORIGINAL IS PUBLISHED BY
BOLD STROKES BOOKS, INC.
P.O. BOX 249
VALLEY FALLS, NY 12185

FIRST EDITION: SEPTEMBER 2020

---

**CREDITS**
EDITOR: CINDY CRESAP
PRODUCTION DESIGN: SUSAN RAMUNDO
COVER DESIGN BY TAMMY SEIDICK

# Acknowledgments

All writers need help and I've received plenty of it in writing *Money Creek*. First and foremost, I want to thank Amin Ahmad and Claudine Guertin-Ceric. The three of us formed a writing group that has been instrumental in the writing and editing of this book. They both give amazing feedback. Thank you to Carol Anshaw for being an early reader, along with Ann Farlee, Beth Brandt, Patricia Barber, Joan Larkin, and Linda Braasch for their feedback. Thanks also to homicide detective (retired) Jim Hennigan who, as always, answers the procedural questions I have. He's very patient. Linda Braasch provided the love and support that got me through the writing of this novel. I say a thank you every day for her.

# Dedication

To Chris, Liz, and Charlie
My wonderful siblings

## PROLOGUE

On a wintry late Saturday afternoon, Clare Lehane found herself in the shabby living room of a shabby house hidden deep in the rural countryside. She sat on a wooden dining chair, chosen over the lumpy, soiled sofa that was pushed against a wall with peeling wallpaper. The hardwood floors were buckled and warped. She smelled mold.

Henry stared at her from across the coffee table, his preppy-style clothing looking particularly out of place. Ray sat on the sofa, a cigarette dangling from his lips. Next to him was barrel-chested Bobby and his girlfriend, Caroline. Her midriff shirt showed off her belly ring. They'd all been making small talk for what seemed like forever.

Clare wished they'd break out the drugs. A social gathering of drug dealers should involve the consumption of drugs. So far it was cheap beer and shots of tequila, and she was getting anxious for something else.

Henry stood and put his phone in his back pocket. "I have to get going." He turned to Ray. "I've got that thing."

Ray nodded.

"I'll go with you." Clare rose quickly from her chair.

"No, you'll stay." Ray stared at her. "We're just getting started here."

"I want to go home."

Henry shifted his eyes from Clare to Ray and back again.

"Clare, just relax and enjoy yourself." She could tell he was anxious she not make a scene in front of his business partners. "I'm sorry I have to leave, but I have something I can't get out of." He gathered his coat and hat and left. The room fell silent and she sat down again.

Bobby took his arm from Caroline's shoulder and leaned forward.

"We want to get to know you better, Clare. That's all."

"Why do you want me here? Can't I just buy some pills and leave?"

Ray stubbed out his cigarette and pulled a joint from his shirt pocket. "You know it's not that simple. You're our customer, yes, but you're also our lawyer."

"This is like a gangster movie. I never signed up to be consiglieri." She was rigid with frustration. Ray ignored her and concentrated on his joint. She stood in disgust.

"I'm going to the bathroom. Down there, right?"

She strode down the hallway, passing tiny, dark bedrooms. She locked the bathroom door behind her and fished a packet of meth out of her jeans pocket, along with a rolled-up dollar bill. Meth was not her preferred drug, but it was all she had right now. She snorted a line and the rush cascaded through her body, a familiar feeling but still exciting. This time it fueled her anger. How could she break free of these people? She couldn't see a way out. She glanced at the mirror and wiped some powder from her nose. Desperation soon replaced her anger. She didn't want her life to be like this. Wasn't sure how it'd gotten so bad.

Just as she turned on the faucet to wash her hands, an explosion erupted. She fell to her knees and gripped the sides of her head. Two more explosions. Four more. Gunfire. She bit her lip to keep from screaming. The shooting continued. When it stopped she remained crumpled on the dirty tile floor.

*Am I next? What the hell is this?*

Heavy footsteps in the living room. She looked at the small window in the bathroom and saw it was low and wide enough for her to fit through.

Then the sound of footsteps running toward the back of the house. She looked out the window. In a moment, a man rounded the rear corner and slowed to a walk. He wore one of those Euro-style vigilante masks with ghastly white skin and a terrifying grin. A gun hung loosely from his left hand, the same gun all the cops used on TV. Tall and lanky, he wore jeans and a camouflage jacket. Beneath the open jacket she saw a green Guns N' Roses concert tee. The same shirt a law school classmate used to wear all the time, from the 2012 concert tour.

The man walked away, kicking dead leaves. Soon she heard the sharp acceleration of a car on gravel. What the hell happened? Was there a way to leave the house without going back into the living room? She was afraid to see what was there. She had to get her phone. Leaving it behind was not an option.

She opened the bathroom door and peered down the dark hall. She smelled something slightly metallic and paused. She stopped at the entrance to the room and her gut clenched.

Bodies sprawled on the furniture, blood pooling beneath them. Ray slammed back in his chair, a bullet hole in his forehead and chest, Bobby sprawled across the coffee table, as if he'd stood to confront the gunman. Caroline draped over the end of the couch. Still alive. She made a low, strangled noise.

Clare rushed to her. Blood streamed from Caroline's stomach, where the bullet had torn into her. Caroline stared straight at her but there was no flicker of recognition, her eyes moving only slightly. Clare saw her phone on the coffee table. No choice: call an ambulance. Caroline might reveal Clare's presence at the party and ruin her life, but at least she'd live and Clare would be able to live with herself.

She moved Bobby's arm to get to her phone. Caroline slumped forward suddenly, her eyes blank, no longer animated. Clare didn't need to check her pulse: she was dead. She slipped her phone into her pocket and moved away from the body. The silence was eerie.

She put her down coat and gloves on and wiped all her fingerprints from the bathroom doorknob, the sink, the toilet seat.

What else had she touched? She wiped the front doorknob as she left the house.

*I'm leaving the scene of a crime.*

She drove to a Texaco station outside Money Creek and pulled up her hood before walking to the phone booth. The 911 dispatcher answered, and she lowered her voice in hopes of disguising it.

"Please state your emergency."

Clare almost lost her nerve. "There's been a murder. Three murders. Timson County, 15264 Lamont."

She hung up and walked back to her car. A family pulled up to the gas pumps, regular folks, two blond kids in the back, and she stared at them as if they were aliens. They occupied a world that was lost to her now. She would never unsee what she just saw, never stop worrying about being caught. All to save her job and reputation and the relationship she was just starting. She couldn't hate herself more.

# Chapter One

*Six weeks earlier*

On Monday morning Clare's phone woke her from a deep sleep. It was her boss, Carlton Henning, calling her at seven to tell her to get in the office on the double. Her stomach soured at the sound of his voice. She grabbed her pillbox from its hiding place beneath her couch and took two tablets of speed with her to the bathroom, washing them down with a glass of water. The thought of facing Henning without some pharmaceutical help was unimaginable. She put on her business suit and heels and left by seven thirty. She'd been in the office all weekend, trying to keep up with Henning's assignments, which was like swimming against Category 4 rapids. It was all she could do not to drown. She was chattel, otherwise known as a first-year associate, and her hours ran from sixty to eighty a week. She was always desperately behind, no matter how much she worked. And for this she'd gone to three years of law school.

She dropped off her briefcase and coat before walking to Henning's corner office. The sound of him barreling down the adjacent hall was like a locomotive. He was a pudgy man, with dimpled fingers and a double chin. He was always out of breath but had the energy of an Olympic sprinter. He caught sight of her.

"Well, it's about fucking time," he said as he passed into his office without stopping. Clare followed him in, the proverbial fly to his evil spider. "Lehane, I just got back from a meeting with Dave

Novak where I was systematically fucked in the ass. He's taken two associates from me on the Walker case. You're not one of them, more's the pity, so now I have to rely on you to do twice the work." He stood behind his massive desk, his crisp white oxford shirt straining at the belly.

She was horrified. "I don't think it's physically possible. I already work seven days a week."

"I don't like complainers. Deal with it or I'll have you transferred to bankruptcy."

From what she'd heard, the bankruptcy department was a killing field, headed by a partner even nastier than Henning. At least in litigation she occasionally got into the courtroom and traveled on document productions.

"I'll give it my best." She tried to sound determined and slightly enthusiastic, but her acting skills fell short of the mark. Her head ached from a mild hangover.

He sat. "What are you working on now?"

"I've got five assignments on my desk, working on them as prioritized. I have to get that motion for extension of time done and also the memo on the new statute of limitations argument."

"Be sure you do the memo. I need it for the hearing on Monday. But before you get to either of those, I'm giving you a top priority, must be done today upon pain of death assignment." Her heart sank. "I want you to create a chart of the actual damages of the five named plaintiffs in the Walker case. Medical bills, lost time from work, you know what to do. Meet me back here by the end of the day."

She fought the desire to tell him she quit. She could almost feel the breeze in her hair as she escaped the building into liberty. But now wasn't the time financially. Her savings were nonexistent, and her money seemed to go primarily to drugs. Her job was less than secure—she'd been written up two months earlier for failing to make a court date after sleeping through her alarm clock. Too much speed had kept her up all night. It was a costly mistake, one she was still embarrassed by.

As she walked back to her office, she saw Alice Parker coming toward her down the hallway. She was a veteran paralegal, competent as hell, and as no-nonsense as they come. How she managed her life with being a single mother and working as many hours as Clare, she'd never know. Clare had a brainstorm and stopped as Alice grew near.

"Alice, how are you?" She smiled as warmly as she could.

Alice stopped because she was unfailingly polite, but her face said she wanted to get to where she was going. "Going crazy with the Walker case."

"Glad you mentioned Walker because I have an assignment for you."

She looked alarmed. "I can't handle another assignment. You'll have to find someone else."

"Sorry. You're the one. Henning just gave me the project and said to find the best paralegal to work on it. That's you."

Flattery wasn't melting the ice on Alice's face. "What is it?"

Clare detailed the project and tried to make it sound as easy as possible. "There's no getting around it. We have to have it done today."

"Christ." Alice was starting to look resigned. "I don't suppose I can talk to Henning about it?"

"I wouldn't go near him if I were you. He's in one of his moods," Clare said, keeping it friendly.

Alice sighed. "I'll do my best."

She returned to her office to get started on her memo, plowing her way through her research, her focus sharp, her thinking clear, her hangover forgotten. She almost didn't mind working. Moments like this, when she felt extraordinarily smart and productive, she was reminded of why she got into law in the first place. She'd been a political science major in preparation for law school, taking her altruistic goal of "helping people" into her first year at Northwestern. Now she was in a firm that represented the corporate bad guys. They paid a ridiculously high salary in return for the vast majority of her waking hours. She had no social life. Golden handcuffs, she'd heard it called.

At five, she walked down the hall to check on Alice's progress on the medical bill chart but didn't find her in her office. She went to her large document room and found it empty. Nor did she see documents on the table that would indicate the chart was being worked on. She called reception and had Alice paged. Two minutes later, she called back.

"What is it, Clare?" She sounded harried, but this was the norm for Alice.

"I'm wondering if you've finished the chart we talked about this morning. Henning will be looking for it about now." She hadn't thought of the chart since she passed the assignment on to Alice that morning.

"I couldn't get to it," Alice said. Clare's gut dropped, as if she'd hit a sudden pocket of turbulence.

"What do you mean? Please tell me you're teasing me."

"Do I sound like I'm teasing?" Alice said dryly. "I got pulled away by Richards. What could I do? I'm not saying no to a name partner in favor of an associate."

"Fuck! You could have told me, for one thing. Henning will kill me." She was approaching panic.

"I tried calling you once, but got interrupted. I forgot to call again. Sorry." Alice didn't sound very concerned. Her position in the firm was much stronger than Clare's. There were partners and senior associates who couldn't do without her. Clare was increasingly expendable.

Maybe she should run away. There was no excuse that would get her off the hook. The real reason the chart wasn't done—that she'd passed the assignment off—would get her into even more trouble. She fished in her pocket for her pillbox and swallowed a Valium dry. Her heart was racing and she was alarmingly agitated. This pill was medicinal. As she was taking a few deep breaths, she heard her name being paged. The receptionist told her to get to Henning's office ASAP. She knew for whom the bell tolled. It tolled for her. She wondered if she could even make the walk down the hallway. Her legs were unresponsive, as if she'd had a mild stroke. Every second she wasn't in Henning's office made the situation worse. It wasn't until she heard her name paged again that she managed to leave her office and walk down the hallway.

The moment she entered, Henning looked up from his desk, his eyes focused on her empty hands.

"Where's the chart?" He stood from his desk, as if getting ready to fight.

"I don't have it." She sounded calmer than she was. She looked around the room, taking in the perks of partnership, which she clearly would never enjoy. The giant mahogany desk, the private washroom, the drinks cart, the couch and chairs. Henning was silent for a moment before he steeled his voice.

"You don't have it as in it's not done?"

"That is correct."

He exploded. "What the fuck? Did I not say it had to be done today? I'm talking to the plaintiff's attorney tonight."

"Yes, that's what you said." She felt physically threatened by his heavy body leaning toward her, his red face and beady eyes. She wondered at this world she worked in, where Mondays were neither the beginning nor end of a work week, where life outside the firm became a tiny part of her existence. Where a partner became judge, jury, and executioner.

"Then what possible reason do you have for not doing it? I'm curious what would cause you to shoot yourself in the head."

She wouldn't throw Alice under the bus. She should have been checking on her progress throughout the day, but she'd simply forgotten to. "None that will make me look any better than I do now."

He ranted and raved for several minutes, even coming around from his desk to stand closer to her. She stood her ground and stared back at him. Finally, he returned to his desk. "I'm writing you up. This'll be your second in a year, if I recall correctly. It'll be up to Novak to decide what to do with you."

The tranquilizer kicked in and she felt a muted euphoria. Whether it was the drug or the possibility of being done with this nightmare of a law firm, she didn't know or care. She smiled pityingly at Henning, as if he were the one in deep trouble and not her.

"You know what? Don't bother, Mr. Novak."

"What do you mean?" he looked at her suspiciously.

"It means I quit, you fucking bastard." She turned on her heel to leave the office, but not before she saw the shocked look on his face.

## CHAPTER TWO

C lare packed the few belongings she had in her office and left without saying good-bye to anyone. There was no sentimentality about leaving, only relief. She grinned as the elevator door closed on her, ushering her into a new life. Perhaps she should have planned her exit. Her bank accounts were low and she'd have to get another job quickly. But she believed things happened for a reason, a helpful creed for someone whose life was filled with mishaps.

Next stop was her drug dealer's, where she had an appointment to replenish her supply. That brought another wave of relief. Happiness was a full pillbox.

She'd first met Casey when she went to Sidetrack, a venerable gay bar in the Boys Town neighborhood in Chicago. She'd been a little queer curious, but unsure what she was looking for, exactly. Did she want to pick someone up? She didn't have the nerve for that. Someone would have to pick her up instead. Men were easy to attract. Piece of cake. Was that true for women? She hoped so but doubted it. It was clear as soon as she entered the bar she wouldn't find the answers at Sidetrack. The clientele was entirely men. She wedged onto a barstool and asked the man next to her whether he knew of any lesbian bars. That was Casey. He wore a patterned, untucked shirt and tight jeans and looked about her age—late twenties—with posture so straight it was as if a yardstick were taped to his back. He turned to her with a smile.

"Honey, lesbian bars are like a new restaurant in Lakeview. They last about a year before shutting down. You girls don't drink enough."

She was tempted to say she drank plenty. "So, there are none?"

"You must be from out of town," he said.

"There're still lesbian bars up and running in New York." She had no idea if this were true.

"Well, it's New York."

She looked around the bar again. "No hope of meeting any women here?"

"Afraid not."

She hesitated. "How about drugs? Could I find that here?"

He put his drink down and stared at her. "Interesting, I wouldn't have pegged you."

"Why?" she asked.

He laughed. "If there's a type, you're not it. It's your eyes. They look halfway intelligent." He leaned in a little closer. "But I may be able to help you out." It was never easy to find a new drug dealer. It was like striking gold.

"You mean I hit it on my first try? My usual dealer is closing up shop, so I've been looking for a replacement."

"You'll have to let me know what you're looking for." The bartender stopped in front of them with a bottle, but Casey put a hand over his glass and waved him away. Clare still had nothing to drink. "I can fix you up with some meth."

"Meth? Do I look like a loser? That stuff's addictive. I was thinking of some speed." She had her standards. Speed helped her work. Meth was for getting as high as possible, and she wasn't interested in that.

"Wise woman. Meth is a staple product for the people in this bar, but I don't like it myself. Come up to my apartment. I'll get you fixed up."

A year later, they were still doing business together. She spent a lot of money buying drugs, but she made a ridiculous salary. Or did. What if she couldn't buy what she needed because of lack of funds? Maybe the decision to quit her job had been rash. She drove from the office to Sidetrack, where Casey lived above the bar, and found him waiting outside his door. He waved her into the living room, which looked like a magazine photo in an article on minimalism.

"You're back soon. Didn't I just see you last week?" Casey said.

Clare blanched. "Is that a problem?" She knew she sounded defensive, but what the hell? Did he want to sell product or not?

"No problem at all. It was an innocent comment."

"You can keep your innocent comments to yourself. I've had the crappiest of crap days."

What did it say when your own drug dealer commented on how much you're using? The thought of cutting down had come and gone over time, but mostly gone. That night was certainly not the time to grapple with it.

He pulled a briefcase from below his black leather couch and opened it, revealing small packets of crystal meth, hundreds of Adderall tablets, a bulging bag of large pills she knew to be Oxycontin, a couple ounces of pot, and another bag of small packets she hoped wasn't heroin. She didn't want to be associated with heroin in any way. Those people were the worst, completely ruled by their addiction.

He peered over the briefcase. "Good shipment of Adderall and it's the real thing. How many do you want?"

"The whole bag?"

"No way. I have to spread this around to keep my customers happy." He was smiling as he dangled the bag in front of her. There must have been a thousand pills in it.

"How many can I have, then?"

"A hundred."

She hid her disappointment. "Done. What else is in there?"

"We have some fresh Vicodin today. I can give you fifty of those."

"I'll take them. Are there any Valium? The last shipment I got from the online pharmacy was pathetic."

He poked around in the case until he found a bag of small white pills. "I can give you a hundred of those."

"Add them to my order. Anything else?"

"Christ. Speed, Vicodin, and Valium aren't enough?"

Her insides tumbled. Casey had never spoken to her that way. No one had ever said anything to her about her drug use, though no one really knew what it was besides Casey. She held her tongue rather than lash out at him. It wasn't wise to piss off your drug dealer. "Add up the bill, please."

She paid the two thousand dollars, money she now needed to live on. Casey offered her a beer and she stayed a half hour to chat. She laughed despite her terrible day and felt reluctant when Casey said it was time to go. Next stop was her neighborhood tap. She couldn't face the silence of her dark basement apartment. There was always someone she knew at the local tavern, someone to distract her from herself and her horrible day.

The last time Clare woke up with a stranger she swore it would never happen again. But here she was, opening her eyes to a room she'd never seen before. She lay on her side, naked in a four-poster bed, as a familiar gut-clenching remorse made her stomach tumble. Her breathing became shallow and rapid. She didn't dare turn to see what kind of man she'd gone home with.

It was still dark out, and only the glare of the streetlight poking through the window blinds lit the room. It smelled faintly of eucalyptus, very tidy except for the pile of clothes strewn near the door. Next to the bed was an antique table and Tiffany style lamp, a pile of books stacked high. She skimmed the titles. What a man read would tell her a lot. There were the most recent releases from Margaret Atwood, Zadie Smith, and Emma Donoghue. Contemporary fiction by women authors. Maybe she'd hit the jackpot and hooked up with a well-read feminist man. She turned to her right and found, instead, a woman leaning on one elbow, gazing at her. She had clear eyes, auburn hair hanging loose around her shoulders, and a crooked smile. Her face was handsome, with chiseled cheekbones and a slightly patrician air. Clare grabbed the sheet and pulled it up to her chest.

"Good morning, Clare," she said in a timbre rich alto.

Clare stared at her with fixed eyes. Hearing her name made her feel more vulnerable. The woman had the advantage over her—Clare knew nothing and she knew everything. She prayed she hadn't done anything mortifying. It was a good sign the woman was smiling at her. Whatever she did couldn't have been too bad. She broke her gaze and lowered her eyes. "Good morning," she said, her throat froggy from sleep and God knows what else.

"You seem uncomfortable."

Clare forced herself to look at her. "I'm a little nervous. I've never been with a woman before."

"So you said last night. I hope it was a good experience for you."

She hoped so too. She wasn't upset at having sex with a woman, something she knew would have happened sooner or later. But she was ashamed she didn't remember meeting her or anything that came after that. Her short-term memory had been on the fritz—when she was in a blackout she forgot everything almost as soon as it happened, which was why drunks so often repeated themselves. At least that's what she'd read in a depressing article on alcoholism. She scooched up to lean against the headboard and winced at the hammering in her head. She was beginning to feel the full strength of her hangover

"How are you feeling?" the woman said. She now sat in a lotus position, facing her. Clare avoided her eyes. She seemed entirely out of her league.

"Not so bad. Yourself?"

"I'm surprisingly good, given how drunk we were last night," she said. "But I have no regrets." She reached over for Clare's hand and held it gently. "I hope you don't."

Can you regret something you can't remember? "No, it was lovely." She looked on the floor for her cell phone. It was nowhere in sight. "Do you happen to know what time it is?"

The woman turned toward her nightstand. "It's six, still time for more sleep." She ducked her head to meet Clare's eyes. "Unless you were interested in doing something else?" Her voice was sultry, as if she really desired her, which Clare found impossible to believe.

"No! I mean, I didn't realize it was so late. I've got to go." She swung her legs to the side of the bed.

"Six is late?"

"I have to get into the office. I work in a sweatshop." Why was she lying? She remembered she didn't have to go to work, that she'd quit the day before, but she was desperate to get away. She looked to where her clothes were scattered near the door. Apparently, they'd been in quite a hurry to get them off.

"I thought you were a lawyer."

"I am. And the hours are ridiculous." Clare took a breath before she slid off the bed and tried to walk in a reasonably dignified manner across the room to her clothes. She could feel the woman's eyes on her.

"You're beautiful. You know that, don't you?"

No, she didn't. Surely her outside looked as bad as her inside felt, a toxic brew of nausea, the hammering head, and a bucket full of recrimination. Her business suit lay crumpled on the floor and she pulled it on before glancing back at the woman. She'd gotten out of bed and stood naked in front of her, as comfortable as a hand in a glove. She was at least six feet, a few inches taller than Clare and a hundred times more confident. Whatever actually happened, she hoped she'd given the woman pleasure. Usually her blackouts erased the memory of behavior she'd rather forget, but she would have liked remembering her first time with a woman. Would like to know whether it was everything she suspected it to be.

Clare had to clear her throat to talk. "Sorry I have to run. I'll let myself out."

"Wait." The woman came closer, her nakedness seemed billboard-sized. "You seem skittish. There's no pressure around what happened last night. Two adults and all that."

"Sure. I understand. It's just I have to get going."

She stared at Clare for a moment before leading her out of the bedroom to the front door. She seemed ready to move on herself. She held the door open, unconcerned at who might pass in the hallway. "The name's Ellen, by the way. I know you don't remember."

"I do remember. Of course, I do."

Ellen raised one eyebrow. "Are you lying to me or to yourself?" She smiled and motioned Clare out the door. "Take care of yourself, Clare."

She flushed as she hurried down the hall to the elevators. Lying about knowing Ellen's name was a white lie, not a lie lie. And she never lied to herself. She was clear on the fact she'd been in a blackout, that she'd gotten shit-faced drunk and acted the fool. The drama of quitting her job made her hit the bourbon more than usual. Mercifully, the elevator door opened as soon as she pushed the button. She could feel Ellen watching from her doorway. As soon as the door slid shut she reached into the pocket of her long wool coat and pulled out her pillbox. It was empty, though there'd been two Valium and a Vicodin in it when she'd gone to the tavern the night before.

Once she was on the street she realized she was a few blocks from her apartment. She wasn't wearing a party dress and high heels, so the walk down Clark Street didn't look like a walk of shame. But that's what it felt like. That she'd slept with a woman? She was relieved her hookup was with a woman. She could have woken up with a great, hairy, Cro-Magnon man in a bad temper. Or worse.

Now she tried to reconstruct the night with Ellen as she walked south to Berwyn. She'd run into her friends Todd and Marty at Hopleaf, a Belgian bar/restaurant a couple of blocks from her apartment and had a few cocktails with them. She also swallowed a Valium, which was her first mistake. She knew better than to mix a night of drinking with benzos, but she hadn't had one that day and how much could one hurt? Todd and Marty were law school friends and the talk was all about Clare quitting her job, something half the first-year associates in Chicago would like to do themselves.

"What are you going to do?" Todd asked. "I hope you saved some of that Dearborn Pike salary. You don't get a package when you quit."

"I'm good," Clare said with a confident smile, even though she had no idea what she would do for money. She hoped her paltry 401(k) would tide her over for a while.

They'd parted ways around nine o'clock. Todd and Marty said they were on their way to a party, but Clare knew they would go straight home to sack out on the couch and watch Netflix. They were only two years out of law school and already settled down, ending their evenings at a reasonable time, still relatively sober. They weren't aware that Clare was still going at full undergraduate speed.

As a rule, she tried to keep her drinking confined to weekends. She wasn't a drunk, mainly because the consequences were usually bad when she drank too much. There was a moving line past which she blacked out, and she couldn't predict how near or far that line was on any given night. When she was on Valium or any of the other depressants, the line was crossed sooner rather than later. After her friends left, the night started to get hazy, but the thought of going home didn't enter her mind. She walked up the street to Simon's Tavern, a drinking establishment more dedicated to the dedicated drinker than the craft beer atmosphere of Hopleaf. The last thing she could remember was ordering a bourbon with a beer back.

How could a blackout start that early? Had she taken only the Valium? Maybe it was more. Somewhere along the way the Vicodin had disappeared. The combination turned her into someone who looked and sounded like her, but wasn't her. It was as if an evil clone stepped in when she blacked out and did whatever she wanted in Clare's body. She'd woken many mornings to learn about what she'd done the night before that needed immediate damage control. She'd broken up with perfectly nice boyfriends, phoned her mother and called her a whore, slept with innumerable strangers, shown up for work still drunk or high, pushed her best friend off a curb, fallen off a barstool.

She turned east on Berwyn and then down the few steps to her garden apartment. It was in a beautiful old gray stone three flat, the interior large and modern and would have been gorgeous if it were a floor or two higher. The windows were small and faced north and the amount of light that made its way inside was so feeble she had to turn lights on during the brightest part of the day. She must have been drunk when she rented it. She kept it very neat as she usually had an abundance of energy. Now she fell on the couch and slept.

When she woke her mouth was so dry her tongue was swollen. She reached for the bottle of water on the table and guzzled until it was empty. Her hangover seemed marginally better, and when she stood she didn't feel queasy or dizzy. She was still crushingly tired. When she dragged herself into the bathroom she forced herself to look in the mirror and saw some ghastly version of herself staring back. The whites surrounding her bright blue irises were shot through with red. Makeup was smudged below her eyes and her skin looked mottled. Her mouth looked bruised and her hair made bed head look like an upgrade. Tears stung behind her eyes. Was this really her? Had things gotten as bad as this felt? She shrank at the thought of her mother seeing her like this. It would break her heart. It was hard to hate yourself this much. Hard to remember a time she'd looked at herself and liked what she saw.

MONEY CREEK

## CHAPTER THREE

By her third day of unemployment, Clare was sick of lying on the couch and brooding. She wouldn't give way to depression. She'd seen friends with depression bad enough to ruin their lives. But the couch time allowed her to think about her future, and she could no longer see it in Chicago. The city was eating her up. She'd have to stay in Illinois if she wanted to continue to practice law—she wasn't licensed anywhere else. What about somewhere else in the state? From her bubble in the city she was barely aware of downstate Illinois.

She was still in her pajamas at one in the afternoon, her coffee table littered with glasses, mugs, beer bottles, Thai take-out, an iPad for watching Netflix. It was time to get into action. She changed into jeans and cleaned up the apartment before sitting at her dining table to fire up her computer. Suddenly, her intercom buzzed. She peered out the window and saw her mother stamping her feet at the entryway. Clare's phone pinged as a text came in. "Don't even think of not letting me in. I can see the lights on in your apartment."

Was there any point in trying to evade her? It was surprising her mother hadn't broken her door down before now. She buzzed her in and opened the door to her apartment before heading to the kitchen to make coffee.

"Where are you?" her mother called, slamming the door behind her. Clare ran water into the coffee carafe. Soon her mother came bustling into the room, her coat flapping open and her knit hat sitting

• 33 •

low on her forehead. The cold came in with her. Before Clare could move she was enveloped in a chilly bear hug. Vicky Lehane was a bear of a woman—tall and wide, strong but not overweight. In her mid-fifties, she had the energy of a teenager, but none of the sullenness. Everything was out in the open with her mother, ready to be dealt with, enjoyed, condemned, or dismissed. Never avoided. She was an intimidating presence when she turned her focus on someone, and right now her focus was like a laser on Clare.

She let Clare go and stepped back, keeping her hands on her arms, appraising her. "What in the name of God is going on with you? I haven't been able to reach you for three days. Two days is a snit or a bad cold or sex with a new lover." Clare cringed. "Three means something's wrong. What is it?"

Clare leaned forward and kissed her on the cheek. "Hi, Mom. Take you coat off and I'll get our coffee."

"I don't want coffee. I want an explanation." She didn't sound angry as much as perplexed. "Is this about that guy you were dating? Jerry? He was a dullard, darling. You're better off without him."

"No, I broke up with him a while ago." She poured the coffee and sat at the small kitchen table. Her mother sat across from her. "It's about my job."

She could see her face pale. Jobs were a trigger for her. She worried herself sick Clare or her brother would lose their jobs, based on nothing. Clare never told her she was having any trouble at the firm to avoid the third degree. Her mother's father had lost almost every job he had, pushing them near poverty, which left a long scar on her psyche. He died unemployed and his death made another woman out of her. Clare had been told many times to not complain about her job and be thankful she had one.

"Please tell me you still have your job." She reached her big hand across the table and squeezed Clare's, who had to pull her hand away to avoid it being crushed.

"Mom, it's not a bad thing. It's good. I was miserable at my job. I've told you that, but I don't think you ever believed me. I mean really miserable. It was affecting every aspect of my life. In fact, it's deprived me of most aspects of my life. I had to quit."

"You quit?" Her mother looked like she'd been sucker-punched. She leaned back on the kitchen chair as if she'd been shoved there. "How is this even possible?"

"I know this'll take some getting used to, but I'm happier already. And I'm leaving Chicago."

Her mother bounded up from her chair. Her voice boomed. "You're not leaving Chicago. No. I won't allow it."

"You can't prevent it. I'm an adult, remember?"

"Why in the world would you want to leave Chicago?"

"I'm too anxious all the time. There's something about the city that puts me on edge."

"You grew up in the city. What are you talking about?"

"I grew up in Edgebrook, which might as well have been the suburbs. It's nothing like down here. I find it exhausting."

Her mother sat down again, frowning. "You're twenty-five years old. How could you be exhausted?"

Clare drank some coffee and spoke quietly. "You don't notice because of the job you have. You don't have to commute when everyone else does, shop when everyone else does." These were irritants, but not her reasons for turning her back on the city. She wanted a fresh start in a place where no one knew her.

"My job, as you call it, is very hard work. I don't think you ever appreciated that." She was the author of a mystery series featuring expert knitter Juliet Cheaves. She was always under contract to produce the next book and she never broke a deadline. "I expect I work harder than you ever have."

Now Clare was pissed off. There was always some point in a visit with her mother when she became angry. It was part of the package deal. But this barb was particularly galling. "You have no idea how hard I've worked. Christ."

Her mother got up and moved into the living room, looking it over for signs of sloth, no doubt. "This really is a godforsaken apartment, Clare. You live like a vampire." She bent down to turn on a lamp. "But better here than somewhere downstate. You'll be throwing your life away."

"Wow. You're a complete city snob. I never realized."

She laughed. "That may be so, but I don't see any benefit to you living outside the city. Where are you going? Will it at least have a coffee shop? A bookstore? Who will your friends be? You can't leave civilization."

Clare walked to the door, hoping she'd take the hint it was time to go. Her mother flopped on the couch instead. She sighed and walked back toward her mother. "I don't know where I'm going. Wherever the best job is, I guess. In fact, I want to start the job search right away. I was just sitting down to the computer when you came by."

"Are you throwing me out?" She raised an eyebrow.

"I'm afraid I am. If you're so worried about me having a job, you'll let me start looking for one."

She heaved herself back up and went into the kitchen for her coat. When she came back she was wrapping a long, multicolored scarf around and around her neck. "This discussion isn't over. Come to dinner tomorrow. We can talk about it with your father."

"Oh, please. Like he'll want to be part of that conversation. You know he doesn't give a shit where I live, as long as it's not at home with you both."

"That's just not true, sweetheart." She had a look on her face that might be appropriate if you came across a shivering puppy or a baby in distress. Clare was well used to her father's indifference. She didn't need her mother's reassurances.

"Well, it's true, whether you chose to see it or not. I'll come to dinner, though."

Her mother picked up her enormous tote bag and stepped toward the door. "You're at a crossroads, Clare. Please don't make any stupid decisions. There are plenty of law jobs in the city."

"Thanks for understanding, Mom. As usual, we're on the same page."

"I love you, sweetheart."

"Love you, too."

She kissed her on the cheek and strode out the door, on to her next errand. Clare was probably sandwiched between meeting a friend for coffee and grocery shopping. She looked out the window and watched her mother marching down the sidewalk to her car. After pouring more coffee, she sat down at her laptop and brought up a jobs website. It wasn't the best way to look for lawyer jobs, but she didn't have any downstate connections. She'd never had to look for a job before. She was recruited right out of law school, which turned out to not be the smartest move.

After two hours, she came across a listing from the law firm of Nelson & Nelson in Money Creek. She looked on Google maps and found the town. It was several hundred miles south of Chicago in Timson County, deep in corn country. She'd been thinking she'd most likely end up in the suburbs, but why not a rural area? It would probably be hard to get into trouble in a small town, and the pace would be much slower than the city. Maybe that was the perfect environment for her to start fresh. No stultifying job and no drugs either. That was part of the deal.

The next day, she drove downstate to interview for the job. Elizabeth Nelson, of Nelson & Nelson, had responded to her email and sounded enthusiastic about talking to her right away. They were looking for a litigation associate, and Clare had all the qualifications. She tried to feel confident coming from a top law school and law firm, but she was almost ill with nerves.

Money Creek had its own exit on the interstate and she drove through a long commercial strip that held fast food joints, hotels, car dealerships, and a Walmart. It didn't seem that small, though the population was only twenty thousand, about the size of her old neighborhood. She followed her GPS to the historic older part of town. She'd read up on Money Creek and knew it was the seat of Timson County and Abe Lincoln had tried cases in its courthouse. As she drove through she saw a lot of businesses named after him— Lincoln Diner, Abe's Tavern, Lincoln Ford. The town itself was named after Robert Money, an early prairie pioneer. The rapid creek ran through its center.

As she got close to downtown she could see the enormous golden domed county courthouse. It was surrounded by a square of nineteenth century brick buildings housing small businesses. If any tourists came to town, they'd call it quaint, but she suspected not many did. She smiled. This was just the right place. She'd enjoy the simple pleasures and new friends who knew nothing of her history. Her mother would be appalled, but she knew what she wanted. The town beckoned. She drove around the square and frowned at the number of empty storefronts, the mark of a moribund town. She imagined a family hardware store run to ground by the Walmart. She was relieved to see a coffee shop called Bean There that looked like one she'd find in Chicago. On the opposite side of the square was a building with a dark green awning and Nelson & Nelson written in large letters. She pulled her car into one of the empty spaces in front of the building.

A woman stood talking to someone in the reception area. She broke away as soon as she saw Clare walk in and approached her with her hand out.

"You must be Clare," she said. "I'm Elizabeth Nelson." She shook her hand firmly. The smile on her face looked genuine. Her short, feathered hair was mostly gray; she wore minimal makeup on her broad face. Her black pantsuit and medium high heels were not unlike what Clare wore herself. She knew from reading the firm's website that she was around fifty years old, but fifty was definitely the new forty in her case. The thin lines around her blue eyes were lightly etched, her neck smooth and firm. She could sense Elizabeth's self-assurance as soon as their eyes met. She looked like the kind of confident woman Clare wanted to be.

They got to know each other over lunch, though from Clare's end that meant a carefully constructed narrative about her legal career to date. She offered as little about her personal life as possible—both parents in Chicago, a brother in Portland, not much else. After lunch, she met with Elizabeth's husband, and by the end of her time there she'd received and accepted their offer. She would move to town as soon as possible and start her new job. The process from thought to job had been so fast it left her anxious. She could barely comprehend the upheaval about to take place in her life, but she felt the first spark of excitement in a long time.

## Chapter Four

Freya pulled up alongside a battered Monte Carlo so that the driver's side windows were next to each other, cop style. She was at a trailhead in Shawnee National Forest, twenty minutes outside Money Creek. The parking lot was empty. Not many people went hiking in twenty-degree weather. She drove her own Jeep Wrangler rather than an official state police vehicle.

"Tell me why this meth lab is different from any of the others," she said without preamble to Jason, her confidential informant. Her clothes looked like those of a tactical officer rather than a detective—jeans and long-sleeved T-shirt, down jacket, shit kicker boots, and a belt with handcuffs, radio, and her weapon.

"Because I think the guy cooking there knows something about the bigger players. His lab is totally upgraded from the one I first saw him operate in." Jason was young, probably no more than twenty-one, unnaturally thin, his past love affair with crystal meth still etched into his scarred face and gnarly teeth.

Freya's partner, Ben, leaned over from the passenger seat. "What's the guy's name?"

"He goes by Morgan. I don't know if that's his last name or what."

"What does Morgan have to say about the change?"

Jason shrugged. "Not much. When I asked him about it he kind of blew me off and said it was time he cleaned things up. I think someone's behind it. There's another lab I've heard of that recently got upgraded."

"We'll follow up on that," Freya said. "But for now, where's Morgan's lab?"

"It's really hard to find. I committed it to memory the time I went out there, so I'll have to take you there myself."

She looked at Ben, who raised an eyebrow. She turned back to Jason. "It's a risk having you with us. We don't want anyone out there to see you."

"Don't worry about it. I'll stay in the car."

An old Mazda 3 pulled into the parking lot with a couple of teenagers on board. They quickly left when they saw the cars in cop formation.

"How often is Morgan out there?" she said.

"A lot. He's cooking a ton, which makes me think he has a big new customer."

"We'll go tonight. Meet us back here at eight."

Being a detective with the Illinois State Police was Freya's dream job, but it had lots of problems. She loved police work—the hunt for a perpetrator, the piecing together of evidence, the thrill of a good arrest. She didn't like the long periods of time she spent away from home when the brass assigned her cases in other parts of the state. She missed her friends in Bloomington. She'd had to give away her cat because of her travel schedule. And worst of all, most girlfriends wouldn't put up with it. But assignment to the state's new drug task force was a plum. Drug traffic had grown sharply in the area surrounding Money Creek. They'd made little progress so far identifying anyone up the food chain in rural drug distribution, assuming there was any food chain to begin with. Anyone who'd managed to get through high school chemistry could pull instructions for making methamphetamine off the internet and start cooking. If they sold their own product there was no one they were reporting to, no higher-ups for the police to train their focus on. But Jason had heard talk about some men who were taking over the market and inching smaller players out of the game. That was her target.

Four hours later, with a search warrant in hand, Freya and Ben followed Jason's directions to the meth lab, ten miles out of town. The route was labyrinthine, a series of increasingly smaller, unpaved roads through vast cornfields. They were followed closely by two sheriff's cruisers and all had turned their lights off. A long dirt driveway led to a clearing with a tiny farmhouse and an RV on blocks next to it. The house was dark and looked uninhabited, but lights glowed from the RV's windows.

They got quietly out of the car, though the music pumping from the trailer was so loud there was no risk of being heard. Four deputies piled out of the cruisers behind them. One leaned in to push Jason down in the back seat, out of sight. Freya motioned to two deputies to cover the back side, while the other two stood with them. One carried a battering ram.

"Ben and I will go in first, you two follow us. Be sharp. There may be multiple people inside and they're probably armed." She looked at Ben, who nodded and drew his weapon. Freya's was already in her hand. She never would admit it, but she was always afraid of blind entries. Who wouldn't be? So much could go wrong.

They moved to the trailer door. The deputy with the battering ram climbed the short staircase, Ben and then Freya right behind him. At Ben's signal the deputy swung the ram at the flimsy door, which shattered on impact. He stepped out of the way and Ben stepped through the door and to his right. Freya went to the left, their guns trained on both ends of the trailer.

"Police!" Ben screamed, but he might as well have held his breath. The pulsating music was many times louder inside. Freya cleared her end and turned to Ben, who had his gun trained on a pudgy young man at the kitchen counter. The air smelled of chemicals. He sensed their presence and turned just as Freya shut off the boom box.

"What the fuck," the man said, reaching behind his back as if to retrieve a weapon. Ben's shot whizzed by his head a comfortable foot to the left of him. Uncomfortable if you're the one being shot at. He screamed and dropped to his knees, his hands over his head.

"This is the Illinois State Police. Keep your hands where they are," Freya shouted.

"Are you known as Morgan?" Ben said. He'd positioned himself so he was between Morgan and Freya.

"That's my name."

"You're under arrest on drug manufacturing charges," Freya said. She looked at a deputy. "You do the honors, okay?" The deputy stepped forward and cuffed him, reading him his rights. Then he hustled him out, leaving Ben and Freya alone in the RV. They would question him later at the sheriff's department.

They looked around and saw a pristine space. The countertops in the small kitchen shone as if they were granite, though she couldn't conceive of granite countertops in a meth lab. Carefully labeled containers of chemicals, glassware, and a box of latex gloves sat neatly on top. What looked like clean butchers' aprons hung by a hook in the wall. Other supplies were neatly stacked at the far end of the trailer.

"It looks more like a chemistry class than the labs we're used to," she said. "Something's going on. I don't see this as self-initiated by the average cooker." Most labs they found were explosions ready to happen.

They left the trailer in the hands of the deputies to process the scene. They'd bring in specialists in hazmat suits to manage the chemicals and dismantle the lab. When they got to Freya's Jeep they saw one of the deputies leaning against it. Jason was plainly visible in the back seat.

"You've got a problem," the deputy said. "Your genius CI was sitting in full view of the guy we marched out of here. I think his cover's blown."

Freya yanked open the back door and grabbed Jason by the collar. "What the fuck did you just do?"

Jason pulled Freya's hand from his shirt. "I was getting cramps squished on the floor. I was going to lay down on the back seat when I saw who you were bringing out of there. It's Morgan, man. And he saw me, no doubt."

"I should make you walk back to town." She turned in disgust and got into the Jeep. She wanted to kick something. Ben got in and looked at her warily. "Let's go back to Money Creek and talk to Morgan. Maybe we'll be lucky and get information worth losing a CI over."

❖

Early the next morning, Ben and Freya stared at each other across the two desks pushed together in their tiny office. They shared temporary quarters at the Timson County Sheriff's Department, in cooperation with the state police.

"Should we debrief about last night?" Ben said.

"We can sum it up in three words—we fucked up." Freya opened the coffee Ben had brought in from Bean There. He reached into a bag and passed her a bagel and cream cheese.

"We should have kept a deputy on Jason." He took a huge bite out of his bagel.

She sometimes wearied of the Sisyphean task they had before them. For every bit of progress they made there was a problem that slowed it down. She put her boots on top of her desk and bit into her bagel as if it were hardtack, her mood sour.

"Let's go to the jail and talk to Morgan again. We didn't get much out of him last night." She stuffed the rest of the bagel in her mouth and followed Ben out the door. They walked across the large open room that held desks for deputies to the front of the sheriff's department. As they entered the hall, Freya saw Joanne Reid talking with a deputy at the reception desk. Her legs were firmly planted, her naturally athletic figure starting to take on body builder proportions. Freya knew her ambition was to be a competitive body builder, and she wasn't far from it. She'd been dating Jo for a few months, but she didn't want to talk to her while she was on the job. Now it was too late to escape. Jo turned her head and broke into a hundred-watt smile when she saw her. They'd had plans the night before that Freya canceled because of the raid. It was the third time in a row she'd canceled plans with her. Jo walked across the lobby to intercept them.

"How'd it go last night?" she said.

"Sorry I had to cancel dinner," Freya said. "Can I call you later? We're on our way to a thing here."

Jo's smile faded. "Sure. I'll talk to you later." Ben was amused, as if he were watching kittens play. They left Jo standing in the middle of the room and made their way to the jail entrance and through the door.

"I don't know why she puts up with you," Ben said.

"Because I'm worth it, of course," she said, smiling brightly. "And she does what anyone dumb enough to date a cop always fails to do. She practices acceptance. What else can you do?"

"You can bitch a lot, which has been my experience."

"Jo's not like that."

Ben stopped in the jail reception room. "How serious do you think this is with her?"

Freya looked up at him. "Not that it's any of your business, but I'd say I simply don't know. The jury's still out."

They checked in at jail reception and went to talk to Morgan a second time, pushing the rock a little up the mountain one more time.

## CHAPTER FIVE

The previous morning, Clare had poured her entire stash of Valium, Vicodin, and Adderall down the toilet. It had taken two flushes and a few deep breaths, but she was determined to quit. She wanted to be successful and happy and she knew she spent too much time and money on drugs. What was a study aid in college had become a necessity in law school. She was overwhelmed with the work and competitive atmosphere in her first year of school and gladly bought up tablets of speed when one of her classmates offered them to her. She'd been used to the way things were in high school and college, when it was relatively easy to stay at the top of her class. Now everyone around her was very smart and her position among them was unclear.

Whether she would have naturally adapted to the stresses of a top law school, she'd never know. With the drug she was able to stay in the top ten of her class. There was no incentive to not take them that she could see. A lot of the first-year students did the same and it didn't feel like she was doing anything wrong. But most of them left the drug behind when they graduated from law school. Clare kept up her relationship with her source until he went out of business and she had to find someone new—Casey. It was business as usual as she started her professional career. Wake up, take a tablet or two, work like a dog, go home and crash. Her life got smaller every day. She occasionally thought of her mother's sister, Alice, who was always in a fugue state from the tranquilizers she took regularly. That wouldn't happen to her.

Her hopeful attitude started crumbling the next day, her first at Nelson & Nelson. It was twenty-four hours since her last pill and she felt shattered. Her body was betraying her—crushing fatigue, extreme anxiety, and growing nausea. If she'd had any drug available she would have taken it. This was not what she'd had in mind by quitting drugs. It was not the way she wanted to present herself on her first day of work. What if she keeled over in front of her boss? She walked the few blocks from her rented house to the office, hoping the fresh, cold air would make her feel sharp.

She had no idea what being a lawyer in a small town would be like. After Dearborn, Richards & Pike, she only knew it had to be better than the life she led there. As she walked through the town square she saw the remaining downtown merchants opening their shops, some sweeping the sidewalk in front. They said good morning as she passed. Should she introduce herself? Probably. She'd be seeing them every morning for who knew how long. But she couldn't bring herself to do it. It was all she could do to get herself through the door of Nelson & Nelson.

She walked into the law firm's small reception room, painted a sky blue. Copies of the *Wall Street Journal* and the *Timson County Times* were on a coffee table in the center of a waiting area. Behind the desk was a middle-aged woman in a motorized wheelchair. She looked up from her computer and smiled.

"I'm Clare Lehane. I believe Elizabeth Nelson is expecting me."

"Right! You're our new lawyer. I'm sorry I missed meeting you when you interviewed." She neatly maneuvered her wheelchair around her desk and stuck out her hand. "I'm Donna, the office manager."

Clare took her hand and hoped her own wasn't trembling. "It's very nice to meet you," she managed.

"I've got you set up in your office. Let me show you and I'll let Elizabeth know you're here."

Just as she moved a throttle on the chair to turn around, a young woman came striding in from the back, carrying a file. She was dressed in a dark gray pantsuit with a crisply ironed Oxford shirt.

Her shoulders and arms were straining at the fabric, as if she were a body builder. She stopped in her tracks upon seeing Clare.

"Oh, good. This is Joanne Reid, the firm's paralegal." Donna introduced Clare, who noticed Joanne's smile looked forced and she didn't offer to shake hands. This didn't bode well. It had been Clare's experience that some paralegals resented the young lawyers they worked with. The lawyers were paid so much more and they often did similar work. She wanted to avoid that kind of tension.

"Do you work in litigation, Joanne?"

"Yes. I'm Elizabeth's paralegal." She was practically lifting her leg to mark her territory. "And I go by Jo."

"Got it. I look forward to working together." Clare hoped her smile appeared more genuine than Jo's did.

Jo tossed a file onto Donna's desk and returned through the door to the rest of the office, letting it close behind her. "Let's go through," Donna said. The door had a lever instead of a knob, placed lower than usual so Donna could reach it, and the door itself had no threshold. Caring people worked there. She followed Donna into a long, wide hallway with offices on both sides. The walls were decorated with Audubon prints of birds and other wildlife, mostly pheasants and ducks. She guessed one or both of the Nelsons were hunters and reminded herself that was normal down here. The first two office doors were closed. Donna stopped at the third and gestured Clare in.

"This is you. Why don't you get settled and I'll find Elizabeth."

She continued down the hallway as Clare walked into her new office and dropped her briefcase on the desk. It was a bigger space than she'd had in Chicago, though not as sleek. Old-fashioned oak furniture gave the room a comfortable feel. Small holes dotted one of the walls where a previous occupant had hung something—maybe a painting or photograph or a giant picture of family or friends, something she'd be hard-pressed to come up with herself. Who'd worked at this desk before her? Why had he or she left? She opened the middle drawer and found office supplies. She was moving the stapler to her desktop when she heard a soft knock at her door. Elizabeth Nelson stood in the doorway, a gleaming smile on her face.

"Welcome," she said. Clare had the same impression she'd had when she met Elizabeth during her interview—gentle, but extremely confident. If Clare were a murder defendant with her life on the line, she'd want Elizabeth to be her lawyer. She looked like she knew how to get things done.

Elizabeth walked into her office and sat in the chair in front of her desk. She looked unhurried, so different from Carlton Henning. "How did your move go?" she said. "It can be rough in winter."

Clare clutched the arms of her chair. She was willing herself past her horrible physical condition and into a conversation with her boss. She couldn't afford to make a fool of herself.

"It was easy, actually. I don't have much stuff, so the truck was only a quarter full."

"Are you a minimalist?" Elizabeth said.

Clare thought of Casey longingly. "I think it's because I'm young. I haven't had time to acquire a lot of stuff."

"Of course. You're in the accumulation stage, while I'm throwing things out right and left. You're in the McClellans' place out there on Oak Street?"

Clare wondered how she knew that since she'd not yet filled out her new employee paperwork. Elizabeth was certainly competent, but she didn't know she was omnipotent. "So, it's true what they say about small towns, that everyone knows everything?" Clare said, smiling.

"Not exactly. More so than the city, certainly. I ran into Tom McClellen and he told me he'd rented the house to a new lawyer at my firm." Elizabeth sat back in her chair, as relaxed as a cat lying in the sunshine.

"Do you live in that part of town also? Will you see me walking to work every morning?"

"I'm usually the first one in the office, so that doesn't seem likely. I do live three streets over from Oak, so we're neighbors."

Clare couldn't think of any more chitchat, so she stayed quiet. Elizabeth roused herself and stood. "Let me take you around. You've met Donna, who keeps everything running smoothly here. It's a wise idea to cultivate a good relationship with her, not that it's hard to do. She's a treasure."

"I also met Jo. Is she the firm's only paralegal?"

"She is. And I'd say an appreciative attitude with her is the way to go. She makes all our lives much easier."

"I'll take that to heart," she said. The last thing she wanted was an adversary.

They walked down the hall to the rear, where she saw a sunny conference room. There were four people in suits standing around a table, drinking coffee. They all turned their heads as Elizabeth and Clare entered the room. "I asked everyone here to introduce Clare at the same time. Thought it would be easier that way."

Easier for her, but definitely not for Clare. Her anxiety grew at all the new faces. She shook hands first with Elizabeth's husband, Hank, the other Nelson. He stood at about six feet four inches and was stocky. He probably played tackle at Money Creek High. His smile was broad in his craggy face. He put his coffee down and took Clare's hand with both of his. She'd met him during her interview two weeks earlier and been immediately comfortable with him. Elizabeth then introduced her to the firm's three other associates and announced they'd all get to know Clare better at a party she was holding for her at the Nelson home that Friday night. Clare had to feel better by then. She couldn't take much scrutiny in her present condition.

Elizabeth took her into her large office next to the conference room where she settled behind her desk as Clare sat in front of her. The room was a light salmon color and smelled of the coffee brewing on a sideboard.

"I know starting a new job can be overwhelming. Why don't we put you to work so you can focus on something?" She reached over to the corner of her mahogany desk and picked up a file. It took two hands, stuffed as it was with a mishmash of papers. "Oleg v. Peterson Agriculture. We're working this up for trial, which may start in several months. You'll have to work fast to get up to speed."

Clare was uneasy. How could she work? She could barely keep her head up. She'd never withdrawn from drugs. It was far worse than she ever thought it would be. "What's it about? I'm eager to get started."

"Our client, Peterson Ag, is the corporate farm that maintains several methane gas lagoons on its properties. Oleg, a farm worker, fell into a lagoon and died. That's the nutshell." Elizabeth was leaning back in her chair, looking closely at Clare. "It's important we get a good result in this case."

"Isn't that true for every case?"

"It is. But Peterson Ag is our largest client. Hank handles all their business matters, and the workers compensation and litigation fall to me. We want to keep them happy."

"Pardon my ignorance, but what is a methane gas lagoon? It sounds post-apocalyptic."

Elizabeth laughed. "You're about to practice the kind of law that we often do here, involving farms and agriculture. A methane gas lagoon holds the waste slurry of the livestock on a farm. For corporate farms this can amount to a large network of lagoons that are literally full of shit. The methane gas from the slurry can be deadly."

"It sounds like a workers comp case to me."

"It is. But as we were investigating his compensation case, we discovered there was a product recall involving the guard railing that failed. Oleg had been standing on a walkway surrounding the lagoon. According to another worker with him, he simply leaned on a gate in the guard rail and it gave way, plunging him into three feet of slurry. Our position is Peterson Ag never received the recall, and if that's so, and the manufacturer knew the gate was defective, it introduces a punitive damages case against them. Ogden Lagoons makes the lagoons. We've brought them into the litigation."

"Why didn't the other guy pull Oleg out?"

"Not everyone's a hero. He said he wasn't willing to go into the slurry and he didn't seem the least bit embarrassed by it. He ran for help instead, but Oleg was dead before anyone got to him. The autopsy showed he'd hit his head hard in the fall, but that wasn't what killed him. He was probably knocked out and then suffocated."

Clare took a deep breath and tried not to slide down her chair as if her bones had been removed. She knew it was possible to get shit cases in a rural county law firm, but she never imagined a literal shit case. The idea of falling face first into that slurry, as they politely call it, did no favors to her stomach.

"I'll take you to the case room. The lagoon manufacturer just produced their documents the other day, and I'm putting you in charge of the review. Jo will help you cull them, but their relevance and attorney privilege status will be left to you to decide. Obviously, we're most interested in finding any evidence they sent the product recall to Peterson."

Elizabeth led her into a room about twice the size of her office. It was lined with worktables against all the walls, with a larger worktable in the middle. At least a dozen boxes were stacked on the center table and the room smelled musty with old files. Reading documents was about as boring as it gets for a lawyer. How would she ever be able to do it without speed? Jo sat at the table with a stack of documents in front of her. Elizabeth introduced them.

"We met out front," Clare said. She turned to Jo. "Looks like I'm on the document review team with you."

Jo smiled weakly. "Great." She turned her head back to her documents.

Elizabeth didn't seem to notice Jo's rudeness. "Jo will show you how we process the documents."

"Would it be okay if I spend some time going through your file before starting in on the document production? I want to fully understand what I'm looking for." Clare needed the cover that reading a file could provide. She couldn't stand the idea of spending the rest of the day with Jo, not in her condition.

"Of course. Let's get it from my office." Clare retrieved the file and hurried to her own office. The first thing she did after sitting down was call Casey. She didn't dare close her door on her first day, so she spoke *sotto voce* when he came on the line. "I need to see you tonight."

Casey snorted. "So much for your new country life. What's the matter?"

"Nothing's the matter. I want to get a bit of a supply from you to transition. Changing everything at once was foolish."

"Do you mean you quit?"

"I threw all those pills away."

"You should have returned them. I would have given you a refund. Why did you go cold turkey?"

"Because I'm stupid. I feel like crap. Turns out you're not supposed to go off Valium all at once."

"I could have told you that."

"Then why didn't you?" Clare could hear a slight whine in her own voice. Pathetic.

"Not my place. But I can't meet you this evening," Casey said.

Real panic washed through her. "Not even for a minute? I'll be quick."

"Not until midnight. I should be home by then."

"Done. I'll see you tonight."

She disconnected and tossed her phone onto her desktop. Chicago was three hours away, so she'd leave at eight and get there early. She poured a cup of coffee in her new Nelson & Nelson mug and resigned herself to reading the file and taking notes until the end of the day. Elizabeth told her during her interview her firm's hours were eight thirty to five, and no one expected her to stay later unless it was something that couldn't wait. She wouldn't try to make an impression by staying late tonight. She didn't think she physically could.

## CHAPTER SIX

Clare left the office at five o'clock on the third day of her new job. She could have worked much longer. In fact, she wished she could work longer, but the culture of the firm discouraged it. You were meant to go live your life. The problem was, Clare didn't yet have a life in Money Creek. Since coming back from her late-night trip to Chicago, she'd spent her evenings at home going mental from boredom. She'd gotten about a week's worth of speed and a fistful of Valium from Casey, but drugs alone couldn't entertain her night after night. She was lonely. She'd also gotten the worst news she'd had in years—Casey was moving out of state, almost immediately, which accounted for his dwindling inventory.

"How can you do this to me?" Clare had asked, holding him by the upper arm as if she could keep him in place.

He gently removed her hand and continued to count out pills. "I'm not doing anything to you. I'm going to Seattle to be with my boyfriend." Clare noticed the moving boxes stacked in the corner.

"What boyfriend? This is the first I've heard of him."

He looked at her with something like pity on his face. "I'm not sure where you got the impression we tell each other everything. I'm your dealer, not your girlfriend."

That hurt. She thought they were close friends and she did tell him everything, though there'd never been much to tell. In Chicago, she'd worked, visited her family on occasion, saw a few friends now and then, and slept. "Give me as much as you can, then. I don't know what I'm going to do now."

"I thought you were quitting?"

"I am. But the Valium has a very long taper down period. I looked it up. Same with speed. But where am I going to find a dealer in Money Creek?"

Casey laughed. "I can't believe you're living in a place called Money Creek. Aren't there a ton of meth dealers down there?"

"I told you what I think about meth. It's evil."

He poured the last of the pills into a ziplock bag and handed it over. "Is there a college nearby?"

"There's Money Creek College."

"That's where you'll find your speed and if you're lucky, some Valium. Rural areas are big on the oxy, and meth, of course."

Clare was desperate. What was she supposed to do? Saunter onto campus and ask the first student she saw whether he had any drugs? Impossible. It was deeply humbling to put herself through something like that because she needed drugs. She vowed to taper off completely and be done with it. She stared at her stash and saw her days of supply were numbered. Her online order of Valium wouldn't arrive for a few weeks. It had to travel from India, somehow make it through customs, and be delivered by the letter carrier. And it was usually terrible quality. She had enough speed to last until the middle of the following week. As she changed clothes she resigned herself to what she had to do. Desperate measures. She'd go to the campus and get the lay of the land. Maybe something would fall into her lap. If she were to quit, it would have to be through a planned approach. She couldn't repeat that first day of work.

She used her phone's map function and headed to the college in her used Subaru Outback, trying to get a feel for where things were in relation to each other. The streets were all residential and one looked much like the other. Money Creek College suddenly appeared on her left as she climbed a small incline. The row of houses on the street were abruptly interrupted by five Georgian style buildings sitting on an enormous snow covered front lawn. The bright sun made it almost painful to look at. The buildings looked relatively new, almost shiny. Everything was crisp and clean. Students wearing down coats crisscrossed between buildings and it looked like a recruitment video. There were two mid-rise brick buildings that she guessed were dormitories. It was the smallest campus she'd ever seen. She parked in the lot across the street and walked along the buildings until she found the student union. Dressed in jeans, a light blue button-down shirt, Frye boots, and her North Face down jacket, she hoped to blend in.

The large room she entered was bright and airy, sun pouring down from a series of skylights. There were several seating areas with tables, others with sofas and chairs. Students took up every seat and she saw right away they were different from the students she was familiar with in the city. They were alarmingly clean-cut. The boys wore button-down shirts and khaki pants, their hair neatly cut, their demeanor more like glee club than hipster indifference. Many of the girls wore skirts and they were all primly made up. Clare wondered if she'd wandered into a Christian college. Students in Chicago seemed scruffy in comparison. The bookstore was off to one side and she walked straight to it. Bookstores made her feel comfortable, and it was likely she'd figure out the religious tenor of the place by what they sold. She found the usual displays of mugs, bumper stickers, shot glasses, and sweatshirts all emblazoned with the college's name. The book stacks were filled with academic texts, but there were no sections devoted to devotion. No bible rack, or Christian fiction, whatever that was. Perhaps the students were dressed exactly the way small town private college students dress. She sure as hell wouldn't be approaching any of them about where to find drugs on campus.

Opposite to the bookstore was the entrance to a café, a Starbucks-sized room with a counter selling coffee, pastries, and sandwiches. There were more well-behaved students at the tables, many of them studying. She took her coffee to an empty seat in the back of the café and worried. She was down to her last twenty-five Adderall tablets, and she often took several a day. Something needed to happen.

After twenty minutes of sipping coffee and fiddling with her phone, she looked up to see a young man sit at the next table, facing her. He looked like the man of her dreams—a stubbled beard, hair tied in a top knot, a black T-shirt with the name of a band she'd never heard of, black shit kicker boots and black jeans. He was tall and lanky, and though his long skinny arms didn't have trace marks on them, she clearly caught the scent of a drug user. He took out his phone and typed a text with blazing thumb speed and then put it down and picked up his coffee. As he took a sip he looked at her, catching her staring at him. He gave her a sly smile that made a worm turn in her stomach. He was going to make this sexual from the first instant. She could see him appraising her.

"Hey," he said.

"Hey." She felt ridiculous.

He shifted in his seat, leaning toward her. "I haven't seen you before. Are you a professor?"

Jesus. Did she look that old? She needed to get back to nightly moisturizing. And who says "Hey" to a professor? Only the supremely confident. "No. Not a professor. I'm just visiting campus."

He took another sip. "Would you like a tour? My apartment's right off campus."

She looked at him incredulously. "You're kidding with that, right?"

He looked amused. "Kidding? No. I can show you around and we can have a beer at my place."

Appalled or not, she saw an opening and was desperate enough to take it. She paused for a moment as if thinking about it. "Maybe. But what if I want something other than a beer?"

A smile spread across his face. "That's what I'm talking about." He looked very young for a brief moment before resuming his laid-back, entitled expression.

"For the record, sex is not what I'm talking about. I don't even know your name, for God's sake. What I meant is whether you had something other than beer to offer."

He looked disappointed but interested. "The name's Evan. What did you have in mind?"

"What do you have?"

He leaned in closer. "I think some weed. Let's go."

Clare didn't move. "Let me ask you this. Do you know of anyone I can talk to about getting some other product?"

He leaned back in his chair and gave her a quizzical look. "Man, I would not expect these words to come out of your mouth. You don't have the right vibe."

"I'm not a druggie," she said impatiently. "I have some specific needs and I'm looking to make a connection here in town. Can you help me?"

He paused to consider. "It depends on what you give me in return." He had the slightly uncomfortable look of someone who thought he might have pushed things too far.

"Let me get this straight. You're saying that yes, you do have a name for me but no, you won't make the connection unless I have sex with you?"

His sly smile returned. "I wouldn't want to put it that way, but yes."

She sighed. Loudly. Could she do this? She thought of her short supply, of Casey's move, of what her physical condition was when she's been without pills for a day. She'd wriggle out of it somehow. Job one was to get in front of a dealer.

"Okay. But before we go anywhere I want you to call your guy and see what he's got. If I'm not buying what he has, I sure as hell am not sleeping with you."

"Sure. If those are your terms." He looked resigned.

"These are not treaty negotiations. If you're going to insist I sleep with you first, I want to make sure you deliver."

"Let me call him." Evan picked up his phone and after a moment said, "Hey. I've got a woman here who's interested in what you might have. Can you tell me what's in stock?" A moment of silence and then "Sure. Got it. We'll be over in a few." He put his phone back on the table.

"What did he say?" Clare said.

"He doesn't want to talk specifics on the phone. He said to bring you over."

"Over where?"

"To my place. We're roommates."

They walked three blocks from campus to the first-floor apartment of an old Victorian frame house. It needed a coat of paint, and some of the shutters were cockeyed. She noticed a few more houses like it and figured it was where off-campus student housing was located. She followed Evan inside and immediately smelled marijuana in the air. A young man sat in the living room, watching something on British television. She heard the plumy accents through surround sound speakers. When he saw them, he snubbed out the joint and clicked off the TV. He wore a heathered gray Henley shirt, new black jeans, and clogs, which gave her pause. His dark curly hair was cut short, his face was cleanly shaven, and he wore an expensive watch. He seemed more like a software designer than a college student.

Clare prayed she wasn't making a terrible mistake. Something about him made her uneasy, perhaps the disarming smile he gave her as he approached. But she was backed into a corner. Taking the risk with a new dealer rather than face being strung out was ultimately an easy decision. He offered his hand.

"I'm Henry. Welcome."

She warily shook. "I'm Clare."

"Follow me. We'll talk in the kitchen." The kitchen was right off the living room. She expected the kind of mess her own college kitchen was always in, but it was sparkling clean. Henry pointed to a round breakfast table. "Would you like a coffee? Beer?"

Clare looked around the room. A Nespresso machine sat on a counter with a carousel of coffee pods next to it. Tempting. But her nerves cried out for alcohol. "I'll take a beer, thanks."

Evan excused himself, winking at Clare as he went out. Did he expect her to look for him after this tête-à-tête and fulfill her end of the bargain? He'd be waiting a long time. Henry put an IPA in front of her and took a drink of his own, appraising her.

"Evan sort of broke the rules by calling me out of the blue to bring a stranger over. Normally we only let in people we know."

"If you're worried about me being a narc, you shouldn't."

"No, you don't look like you could be undercover. You're kind of old, for one thing."

Christ. It seemed the price she had to pay for getting some product was to feel ancient. "I was hoping you could help me. I'm looking for some speed and any kind of downer you have. I've got cash with me."

He stared at her as if she'd just laughed at a funeral. "That's not the way it's going to work. We're going to relax and get to know each other first." He put his beer down and spread his hands flat on the table.

Clare sighed. "Sure. Ask me whatever you'd like"

"Tell me where you live in Money Creek and who you know."

"That's easy. I live on Oak near downtown and I don't know anyone. I just moved to town."

"Are you working?" Henry said.

"Yes." Clare shifted in her chair.

"Then you know the people at your workplace. Where would that be?"

"I'm a lawyer at Nelson & Nelson," she said.

Henry took another drink. "I know the place. I'm trying to figure out why a clean-cut lawyer from the best firm in town is in my kitchen asking for drugs."

Clare stared at him. "Are you asking why I do drugs? Is this a counseling session?"

Henry smiled. "I'm cautious, Clare, which benefits you, too. I don't think you'd want news to leak that the new lawyer at Nelson & Nelson was a drug addict."

"I'm not a drug addict," Clare said, putting her beer down hard. "Why would you even think that?"

"If you weren't I don't think you'd put yourself in this situation. It's too dangerous. What if we blab all over campus that a pretty lawyer from Nelson & Nelson was trying to score drugs at the college. What if I told Nelson & Nelson?"

"Why would you do any of that? It doesn't make sense," she said.

"I don't know you. Maybe you'll tell people about me. Think of it as insurance that you'll keep your mouth shut." She considered the increased vulnerability in buying and selling drugs in a very small town. It was information that could be used as a weapon, as Henry seemed to want to do. But she didn't care. The worry over being exposed paled against the worry of not having any drugs at all.

"I'm not an addict," Clare insisted. But Henry stayed quiet. She filled the silence. "You go ahead and think what you'd like. Now, can we talk sales here? I'd like to be on my way."

Henry looked satisfied. "Good. You're looking for speed, which is a staple of my business, as you can imagine on a college campus. Even the appallingly straight students at Money Creek want to cram at exam time. But I'm afraid I don't have any in stock. We're expecting some next week." Her face fell in disappointment. "I have some in my personal stash I can give you. It'll keep you going until the shipment comes in."

"How much are you talking about?"

"Around ten tablets. I hardly touch the stuff," he said.

Clare knew the amount was cutting things close, but she had a reprieve. "Thanks. But I'll pay for them. I don't want to owe you anything."

"Do you have a hard time letting people be nice to you?" He looked as if he really cared whether she did or not.

"Is this more of the therapy you seem to want to give me?"

Henry laughed. "I find people interesting and you're an interesting puzzle. What else do you want?"

"As I said, any depressant you have in stock. Valium or any benzo, Vicodin," Clare said, looking at him hopefully.

"I understand. You need something to take the edge off the speed. This isn't a town that's big on Valium use. There's not that much anxiety in Money Creek. But I can look into it for you. I never have had any Vicodin, but the oxy is usually available." He finished his beer and stood from the table. "Let me go look and I'll let you know what I have."

Relief flooded her. Now she could start to moderate her intake without having to go cold turkey. She drank her beer and enjoyed it. Henry came back into the kitchen and put a plastic bag of pills on the table.

"Ten Adderall and twenty oxy. Will that hold you until we get more in?"

Clare raised her eyes from the bag. "It depends on when that is."

"I can't be certain, but it's supposed to be Wednesday of next week."

That was six days away, which should be fine. Henry watched her.

"I have some meth if you want to have something more to tide you over," he said.

She raised her hand as if she were pushing the meth away. "No, I don't do meth."

"Wise woman." He looked down at the bag. "That'll be one fifty."

She reached into her backpack and pulled out her wallet. The cost was about half of what she'd pay in Chicago. Maybe her current salary would cover her drugs. She paid him and stood to put her jacket on. "Thank you, Henry. You've really helped me. What's the best way to get in touch with you next week?"

"Grab your phone and I'll send you my cell number. You can call me, but never say anything specific on the phone. You're smart enough to remember that."

He saw her out the door and Clare took a deep breath of the cold air. The walk to her car was refreshing. The terrible stress of where to find a regular supply was lifted like a yoke off an ox. Henry was patronizing and judgmental, but he was a source. That was all that mattered.

## CHAPTER SEVEN

Freya and Ben walked into their tiny office following a brief meeting with the sheriff to bring him up to speed on their investigation. She knew that working with local law enforcement was often confrontational, the fight for jurisdiction seeming to be a matter of honor rather than anything having to do with effective investigations. But the sheriff, Mark Phillips, welcomed the help in trying to control drug activity in his county. He was young, college educated, and knew the limits of his department. He vowed to assist the state police in their operations. In return, they made the sheriff an official part of their task force on drugs. It was all working out well.

Ben leaned back in his chair and pushed the door to their office closed. Freya drank her coffee. He pulled a pad of paper in front of him and looked at her.

"We've got the phone conference with the lieutenant at three. We need to figure out what and how to report to him."

"We report everything. Don't we?" she said.

He leaned toward her. "I'm not looking forward to telling him the undercover operation was blown."

She shrugged. "It happened. We have to tell him." She unwrapped a cherry Danish and took a huge bite.

"I know. I was wondering if there was any spin we could put on it."

She looked at him curiously while she finished chewing. "Here's the spin—both our man Jason and Morgan had good intel.

Real information that changes everything. We're much closer to identifying those who are running drug distribution in the area than we were before."

During their interrogation the night before, Morgan said he'd been approached by a man who told him he was now going to sell exclusively to a group of businessmen. He had to conform his lab to their standards and the man had given him supplies, ingredients, and a day's training on how to cook meth and maintain a laboratory. All he knew about the man was he arrived once a week to pick up product. Morgan's other buyers were pissed he'd stopped selling to them.

"You're right," Ben said. We knew there were several major players in the area, but a cartel? Are we in Columbia?"

"Cartel might be too big a word for what's going on here. One thing it will do for us is clear out the small meth labs all over the place. They want a monopoly on production. That'll leave us with clearer targets." She took another bite of the Danish.

"If we can identify the members, that is," Ben said. "I'm worried the level of violence will go way up. Look how scared Morgan was when we interviewed him. He was terrified."

"He was. He has more information to give us. I'm supposed to talk to the state's attorney at eleven thirty to see if we can offer him a deal. Maybe that'll help his recollection."

Ben opened the door. The little office had quickly become stuffy and overheated. "Why don't you take lead on the phone call this afternoon?"

She was surprised. Usually Ben liked to be the face of the task force whenever possible. "Why?"

"You sound more optimistic than I do."

She settled in to make notes for the conference call. She saw that Ben was alarmed at the idea of taking down a big organization. She should be too. They could call in the DEA and give the case away, but the challenge was too alluring. She tried not to think about the fact that even if they did take down the organization, it would only briefly interrupt drug sales in the surrounding rural counties. Meth labs would spring up like dandelions and they'd soon be back to where they were now. If she thought about that, she'd not be able to go to work every morning. She could have been a lawyer. She took all the pre-law courses in college and her LSAT scores were good. But the promise of action drew her to law enforcement. She hadn't anticipated how frustrating it would be.

At eleven thirty, she walked to the nearby courthouse. There were entrances to the building on all four sides, each leading to the rotunda inside. Two of the entrances were closed off and the other two had sheriff's deputies manning security posts. She breezed by the guard and into the rotunda, up the grand staircase to the second floor where the state's attorney was.

Don Golubivic's office was at the end of the hallway that ran behind the large reception room. On her way there she passed a couple of offices occupied by assistant state's attorneys. One of them was Lorell Stoker, who was the first stop Freya should have made. She bypassed Lorell to get to Don who was the top dog. She wanted to get a quick decision on what they could offer their witness to induce him to give up more. She knocked on his closed office door and went in. Don sat at a desk overrun with files and boxes and he looked a little harassed when he glanced up at her. He was middle-aged and gaunt, his love of running having turned into a bad habit.

"Freya Saucedo. What a great way to start the week," he said. Surprisingly, he seemed to really mean it.

"Thanks. You may not think so after I tell you why I'm here."

He gestured her to the chair in front of the desk. "Let me hear it." He took a drink from his ISU coffee mug.

"We talked to the guy we busted at the meth lab last night. He's tipped us to the fact he sells his product exclusively to one buyer and he's heard that buyer is part of a larger organization. I think our drug problem is a lot bigger than we thought."

He placed the tips of his fingers together and nodded, like a priest handing out a benediction. "You want a deal? Isn't it a bit soon to offer one?"

"We need names and Morgan isn't motivated enough to give them to us. I'm asking that you drop all charges in exchange for his giving us those names."

He leaned back in his chair. "I'm fine with that. Another dude in prison doesn't advance our game much. I'll tell Lorell to expect your call."

Freya walked out before he could change his mind. He hadn't seemed particularly concerned about the amount of drug trade in his jurisdiction, probably because he was moving on soon to private practice. Twenty minutes later, she and Ben were in the interview room with Morgan. He looked rough after his night in jail, but not much worse than he looked the night before. He was clearly a prime consumer of his own product. His thin face made his brown eyes appear to bug out and the skin was peppered with acne. His stringy hair was combed straight back from his forehead and fell in greasy clumps to his shoulders. He was with his court appointed lawyer after having been arraigned earlier in the day.

"My client wants a deal," David Ricketts said. He sounded unenthusiastic, like a government clerk in his fortieth year of service, though he appeared to be under thirty years old.

"I'm sure he wants a deal," Freya said. "With two previous tags, he'll be making a return trip to Pontiac."

"My client is in fear for his life. In exchange for the extent of what he knows, we want the charges dropped and entry into a witness protection program."

"Let me see what the DA's office says," Freya said. They stepped out in the hall.

"You've got the okay to drop the charges, but it's a no-go on witness protection. This is Timson County, not the FBI," Ben said.

"I suppose we could see if the state would provide witness protection."

"Forget it. I don't want to use up our resources on this guy. Let him run if he's scared he's going to get killed."

"You're all heart, Ben. Let's hear what he says before saying no."

He turned quickly to re-enter the interview room, a quick flash of annoyance on his face. He never liked it when they disagreed. They settled into their chairs facing Morgan and his lawyer.

"If your client has quality information, we have authorization to drop all charges," Ben said.

"And the witness protection?"

Freya pulled her notebook out and picked up a pen. "That all depends on how helpful he is."

"I'm not saying anything until I get protection," Morgan said. A front tooth was missing, making his words slightly sibilant.

"Fine. Then you're right back to the manufacturing charge."

There was a silence as Morgan considered his options. If he betrayed his customer, he'd be a sitting duck for retribution once he was in prison.

"Fuck it," he said. "I hardly know anything."

"Give me the name of the person you sell your product to," Ben said.

"He goes by Stingy."

"His real name."

"The fuck if I know. I know him as Stingy. He buys anything I make and pays me a bonus for not selling to anyone else."

"And do you sell to anyone else?"

"Hell no. He made it pretty clear he has the muscle to mess me up if they find me selling elsewhere."

"What did Stingy say, exactly," Freya said. "Who's the muscle?"

Morgan shifted in his seat and looked at his attorney, who nodded for him to continue. "All I know is there's three different guys. Stingy said they have a big organization and plenty of ways to keep everyone in line. And that's it, man."

"What are the names of these three men?"

"You think they're going to let someone like me know that?"

"How do you get hold of Stingy?"

"I don't. He calls me every Monday and says he'll pick up product on Thursday. I mean, I don't sell to him every week. Sometimes they don't need it, and sometimes my batches don't come out too good."

"I can only imagine," Freya said. They drilled him with more questions until satisfied he had no more to tell. She looked at Ricketts, who appeared half asleep. "We'll drop the charges against your client."

"Right on," Morgan said.

"But no witness protection. There's nothing holding you here. If you're truly afraid of reprisals, I'd suggest you leave town." She pushed back from the table and led the way out the door.

They left the jail to return to their office. "That's good intel. Now we know the scope of the organization," he said.

"Now all we have to do is find Stingy."

He popped a stick of cinnamon gum in his mouth. "Piece of cake."

Clare and Elizabeth went through the rear door of the office into the firm's parking lot. Elizabeth unlocked her Lexus GS with her fob and Clare got in. She glanced around the other cars in the lot—two SUVs, an Audi, and a Mercedes E 300. It seemed the lawyers of Nelson & Nelson spent their money the same as city lawyers did. She wondered if the other associates were as laden with student debt as she was. Between student loan payments, rent, and her drug supply, a used Subaru was a stretch.

Elizabeth pulled out of the lot and headed to the Peterson Agricultural property where the methane lagoon swallowed up Mr. Oleg. She drove west onto Woodlawn Avenue, the commercial strip in town where everyone did their shopping. As the county seat, Money Creek drew shoppers from the large surrounding rural area, which rated them a Target in addition to a Walmart. Elizabeth pulled up at a light in front of a huge Kroger grocery store.

"Have you gotten familiar with the town yet?" Elizabeth said, glancing at Clare. She was relaxed at the wheel, the sunglasses she'd slipped on giving her a flashy, out-of-the-office look she hadn't seen before.

"I'm comfortable along this strip, but still get confused in the streets around downtown."

"It'll be back of your hand before you know it. There isn't much to remember once you get the hang of it." Elizabeth accelerated onto the interstate and drove south. "The farm is about a twenty-minute drive, so why don't you tell me where you're at in the document production."

Clare shifted in her seat. She was completely on top of things—up to speed on the case file and comfortably in charge of the documents.

"Jo and I are working our way through. I'm sifting through correspondence and she's looking for any prior incidents with the faulty gate."

Elizabeth nodded. "That would kick up the punitive damages about threefold. Keep your eyes peeled."

She usually found it irritating when bosses told you to do the very thing you just said you're doing, as if they'd thought up the idea. But she was inclined to like Elizabeth and gave her the benefit of the doubt. She was about as opposite of Carlton Henning as was possible.

"How is it going with Jo?" Elizabeth asked. "Is she helping you? Giving you attitude? She has a perfectly nice side to her, but can be a little prickly."

"She seems completely neutral—neither friendly nor unfriendly. She knows what she's doing, so she's a big help. We should be done by next week." So far, Jo had remained aloof around Clare and kept their talk strictly to business, which was fine with her.

She looked out the window as the car sped silently along the highway. Everywhere she looked were empty fields, waiting for the spring planting of corn and soybeans. It seemed endless. She thought about living in an area whose whole purpose was to feed the country and in many ways was more profoundly important than anywhere else. She found her attitude adjusting from judging the area as unsophisticated to appreciating the perfect function it served.

Elizabeth exited the interstate and drove for another ten minutes along rural roads. She stuck to talking about the trial preparation for the case, not interested in grilling Clare about her personal life, which was no small blessing. She pulled into a gravel lot that fronted a squat brick building. It was nearly surrounded by more empty fields as far as she could see. Inside the building was a front room with two desks and a dozen file cabinets. They could hear what sounded like a large machine running behind the room. A man sat at one of the desks.

"Hey, Mrs. Nelson," he said, getting to his feet. He was around retirement age, dressed in jeans with suspenders. "I didn't expect to see you today."

"I'm here to show the lagoon to my new associate, Charlie. You don't have to come with." Elizabeth said the last with some emphasis.

"Whatever you say," he said, sinking back into his chair. He turned to the papers on his desk as Elizabeth and Clare walked out of the building toward the lagoon in back. Clare had a hard time taking in what she was seeing. There were about three acres holding an octagonal shaped pond covered by a tarp. Pipelines ran both vertically and horizontally through the lagoon, leading toward an enormous tank that then led to the rear part of the brick building. A cement ledge ran around the pond's circumference with a metal railing acting as a safety fence. She expected to be overpowered by the smell of animal waste, but it was minimal.

"I don't understand," Clare said. "How did Oleg die falling into a tarp?"

"After the accident they decided to finally spend the money on covering the lagoon, as most of the larger farms had already done. This was wide open when Oleg fell in and the gate's been since removed. He fell face first and died before anyone got to him."

"Seems to me putting the tarp on is acknowledgement of the previous danger," Clare said. She gingerly followed Elizabeth up a short ladder to the four-foot-wide ledge. Tarp or not, she didn't want to fall in.

"We're hoping a jury will find they didn't know of the danger at the time." They stared at the huge lagoon for a few moments. Elizabeth looked at her. "Do you understand more how the accident happened?"

"This helps a lot. Was anyone in the building when he fell in?"

"Charlie was working that day. He called for an ambulance when the other man ran into the building to let him know what happened and went into the lagoon to save Oleg, but it was too late."

They walked to Elizabeth's car and started the drive back.

"Are you looking forward to the party tomorrow night?" Elizabeth said.

Clare had been trying to forget about the party the Nelsons were throwing on Friday night to mark her signing on with the firm. She couldn't absorb the trouble they were taking to make her feel welcome. All week, Elizabeth and Hank had been going out of their way to include her in the firm's activity. They took her to lunch with the other associates, introduced her to clients, had her sit in on conferences on other cases. As a lawyer she was thrilled with being made such a part of the firm. It was so differentfrom being a mere cog at Dearborn Pike. But it was almost overwhelming. So much attention also meant scrutiny. She couldn't withstand much scrutiny.

"I'll be there," Clare said, trying to sound cheerful.

"I know you just got to town, but feel free to bring a date. Everyone's significant other will be there."

Clare almost laughed. "A date? I'm afraid I don't operate that quickly."

"Did you leave anyone behind in Chicago?" Elizabeth sounded more conversational than nosy.

"Nope. I'm about as single as you can get."

"I don't think that will last very long."

"It will if I have anything to say about it," she said lightly. "There's been enough change in my life recently."

Elizabeth turned into the town square. "You're young. You'll adapt quickly. My main concern is you're happy with your work."

"Oh, I am. Thank you so much for giving me this opportunity." She didn't have to fake her enthusiasm. She knew she was lucky to have ended up with someone like Elizabeth. For the first time, she felt she had a future.

They stopped for lunch at the Lincoln Diner and Clare struggled to eat a respectable amount of her salad. It seemed like no matter how much she ate, the salad still filled the bowl. Her appetite was suppressed, as usual. She had to work to keep her weight up when she was using speed, which was basically all the time. Maybe she'd lay off speed tomorrow so she'd have an appetite at the dinner party.

That was a situation that called more for Valium than anything amping her up.

Back at the office, Clare settled into the empty case room and began reading where she'd left off. Jo walked in carrying a cup of coffee and sat at the other end of the table without saying a word. What was it with this woman? Was she socially inept or did she actively dislike Clare?

"Hi, Jo. Did you grab some lunch?"

Jo looked at her in surprise. "Yeah, I always bring my lunch to work."

"That's a good way to control what you eat, nutrition wise, I mean. It's not like you have to watch what you eat." Oh, God, she was fumbling her way further from Jo's good graces.

"It's also a good way to save money," Jo said. "I don't get paid like an associate." She turned back to her documents.

Was that it? She was resentful that lawyers made more than paralegals? Welcome to reality, Jo. Go to law school for three years and then bring up equal pay. They were currently doing the same job, but the responsibility for it was on Clare's shoulders. The decisions as to relevancy and attorney privilege were hers to make. She didn't understand why Jo would take this out on her.

Clare stayed silent and went on with her work. At length, she said, "Are you going to the party at the Nelsons' tomorrow night?" She sounded like she really cared if Jo went, when in fact it would be great if she didn't.

Jo relaxed a little. "The Nelsons give great parties. I wouldn't miss it."

"Elizabeth told me I could bring a date, which is laughable. I don't know anyone. Are you bringing someone?"

"I'm bringing my girlfriend, Freya." She looked at Clare as if expecting a reaction to that, as if she didn't come from Chicago, where there were more gay people living in her neighborhood than the entire population of Money Creek.

"That's great. How long have you been together?"

Jo smiled at her for the first time. This was something she wanted to talk about. "Only three months. It's new, but I think it's the real deal."

"Lucky you," Clare said. She tried to keep things going. "What does Freya do?"

"She's a cop. Illinois State Police detective."

"Really?" Clare said, as if Jo had told her she's a troll under the bridge.

Jo laughed. "Really. She and her partner are stationed here while they work on their drug task force, but she lives in Bloomington."

Drug task force? That didn't sound good. She kept a neutral expression. "Wow. I think the most exciting person I ever dated was a cameraman at Wrigley Field. Does she ever tell you about her work?"

"She can't, really, not that I'd betray a confidence. I get the broad outlines, but no details," Jo said. She took a sip of her coffee and turned back to her work.

"I'm looking forward to meeting her."

Jo looked at her again. "What's your story? Straight? Gay?" Apparently, the floodgates were now open.

"Straight. Boring." Clare leaned back in her chair. She was always uncomfortable when this question was asked of her, which seemed to be frequently. Did she even know if she was straight or gay? She slept with men, and what little bit of dating she did was with men. But an interesting woman could occupy her thoughts, make her want more. She'd been too stressed and busy since law school started to do much more than think about it. Too timid. Maybe now that she lived in Money Creek it would become clear, though there couldn't be that many lesbians in town to help her figure it out. Jo might be one of the only two, thrown together out of sheer necessity. She wasn't about to share her complicated sexual identity with her.

Jo laughed. "That's a funny way to describe it, not that I disagree with you. I'll keep my eyes peeled for any non-boring men I come across."

"Please don't," Clare said quickly. "I don't think I can handle anything else new right now."

They both picked up their documents and started to read. The atmosphere was relaxed, at least compared to previously. Nothing like a little talk about romance to thaw the air. Jo left for the day at five, along with the rest of the staff and most of the lawyers. When she went to the break room to get a LaCroix, she saw the lights still on in both Elizabeth's and Hank's offices. No harm in working late to impress the bosses. The documents were incredibly boring and she wanted to stop, but what came after work seemed worse than continuing it. She'd spent every evening at home, cooking dinner, watching Netflix, reading. Not a bad way to spend an evening, but not every evening. Her life outside of work spun out in front of her in a monotonous fashion, and it made her nervous.

Hank and Elizabeth left at six. Hank ducked his head into the document room and told her not to burn herself out, which was comical given the hours she used to work. She stayed another hour before locking up and walking home in the cold air.

She knew she was going to have to learn to cook. There was no Thai restaurant on the corner, no Grubhub to deliver her dinner. She could drive out to Woodlawn Avenue every evening for her choice of Olive Garden or Red Lobster, but the thought depressed her. She'd stocked her kitchen with chicken and steak and vegetables, along with a fair number of frozen dinners, and cobbled together some meals with the help of internet recipes.

She changed into jeans and a long sleeve T-shirt, her moccasins on her feet. Her house was neat, the kitchen sparkling. She pulled a steak out of the fridge, along with some green beans. She snapped the beans and washed them in a colander before putting them in a pan on the stove to steam. Then she seasoned the steak and threw it onto a grill pan at a high temperature. This, she'd learned, would sear the steak and lock in the juices. Who knew? She set the table, and when the dinner was done sat down with a copy of the *New Yorker* by her plate. She hadn't eaten since breakfast. She enjoyed the food, found some satisfaction in having cooked it. The idea that this is what normal people did made her feel safe somehow. As if the trappings of a home life would make her content with one. She wanted to be normal, without the chaos of her former life. But it was a little dull.

She washed the dishes and saw it was only eight o'clock, a full three hours until her bedtime. She thought of calling one of her few friends in Chicago, but couldn't get over her irritation that no one had called her since she moved. She decided to go for a drink. She needed to start making friends. She only knew of one bar in town because she passed it on her way to work every day. Abe's Tavern was located in a storefront on a street off the town square. Its old-fashioned neon beer signs for Pabst Blue Ribbon and Old Style had attracted her each evening as she walked home, but she'd not yet stopped in. She bundled into her down coat and walked toward the tavern. When she got downtown she saw the glow of the bar in the dark, a beacon to anyone needing to be with people, strangers even, to feel a part of something.

She pulled the door open and saw the drinkers at the bar turn to see who'd come in and turn back to their drinks, an autonomic response to the sound of the door creaking. The long, rectangular room had several empty stools at the bar. The right side was filled with scarred wood tables. At the far end were two pool tables with a small crowd gathered around them. The room smelled like burgers and fries, and about half the tables were filled, some with families with children. Clare sat at the bar.

The bartender approached and wiped the space in front of her. "You're new here," he said matter-of-factly. "What can I get you?" His smile was friendly.

Clare pulled her wallet out of her jacket pocket. "Give me a shot of Four Roses and a beer back. I don't care what beer." He brought her the drinks and took her money, remaining in front of her as if expecting more.

"I'm Clare. I just moved here last week." She took a sip of beer and hoped he'd stay to talk longer.

He stuck his hand out across the bar. "I'm Danny. I own the place. Where did you move from?"

"Chicago. North side."

"Go Cubs," he said with a smile. "Why Money Creek?" Danny looked to be in his forties. He wore an ISU sweatshirt and jeans and had a thick wedding ring on his finger.

"I took a job with a law firm."

"You're a lawyer?" He sounded genuinely surprised. Maybe they didn't get many of the professional classes in the bar. "I never would have guessed."

"Why? Because I'm young?" She smiled, keeping it conversational. She was trying to figure out what was unlawyerly about her, other than everything.

"I suppose that's it. We love having new young people in town." What was the average age in Money Creek? Usually her age was something used to make her feel inadequate, especially in the practice of law. Lack of experience, seasoning, common sense. Money Creek must be like so many small towns where the young people move out and only the rare few move in.

Country music blared from the jukebox, and she tried not to cringe. She generally disparaged the genre, though she knew nothing about it. She needed an open mind or she wouldn't be at all happy in Money Creek. Hunting, country music, lots of churches—she'd have to get used to it all.

Danny took care of another customer and then wandered back. "We have bands here Friday and Saturday nights. You should check it out if you're looking for something to do."

She looked at him brightly. "I might do that. How else do people entertain themselves in this town?"

"Oh, you know. Drinking. There's a car track west of town and folks like watching the races. Lots of parties. Most stay in and watch cable these days, but there is a movie theater."

God. What was she going to do here? She needed a hobby. Maybe painting. She'd always wanted to try that, though there was no evidence she was the least bit talented. Genealogy? Building doll house furniture? There were no pastimes that jumped out at her. She ordered another shot. A man climbed onto the stool next to her and Danny turned to him with a smile. "Hey, Ben. How you doing, man?"

Ben reached across the bar and their hands slapped together with a loud crack before they shook. Danny brought him a beer and a bag of peanuts while Clare looked down at her drink.

"This is Clare," Danny said. "She's brand new in town."

Ben was very good-looking, with thick wavy hair that was nearly black, a long, slender build, dark eyes under thick lashes, and features just off kilter enough to be interesting. He turned to her with a smile. "Welcome to Money Creek."

Clare met his eyes and looked for that spark of interest that meant she'd have to handle him in some way—either ward him off or reel him in. She didn't see any. "Thanks. This is my first time in Abe's. Are you a regular?"

He looked amused. "I'm pretty lightweight with the drinking, but I stop by often so Danny doesn't worry about me."

Danny pointed at Ben while he addressed Clare. "He's a heartbreaker. Consider yourself warned."

Clare drank her Pabst and watched as they exchanged a little news before Danny moved down the bar again. Ben picked up his beer for the first time and drank a small amount. Definitely not a guzzler. She took a sip of her own beer and left her shot of bourbon untouched. She was tired and her spirits were starting to slump. The speed she'd taken that morning had worn off. But she was interested in talking to Ben. She wanted to see if he was going to try to break her heart. She told him she'd moved to town to work at Nelson & Nelson.

"You're the one Elizabeth's throwing a party for," Ben said, not at all amazed, though Clare certainly was. Who all was coming to this party?

"I wish she wasn't doing that. It makes me self-conscious."

"It's a good thing, really. If you're new here people are going to notice you. It's better to have a jump on getting to know them. Besides, the Nelsons throw a good party."

She smiled. "I've heard."

"Here's a tip, though. Don't let Danny know you're working for the Nelsons. His uncle is the man that died in that slurry lagoon. He's not a big fan right now."

The town was even smaller than she thought. Everyone knew or was related to everyone else. It made her uncomfortable saying anything to anyone, afraid it would get back to the wrong person. She picked up her bourbon and sipped. "Danny will find out eventually. Seems like there are no secrets in this town." She thought of what Henry had threatened. Would her drug use remain a secret?

He tipped his beer toward her. "It sure feels that way sometimes."

"Do you know the Nelsons well?"

He opened his bag of beer nuts and offered them to her. She took a handful. "Anyone connected with the law knows the Nelsons. They're the premier law firm around here, and they make it their business to know everyone. They're good people."

Clare nodded agreement because it certainly seemed to be true. "What do you do that's connected to the law? Are you a lawyer as well?"

"Hell, no," he laughed. "If I had to defend some of the scumbags I help arrest I'd kill myself."

"You're a cop?"

"Yeah. I'm a detective with the Illinois State Police."

"You're the second state cop I've heard mentioned. Do you know a woman named Freya?"

Ben laughed. "I know her very well. She's my partner." Of course, she was.

"I don't understand. I thought there was a sheriff's department in Timson County. Do you work with them?" She sipped her bourbon.

"I'm actually stationed out of Bloomington where the ISP has a post. We're here as part of a task force on drug activity in the area."

This wasn't good at all. Clare had officially become part of the drug activity in the area. Did they know about Henry? Was he under surveillance?"

"Where are you from?"

"Chicago."

"The city has every kind of drug imaginable, while here we're mainly after meth and Oxycontin suppliers. They operate over hundreds of miles of rural land. It's not easy pinpointing any dealers of significance. They have retreats so far hidden down tiny rural roads that we have no way of finding them."

"Sounds like it's hard to be successful at what you do," she said, hoping it was true.

He shrugged. "We regularly take down small meth operations, the kind that often blow themselves up and do the job for us. But let's not talk about work. That's all cops do and it's refreshing to hear from someone else." He was turned fully toward her, but she could tell he was a gentleman, the kind that wouldn't make a move unless he clearly got a signal from her. Did she want to send one? Her heart wasn't in it. Besides, a relationship with a cop would be among the stupider things she could do, and she could do plenty of stupid things. She drank the rest of her bourbon and reached for her jacket.

"Sorry I can't chat longer. It's a school night."

"Understood. I'll see you tomorrow at the Nelsons'. It was nice to meet you, Clare."

She shook his hand and headed toward the door, waving to Danny as she passed. The blast of cold air that greeted her outdoors was a balm. She'd found herself getting overheated inside from the closeness of bodies, an overactive furnace, and the reality of now knowing a cop on a drug task force. Of all the things. She got home and took a look at her stash. She'd have to quit when it ran out. Continuing to buy was too dangerous now that her name and face were known to the state coppers. And that was what she meant to do anyway, wasn't it?

# Chapter Eight

Clare stared at her closet, trying to select something for the Nelsons' party. Her work clothes were too stiff and her casual clothes were too casual. More tavern wear than party wear. She went into her sweater drawer and found a wrinkled blue knit tunic. She steamed it while taking a shower and then paired it with the expensive jeans she'd bought cheap at a consignment shop. She pulled on her Frye boots, put earrings and a necklace on, and looked in the mirror. Not bad. She applied a little eye makeup, a hint of blush, and a touch of perfume. It would have to do.

The party started in half an hour. She wasn't sure what the etiquette was in Money Creek—did one arrive on time or fashionably late? Was there a different rule when the party was being thrown in her honor? It seemed a lot of fuss and focused entirely too much attention on her. Her tastes ran from dark tavern to dark apartment. A cheery home, nice people, normal family, generosity—the Nelsons disturbed her equilibrium. Her bombastic mother and silent father taught her to keep her head low. She knew the Nelsons had a son, and she imagined them as parents—engaged, curious, protective. Her eyes stung.

She took two tablets of Valium, knowing that would calm her without intoxicating her—as long as she stayed away from too much booze. Her biggest fear was to act foolishly at the party. At seven, she left for the five-minute walk to the Nelsons'. As she walked up Oak Street, the houses started to get larger, the front yards expansive, the architecture elaborate. Enormous oak trees loomed along the street, dimly lit by pseudo-Victorian gas lamps, so unlike the blazing phosphorescent streetlights in Chicago. When she reached the Nelsons', she wasn't at all surprised to see a massive Victorian house, painted a fresh olive green with black shutters and a deep red door.

The door swung open before she could ring, and Hank Nelson pushed the screen door out to let her enter. "There she is! Now the party can start." He gave her a hug and she wrapped her arms tentatively around his broad back. "Let me take your coat," he said as he stepped away. She stood awkwardly in the foyer as he hung it in the closet. She could see some people gathered in the living room to the right of the entry. To her left was a large dining room with a table set for for a crowd. A floral centerpiece spread across the middle of the table, which had multiple wine glasses at each setting. She saw Elizabeth emerge from that direction, a warm smile creasing her face when she saw Clare.

"Welcome, Clare. We're so glad to have you here, aren't we, Hank?"

"Before we lose you to the rest of the party," he said, "we wanted you to know how pleased we are you've come to work at our firm. We already can see what quality of lawyer you are. We're lucky to have you."

Clare blushed, unused as she was to hearing compliments. "I'm the lucky one," she said. "Thank you so much for taking me on. I won't disappoint you."

Elizabeth took her by the elbow and headed to the living room. "I'm sure you already know some of the people here, but let me introduce you around." The room was a large square, centered on a hearth big enough to roast a pig. Several people were arrayed in front of it. Her next-door neighbor Sally, who was the county's recorder of deeds, was one. She'd introduced herself on the day she'd moved into her house. There was the county clerk, the county treasurer, the sheriff and Ben. Elizabeth introduced her to each one, and she promptly forgot each of their names.

"There are a bunch of people in the kitchen, naturally," Elizabeth said. "I'm going to shoo them out here. What can I bring you to drink?"

"A beer, please." Clare wanted to grab Elizabeth's arm and follow her out of the room. She was shy about talking to Ben, but the others were an even greater challenge. Hank let in a woman she'd not seen before who made her way to Ben's side. She had long dark hair kept back in a ponytail, an athletic build, and a tentative smile. She felt a flicker of attraction and wondered if she was Ben's girlfriend. He brought her over.

"Clare, it's nice to see you again," he said.

"You too. Have you taken down any meth labs since I last saw you?" She smiled, pleased to have mentioned something that he'd told her in their previous conversation, demonstrating how attentive she'd been. But Ben's face colored, and the woman he was with turned and gave him a funny look. She then turned back to Clare and extended her hand.

"I'm Freya Saucedo," she said. "I work with Ben." Jo's girlfriend. That made things interesting.

Clare realized it probably looked like Ben had been talking out of school with her. "Ben didn't tell me anything the other night, only that he's on a drug task force. I don't want you to think he spilled any secrets." She realized she was making things worse. "I take it you're Ben's partner?"

"That's right." Freya looked her in the eye. "I heard about the new lawyer at the Nelsons. I'm glad I got invited."

"Does your girlfriend work there by chance?"

Freya looked surprised. "Do you mean Jo?"

"Yes, she told me you'd be here." She had to give Jo credit for having a cool girlfriend.

Freya exuded self-confidence. Clare had always been attracted to assured, powerful women. She was dressed in jeans and boots, with a white cotton button-down shirt and thermal vest. She wore no makeup and Clare guessed her to be about thirty. Her tight ponytail attenuated the strong features of her face and her sparkling brown eyes. She was quite beautiful, with a slightly masculine edge Clare was drawn to. She looked like a woman Clare knew in law school who'd occupied her thoughts throughout her second year. Very distracting. She was beginning to rue that Freya was already in a relationship.

Elizabeth came back and handed Clare a beer. "Freya, Jo's in the kitchen if you want to see her."

They all looked at Freya, who turned to Clare and excused herself. Was that a hint of disappointment she'd seen in her face? More people came in the room, and Elizabeth maneuvered the crowd so they all faced Clare. They may as well have been a firing squad. With Ben still at her side, she somehow managed to make small talk and look like she was having a good time. One of the associates at the firm approached. Thomas was not much older than Clare, good-looking in a blond, surfer-boy way. He wore tight black jeans and black boots along with an expensive looking hoodie. It was a modified hipster look. He even smelled faintly of patchouli oil, or he'd smoked a joint on the way to the party. He seemed out of place in Money Creek, but then so did she. Could he be a misfit also? They worked together on the methane gas case and she was comfortable with him.

"I'll be done with that brief by Tuesday," Clare said, referring to her most recent assignment from Elizabeth. "I wouldn't mind if you took a look at it before I turned it in."

Thomas took a sip of whatever dark liquid filled his glass. Bourbon, Scotch? Rye was making a comeback. Whatever it was, she wanted some too, but didn't dare. She shuddered at the thought of what losing control could result in. What if she were so drunk she made a pass at Freya? Or worse, Elizabeth. Whatever was most inappropriate was what she'd most likely do.

"I can't imagine what I'd have to offer a hotshot lawyer like you," he said with a smile. "And anyway, we shouldn't talk about work. Elizabeth wouldn't like it."

"I never imagined working for a partner who made it her business to have me work less. That is so opposite from where I worked in Chicago."

"We're both lucky we landed here," he said. He was about to say more when Elizabeth reappeared and took Clare's arm. "Time for dinner, and I want to sit next to you." She looked at Thomas. "Are you coming, Thomas?"

"Certainly," he said. He looked amused.

Elizabeth led her into the kitchen, where a buffet was spread out on the giant granite island. The room didn't have the latest finishes. They were the next to the latest and still impressive. High-end appliances, elaborate vent hood, Italian cabinets. It looked very much like a Chicago luxury kitchen. It was starting to sink in that living in Money Creek didn't mean everything was Walmart and Menards. Wealth and taste ran the gamut here, same as they did in the city, but in a miniature frame.

A line had formed at the buffet, with Freya and Jo a few people ahead of Clare and Elizabeth. She watched them closely, curious about their relationship. Jo was behind Freya. She leaned forward and whispered something to Freya, who turned her head, her smile fading as she saw Clare. She said something briefly to Jo and turned around again. What was that? Why did she stop smiling when she saw her?

After she joined the others at the dining room table, Clare relaxed some—the food and wine gave her something to focus on and talk about. The smell of rosemary wafted up from the pork tenderloin on her plate. Her wine glass was full of a wonderful shiraz, and she was enjoying every tiny sip. Elizabeth was on one side of her, Ben had somehow maneuvered himself to the other, and Jo and Freya were across the table. Freya was busy talking to the sheriff on her other side while Jo quietly ate her dinner and didn't look up from her plate.

Clare turned to Elizabeth and saw her looking toward the entrance hall with bright eyes. She followed her gaze and dropped her fork. Henry stood at the entrance to the dining room, wearing a long black coat and scarlet scarf. He was smiling apologetically as Elizabeth waved him over. It was everything she could do to keep her expression neutral. Henry saw her and did not react.

"Henry, you fox," Elizabeth said. "I didn't think you'd make it tonight."

"I didn't think so either, but then I became curious about your new associate."

"Well, here she is. Meet Clare Lehane. This is my son, Henry."

He winked as he shook her hand and pretended to never have seen her before. Why should she be surprised her drug dealer was the son of her boss? Why not? That's how small the town was.

"Henry's in his senior year at the college here." She smiled up at him. "We'll have him around only a short while longer."

"What happens then?" Clare said.

"You'll have to ask him, but I can't expect him to stay in Money Creek."

"I'm sure Miss Lehane isn't interested in all that, Mother." He turned to Clare. "I'll leave you to your dinner. Perhaps we can chat afterward?"

What twenty-year-old kid called anyone "Miss"? Or talked like he's attending Cambridge instead of Money Creek College. "Of course," she said. "I look forward to it."

Henry moved away and Elizabeth turned to talk to her.

"I'm so glad Henry showed up," she said. "I wanted you to meet him."

"He seems charming. Are you close?"

"Very. He's our only child, so we dote on him." She glanced down the table where Henry was taking a seat.

"He certainly is well-mannered," Clare said, hopefully without irony.

Elizabeth laughed. "He watches too much British TV. It's rubbed off on him." Then she turned to the person on her other side.

"More wine?" She looked up to see Freya leaning across the table with a bottle in her hand. She knew she should put her hand over her glass, but she let Freya pour. She hardly felt the Valium she'd taken, and her level of anxiety had just been kicked up with the appearance of Henry. Freya sat and leaned forward across the table. She wore a bold smile. It seemed she was about to say something when Jo interrupted her.

"Let's take our plates in and get some coffee," she said. She ignored Clare, who didn't miss the expectant way she stood and took Freya's plate, waiting until she rose to join her. Freya looked once more at her and smiled apologetically. Clare didn't sense the slightest connection between Jo and Freya. She wondered how much of a relationship they really had.

After the meal, she found herself standing in the large kitchen with a cup of coffee, which she'd surely regret when it was time for sleep. But she wanted a prop in her hand. Henry made a beeline to her after depositing his plate.

"Hello, Clare. Are you surprised to see me?" He looked smug. He knew all along he'd see her at the party but wanted to surprise her, and not in a good way. Her uneasiness about Henry grew deeper.

"This is messed up. I don't know whether I can do business with you." Who was she kidding? Uneasy or not, she wasn't about to cut ties with the only dealer she was likely to find in town. But it was better if Henry didn't know that.

"It'll be okay. I'm still willing to sell if you're interested in buying. No one has to know. I don't think either of us is going to tell my mother."

She looked at him, considering the situation. "I suppose that's true. I have to be careful."

"Of course. We always have to be careful."

Clare looked across the room and saw Elizabeth watching them with a smile on her face. She waved at her. "Do you know how long your mother would expect me to stay at the party? My nerves are shot."

Henry laughed. "I have a joint we can share, if that'll help calm you."

"That's all I need. Elizabeth would smell the weed in a second. Do you have anything else?" She looked at him hopefully. Some kind of downer would be very welcome.

"Only some mushrooms."

"Mushrooms? I don't think so."

Henry raised his hands. "Understood. I think if you go and have one more conversation with my mother, she'd be fine with you leaving. People will start heading home soon anyway. This is an early to bed kind of crowd." He reached out his hand. "I'll look forward to seeing you again. I think we'll be great friends."

There was something creepy about Henry's exaggerated politeness, but she quickly thought past that to how she could get out of there. The only time Clare enjoyed a party was when she was drinking and drugging with abandon. No constraints, simply pleasure. Absent that, parties were like this one—something to flee as soon as possible. She was looking for an opening, a worm hole through which she could shoot herself out the door. As she walked toward Elizabeth she was waylaid by Freya, who held up her hands like she was stopping a train. Clare stood where she was.

"Sorry to intercept you. I wanted a chance to talk to you before you left," Freya said, relaxing her stance.

Clare looked around the room for Jo, her instinct telling her she wouldn't be happy to see her having a private conversation with her girlfriend. "What would you like to talk about?"

"Your boots, mainly. I've been looking for that style and haven't found them anywhere." Freya wasn't looking at Clare's boots. She was looking straight at her, trying to catch her eye.

"I got mine at a store in my neighborhood in Chicago. Alamo's. You could call them to see if they have them in stock. Or you could check the Frye website." It didn't seem likely that Freya couldn't figure out how to get the boots she wanted.

"Alamo's. I'll do that. What was your neighborhood like? I have to admit I don't know Chicago well."

Clare smiled at the thought of it. "It's great. Like a little village with its own unique shops. Diverse and liberal, which I liked a lot. You know your neighbors, see them at the coffee shops. Most of my friends live there."

"It must have been hard to leave," Freya said. "I mean, it doesn't sound like you were unhappy living there."

"Well, neighborhood isn't everything. There were many things that were easy to leave." She hoped she wouldn't have to enumerate them. Being fired and leaving Chicago on a whim weren't the things she wanted to share with Freya. "You live in a small town, so you probably know the things about a big city that aren't so attractive."

"Bloomington's no Chicago, but it's a lot bigger than here. It's a university town."

Clare wondered what Freya was leaving behind in Bloomington. Apparently, she was settled enough in Money Creek to get a local girlfriend. Jo was still not in sight.

"I was wondering if you'd like to have lunch or grab a drink sometime," Freya said.

She became still. What the hell? "What about Jo?"

Freya laughed. "What about her? I'm not asking you on a date." Clare's face colored. She found she couldn't say anything. It all seemed like a minefield. "Look, it's good to have someone new in town who's my age and has a brain in her head. I thought we could be friends."

"Of course. I didn't mean to presume anything," Clare said, looking down at her coveted Frye boots. "I work with Jo and didn't want her to think the wrong thing."

"Let me worry about Jo. Why don't I call you sometime and we'll see what happens?"

Clare saw Jo enter the room with two coats in her arms. "Sure. If you'd like. You'll have to excuse me, but I need to get home." Jo approached them just as Clare turned and sped out of the living room, intent on finding her coat and getting home to her safe house. And a stiff drink. In addition to everything else, she now had Freya to think about, and that didn't seem like a bad thing. She couldn't help but sense it was more than friendship she was interested in.

Henry got into his car to return to his apartment. Of the many dinners and parties he'd attended at his parents' home, this had been the most interesting. From the moment Evan brought Clare into his home, Henry was drawn to her. She reminded him of some of his customers at Princeton—pulled together, smart, sure of themselves. Unlike his customers at Money Creek College, who were, in a word, unsophisticated. He was forced to deal with the Money Creek students after being tossed out of Princeton following a drug charge.

His parents wanted him close to home after that, and so Henry returned to bide his time. It was a bitter fall from the Ivy League to a no-name college. His growing drug business in Money Creek kept him from going stir-crazy.

When he got home he saw Evan sprawled on the secondhand leather sofa that dominated the living room space. The smell of marijuana was redolent. Evan leaned toward the coffee table and squashed out the tiny roach in his hand. "Hey, man. How was the party?"

Henry shrugged off his long coat and hung it on a coatrack near the front door. "Good. Clare was there."

"Oh, wow. What was she like?" Evan was sitting up now, his unfocused eyes on Henry.

"Like?"

"You know. Was she friendly? Flirty?"

"She was definitely not flirty. I think she's in shock to learn her drug dealer is her boss's son. It's a lot to take in." Henry walked toward the kitchen and Evan followed. He grabbed a bottle of red wine from a case shoved into a corner of the room and poured some into a fine stemmed glass without offering any to Evan. They took a seat at the kitchen table. Textbooks and drug paraphernalia littered the center, and Henry started straightening up.

"Get this drug shit out of here. Haven't I said I don't want this out when we're not using it?"

Evan smiled and started sweeping up the rolling papers, pipe, and mirror. "Yes, Your Majesty."

Henry didn't smile back. Evan took the paraphernalia away and grabbed a beer on his way back. "What did Clare say?"

"I think her main concern was whether my being her boss's son meant she can't buy drugs from me anymore."

"I think she's pretty desperate for a connection. Who comes on campus without knowing anybody, randomly looking for a student to buy from?"

"And you were the first scruffy student she saw."

"I guess." Evan drank down half his bottle of beer.

"What I find interesting is now Clare and I both have something on each other. If I tell my mom about Clare, she's in big trouble."

"As in, her ass is fired."

Henry nodded. "Yes. And she hopes I'd be in big trouble if she tells her about me."

"Will you be?"

"Not much, I don't think. My parents already know I've been involved with drugs. If they heard I still am it wouldn't shock them."

"They'd be pissed off, though."

"Very pissed off. But what are they going to do? They're not going to turn me in to the cops. They want me to graduate from somewhere."

At Princeton he'd hung around some of the most well-connected young men in the country, people so rich they'd spend more in a weekend than most students spent all year. He wanted to keep up with them, but it was impossible, at least until his roommate hooked him up with a compromised physician who started to write prescriptions large enough for Henry to sell to others. The addled doctor drove a pickup truck bearing the sign: *Ernest Jeffries: Neurosurgery and Light Hauling.* He was not hard to manipulate. Henry discovered he was very good at growing a business. He expanded his product line to include cocaine, which solidified his new role as one of the most popular members of the group he was so desperate to be a part of. He was invited into one of the elite dining clubs, taken home for weekends in Newport and the Hamptons. Returning to life in Money Creek had been crushing.

Evan rolled his neck around until it popped. Henry scowled. Evan was a great right-hand man, but sometimes he annoyed the hell out of him. He cracked his knuckles and burped. "I kind of like Clare." Henry kept the scowl on his face until Evan looked at him and noticed. "What?"

"Don't get any ideas about Clare. She's not going to give you the time of day."

"Hey. I almost had her talked into sleeping with me if I introduced her to you."

Henry looked at him coldly. "You're disgusting."

Evan shrugged. "I thought better of it once we got here. But I'm pretty sure she would have done it."

"And that reflects well on you how? You really are a fool." He got up from the table and picked up the textbooks. "I'm going to my room. I'd rather not see you for a while."

Evan looked hurt and confused. "I didn't do anything, man."

"You tried to coerce a woman into having sex. That makes you a predator in my book."

"Predator?"

"Look it up and let's see how well you sleep tonight," he said as he left the kitchen. He heard Evan mutter, "I sleep fine." He got to his room and threw himself on the bed. The idea of Clare being coerced into sex disturbed him, but if he was honest with himself, he knew it was because it meant Clare would be with someone else. She interested him, and that was rare in Money Creek, where he'd known most of the people his whole life. He wondered whether she could return these sudden feelings of his, how he could encourage it.

## CHAPTER NINE

Clare finished doing the dishes after her dinner of roast chicken thighs with rosemary, lemon, and new potatoes. She'd sautéed some spinach on the side, being convinced she'd been lucky to not contract scurvy the way she used to eat.

She sat on her couch and turned on the TV to watch a couple more episodes of *Orange Is the New Black*. She'd power-watched the first season over the weekend, and by Wednesday was well into the second. It was woman-centric, which was so refreshing. She popped a Valium and sipped at a bourbon and snuggled down. Life wasn't too bad. Sometimes boring, but she could also feel surprisingly content. The shock from the week before of discovering Henry was Elizabeth's son had worn off. As long as he kept her supplied she could deal with the rest. Who said you have to like your drug dealer?

Her phone rang and she took the call.

"Clare, it's Henry Nelson." She wasn't upset to hear from him. Maybe he had news on the shipment of speed.

"Hello, Henry. I was going to call you soon."

"Good. Now that we have this special connection through my mother, I hope we can be friends."

"Don't you think your mother would be suspicious of a friendship between us? I must be five years older than you." Henry seemed surprisingly mature for his twenty years, but at that age a five-year difference was huge. "But you have what I want, so I'm stuck with you."

Henry laughed. "You wound me. I thought you'd like me a little more than that."

"I don't know you well enough to like you. You'll have to earn that." She knew she was being hard, but she didn't want to let him feel in control of the relationship.

"Maybe this will help. If you come over to my place now, I can offer you a special deal on a few products."

"Are you having a Mary Kay party?"

"You're a riot. It's Tupperware, not Mary Kay. Sheesh."

"I'm all settled in for the night. Does it have to be now?"

"I have other customers, you know. I'm doing you a favor giving you an early peek."

She couldn't yet feel the Valium in her system, but that would be a matter of a half hour or so. If she didn't have any more to drink, she should be okay on the road. "Okay. Can you give me the address? I don't remember it from when Evan walked me over there."

Henry gave her the address and hung up. She changed out of her sweats and then pulled out her pillbox, where she saw her dwindling supply. Ten minutes later, she was sitting in his neat living room, watching as he reached into a leather bag and pulled out several baggies full of pills. He tossed them on the coffee table.

"What's your pleasure? I got some Valium for you." He picked out one bag and put it in front of her. It contained small yellow pills with Roche imprinted on one side, the real pharmaceutical five milligram Valium. This was a vast improvement over the supply she usually ordered from online pharmacies. The bag was filled with at least a hundred pills. She tried to act cool, but her insides were jumping with excitement.

"Nice. I'll take what you have."

"Sold."

"What else?"

He showed her the bag of Adderall and a few ounces of marijuana. She took as much as he'd sell her, but passed on the weed. It had never been her thing. When he told her the price, she blanched. A thousand dollars was all of her ready cash. But she couldn't bring herself to pass up any of the quantity that now sat in a neat pile in front of her. She pushed aside the thought that she was supposed to be quitting. She asked Henry to let her pay the next day and he readily agreed, something that Casey rarely did. Her salary had gone from $175,000 a year to $70,000, but living in Money Creek was cheap and there were few things to spend her money on.

She put the plastic bags in the big pocket of her deep green coat. It was a coat built for Chicago winters, but she was discovering the weather was even harsher in this part of the state. It was five degrees out and windy, the sort of cold that froze her sinuses and hurt her eyeballs. She took a drink of the beer Henry had poured for her.

"This connection with your mother gives us both something to use on the other." She looked at him for confirmation.

"Maybe. Or it's something that binds us. It's all in how you look at it."

"True. But if it came out that you were dealing drugs, your parents would be devastated."

"Certainly. But my parents would still love me. They'd fire you."

"Bad for both of us, but there's no reason either of us would tell, is there?" she said.

"None at all. But you're right to bring it up. I look at you as a new and valued customer. I hope you'll never give me cause to tell my parents about you."

"What's that supposed to mean?" A prickle of fear came over her. Underneath Henry's polish and charm was a hard streak she'd need to be wary of. Should this even be surprising in a drug dealer? "I'm not planning on saying anything about you to anyone."

"Then we understand each other," he said, a smile back on his face.

"You're the only dealer I have."

"There are others, but they're not people you want to buy from. You're better off with me."

"What do you mean?"

"I can't cover the huge area around here. I'm not big enough. There are other dealers who share the same territory. They're not all upstanding individuals." Henry put the remainder of the drugs into his bag. "Most of them deal in crystal meth. I cover the college and town, so meth is far less in demand."

He stood up to end the meeting and Clare rose to put her coat on. She couldn't quite get a handle on Henry. His tone was friendly, but he carried a big stick to whack her with if he had a mind to. It hung like a threat over her head, like Carlton Henning's voice. As she drove home she noticed the Valium starting to flow through her system, a feeling of well-being so calming she stopped thinking of the problem of Henry Nelson altogether. She decided to stop at the Shell station to pick up a six-pack of beer. When she reached the door of the store, Freya walked out and stopped short when she saw her.

"Clare." Freya seemed almost shocked to see her.

"Hi, Freya." She was shuddering inside her coat but didn't want to break away from her.

"Are you filling up?"

"Pardon me?" Clare said.

"Filling your car up with gas." Freya sounded awkward, as if she'd never made small talk before.

"No, I was stopping by for some beer." She looked at Freya a moment. "Would you like to have one with me?"

"Sure. As long as we get out of the cold."

"How about my car?"

"I don't know how it will look for a cop to be drinking beer in a parked car."

"The car's not moving. We wouldn't be doing anything wrong. Come on in with me and I'll get the beer." She was surprised she made the invitation. But she liked Freya, and she didn't want to miss an opportunity to be with her without Jo around. They went into the store, and when they came out Clare led the way to her car, taking some files and empty bags off the passenger seat so Freya could sit.

"At least leave the parking lot and pull over on a darker street. The store's cameras are pointed at us right now."

Clare pulled into a residential street a block away and parked between streetlamps. "This isn't how I imagined our first time out together," she said. "We could go to my house."

Freya raised an eyebrow. "You were imagining us out together?"

"You brought it up—that we might see if we could be friends. I tried to imagine what that would look like." Warmth flooded her cheeks and she hoped Freya couldn't see her blush.

Freya smiled and took a beer from Clare, who put the rest of the six-pack in the back seat. "How did you imagine it?"

Clare cracked open her beer. "Maybe sitting at Abe's for a few drinks or out to dinner. I'd lean on you for restaurant suggestions."

"There aren't many to choose from. But I'd be happy to be your guide." She clinked her beer can against Clare's and relaxed against the car door. "Tell me a little bit about yourself."

What to say? She wanted to give a good impression, but the whole truth would make Freya either run or arrest her. For a fleeting moment she thought how it would be if she had nothing to hide. Would that be the freedom she was after? "I wouldn't know where to start."

"How about why you moved to Money Creek?"

"Practicing law in a big Chicago firm almost did me in. I wanted a complete break, and the job at Nelson & Nelson sounded perfect for me. I'm not sure what they think, but I'm really glad I'm there."

"I think it was clear at the dinner party Elizabeth thinks highly of you. I wouldn't worry on that score," Freya said.

Clare shrugged. "What about you? Is the drug task force where you want to be?"

Freya took a long drink before answering. "Technically, I'm a detective, which is what I've always wanted to do. Solving murders was the ultimate high in police work. But then I got transferred to the task force and I'm glad I was." She sat up straight and looked at Clare. "I hate drugs, and I hate people who sell drugs, and I kind of hate the people who use drugs."

She tried not to wince. "Sounds like you're in exactly the right place."

"For now, anyway." She tilted her head back and emptied her can of beer.

"Do you want another?" Clare asked.

"No, I've got to go. I have an early morning tomorrow."

She really should be running the other way from Freya, who would hate her if she knew the truth about her drug use. But there was something about her passion for her work that attracted as much as alarmed her. What an idiot she'd be to let herself be drawn into Freya's orbit.

"I'd love to get together for dinner, though. Can I call you?" Freya said.

Clare didn't know how to say no, nor did she particularly want to. They could be friends. Maybe she'd be able to keep hiding her drug use until she quit. She dropped her off at the gas station and drove away smiling. The evening had been productive. She'd replenished her supply and possibly made a new friend. She didn't dwell on the irony of it.

## CHAPTER TEN

Clare arrived early to take the deposition of the fence manufacturer's quality control manager. She was in Carbondale, about a three-hour drive south of Money Creek in the southern tip of the state, at the law firm of the manufacturer's attorneys. A receptionist led her back to a conference room and she could see the sleek design of the offices, the bustle of lawyers and paralegals walking about.

She was coming to love the freedom she had at the Nelson firm to actually practice law. Elizabeth was trusting her with more responsibility, and so far, she'd been up to the task. It helped to not have a dragon breathing fire down her back all the time. The witness she was going to depose was a potentially significant one and she didn't want to let Elizabeth down. It was her first deposition and she was more than a little nervous.

As she put her briefcase on the table, a young man entered the room. He flashed her a killer smile as he offered his hand.

"I'm Dane Michaels," he said. "I'll be sitting in the deposition with you for the manufacturer. Can I get you some coffee?" He pointed to a thermos on the room's credenza, along with a plate of bagels and donuts.

"Where would you like me?" Clare said.

"Anywhere is fine. The witness is here, but we're still waiting on the stenographer and the plaintiff's attorney. It's still a couple minutes early."

Clare made herself comfortable at the table. "I see both our firms have passed this deposition off to younger lawyers."

"Not really. I take depositions all the time." Wonderful. Experience versus complete innocence. In depositions the rules of evidence are treated loosely, so she wasn't too worried that any mistakes on her part would prove fatal. Her job was to get as much as she could from the witness.

Bob Highsmith, an associate at the plaintiff's attorney's firm arrived, followed by the stenographer. The witness, Robert Lyons, was sworn in. He was a big-bellied man who wore a suit that clearly had been purchased in earlier, thinner days. His dress shirt looked like it would pop a button at any minute.

"Mr. Lyons, I'm Clare Lehane, counsel for Peterson Agriculture. I'll be asking you some questions today about the equipment sold to my client by your company."

Lyon's eyes were a bright blue, a feature nearly overwhelmed by his puffy cheeks. He nodded.

"You'll be required to give audible answers to my questions so the stenographer can record them. And I want to also remind you that you are under oath, required by law to answer truthfully and completely. If it is found that you've given false testimony, perjury charges can be brought against you. Do you understand these things, Mr. Lyons?"

"I understand." For such a big man, Lyons had a tiny voice.

Clare began the deposition by having him describe his duties and responsibilities at Ogden Lagoons. She had to ask him to speak up several times. He described a typical day on the job, the process of quality control, and the amount of times incidents occurred when the department failed to discover a problem in one of their products.

"Mr. Lyons, are you familiar with the fencing system that's designed to cordon off methane lagoons?"

"I am." Lyons looked relaxed and confident. The questions had been easy.

"Did that system include a gate that would allow access to the lagoon should that become necessary?"

"Yes, but as a practical matter there shouldn't be any reason to access the lagoon."

"And does that system, including the gate, fall within your responsibilities as a manager? Were quality control procedures followed for that product?"

Lyons took a drink of coffee. "Yes."

"Had you at any time been made aware that there was a safety problem with that fencing system?"

"Objection," said Michaels. He was leaning back in his chair and seemed barely interested.

Clare looked at him. "Are you going to state the nature of your objection, Mr. Michaels?"

"I'm preserving the objection for the record."

"You can answer the question, Mr. Lyons." She was fantastically alert and focused.

"I think I heard of a fellow falling through the gate into a lagoon."

The three attorneys sat up straight. "You mean someone other than the plaintiff?"

"Yes."

"Do you remember when this was?" Clare said, her pen poised over her notepad.

"Nah. I don't remember."

"Do you remember whether it was before or after the death of Mr. Oleg, who also fell through the gate?"

"Objection. Asked and answered."

Lyons looked at his attorney, who nodded. "It was before." Clare remained silent until he spoke again. "I remember it was before because that's when my bosses started talking about a recall. The guys in my department thought it was bullshit, pardon my French. If a man is standing on the edge of a methane slurry lagoon and leans against the gate, well, that's a stupid man. Can you do a product recall on stupidity?"

"Objection!" Michaels placed a hand on Lyon's forearm. "Don't say another word."

Clare laughed. "That's a bit like closing the barn door after the horse has got out." Why was she using farming metaphors? "Mr. Lyons, I'll ask you again how long before the product recall this incident happened—either when you talked about it with your co-workers or heard about the incident itself?"

Michael still had his hand on the witness's arm. "Don't say another word. I object to this line of inquiry as being irrelevant and beyond the bounds of this deposition."

She looked at him as if he'd announced the end of sunrise. "Your ridiculous objection is noted. Now, Mr. Lyons, was it common knowledge among the workers at Ogden that people were falling into methane lagoons because of a faulty gate?"

"I'm instructing my client to not answer any more questions along the lines of this inquiry."

"You've got to be kidding. Any judge would allow this testimony. It strikes right at the heart of what Ogden Lagoons knew prior to the issuance of the safety recall. Please tell your client to respond to my question. Would you like it to be read back to you?"

"I'm not allowing him to testify. You can continue the deposition with any questions not related to what Mr. Lyons and his co-workers talked about."

Clare glared at him before pulling her phone out of her jacket pocket. "Fine. We'll have the judge decide."

Michaels looked exasperated. "You can't call the judge over this."

"Of course, I can. Will you please ask the witness to step out while we talk to the judge?" Michaels told Lyons to wait in his office and closed the conference door behind him. The stenographer stayed in place. Clare googled the Timson County courthouse and rang the general number to be put through to Judge Carruthers's chambers. His clerk answered and said the judge was in recess in his office and he'd put her through.

"Judge Carruthers, thank you for taking my call. This is Clare Lehane."

"Of course," he said. "The new associate from Chicago." He sounded relaxed. They'd met at Elizabeth's party and she was glad he remembered who she was.

"Judge, I'm going to put you on speaker phone. I'm in the middle of a deposition in the Oleg v. Peterson Ag case, down in Carbondale. I'm here with Dane Michaels, counsel for the lagoon manufacturer."

"Good morning, Judge," Michaels said.

"We've asked the witness to step out of the room while we see if we can get a ruling from you on a disagreement Mr. Michaels and I are having." Clare continued by describing the impasse. She heard confidence in her own voice.

"Mr. Michaels," the judge said, "I think you know you must allow your witnesses to answer Ms. Lehane's questions. They go to the central question of who knew what when." Michaels made a lame attempt to argue that the testimony was hearsay. "I'm allowing the testimony and admonishing Mr. Michaels for making this call necessary. Your objection is noted on the record and you'll have a chance to argue it in court. You know how this works."

"Thank you, Judge," Clare said. She hadn't even had to make an argument, which she was prepared and eager to do. Nothing seemed beyond her at the moment. If she'd argued the world was flat, she was sure she'd win the debate.

The judge hung up and Michaels went to get his witness. Clare looked at her phone and saw a message from Freya, asking her to lunch. She sent a quick reply that she wasn't in town and asking for a raincheck. What would Jo think of them having a meal together?

Clare continued her questioning of the witness once he was back in his chair. "Mr. Lyons, did the opinion of the people in your department of the intellectual abilities of those using your product affect how you administered the safety recall?"

"Objection," Michaels said, with no enthusiasm in his voice. "You can answer the question."

"Of course not. We sent the recall notices out to all our customers, and as far as I was concerned, that was the end of it." Clare could practically hear Michael's groan.

"You sent one written notice and didn't follow up to be sure your customers received it?"

Lyons looked uncomfortable, as if he knew he was burying his employer but not able to stop it. "We never received instruction to do follow up. As I said, the notices went out and that was the end of it."

"It's possible that Peterson Agriculture didn't receive the notice at all, correct? The post office may have lost it, for instance."

Lyons shifted in his chair. "I guess that's possible."

Clare had what she wanted but continued her questioning until she was sure she'd drained him of information. She gathered her things and left, sorry only that she couldn't depose others in Lyons's department right away. On the trip back to Money Creek, she was drenched in well-being. She was good at her job, she'd score some points with Elizabeth, and she'd had fun. She called Freya and asked her out to dinner. She wasn't sure what she wanted from her, but she guessed Freya wouldn't make any move until she'd ended things with Jo, and she had no way of knowing whether she intended to do that. She didn't have to guess at her integrity. Dinner tonight would be safe. She needed time to think about where she wanted things to go, though her body was starting to make that very clear.

## CHAPTER ELEVEN

When Clare got back to the office, she found Elizabeth in the conference room, a file full of papers spread in front of her, typing on her laptop. She looked up when Clare entered the room.

"You're back. I didn't know if we'd see you today."

She almost didn't. Her body started to flag on the long drive back from Carbondale. She'd popped another tablet of speed, annoyed at anything interfering with the day's triumph. It was a little after five o'clock and the other lawyers had left for the day. "I wanted to let you know about the deposition."

She filled Elizabeth in on what had occurred. Would Elizabeth be pleased? She hoped so, though she was simply doing her job. The deposition had required she think on her feet, something she was not always confident she did well.

"That's excellent, Clare. It's a significant piece of evidence. Will you arrange to depose others in Lyons's department? We'll want corroboration of what he said."

"Sure. I'll start on that tomorrow." She'd been hoping for a little more praise. She was speedy and a little on edge. Her mouth was dry and her heart was noticeably beating, her right eye started twitching. She tried to recapture the good feeling she'd had after the deposition.

Elizabeth closed her laptop and started packing up the papers. When she looked up, Clare was still standing in the same spot, her hand to her eye. "Looks like you have a tic," she said. "Are you feeling okay?"

"I'm fine." She pushed down next to her eye, trying to stop the twitching. Her head began to ache. "It must be the long drive in the bright sun."

She turned to leave, before Elizabeth stopped her. "You did good work today."

Clare flushed with pleasure, the way she always did when she received a compliment. And just as quickly, the good feeling was gone. "I don't know. I probably could have gotten more out of the witness."

"Doesn't sound like it. Before you go, draft an expedited motion for a continuance and we'll file it first thing in the morning."

She went back to her office and quickly wrote up the motion. She didn't feel like working any longer. She drove home, changed clothes, and sat in her living room. A few calming breaths failed to ease her jitters. She pulled out her pillbox and took a couple of Valium, which would do the trick. While she waited for those to kick in she thought about her dinner with Freya. They were scheduled to meet at seven. If something did develop between them, Clare would have to quit using drugs. There was no way Freya wouldn't know she was using. Maybe that would be the catalyst she needed to finally quit. She finished her beer, put a couple of extra Valium in her pocket just in case, and headed out to Woodlawn Avenue and the Red Lobster.

Freya sat at the front of the restaurant and rose to greet Clare when she entered the room. Clare smiled as she sat and shrugged out of her coat.

"I haven't been in a Red Lobster in years," she said. "They don't have many in Chicago."

"Here it constitutes fine dining, so I imagine you'll be back. Olive Garden and Outback Steakhouse are also among the premier restaurants in Money Creek. Bet it makes you miss the city."

"Not yet, it doesn't."

"It's a different story in Bloomington. We have great restaurants there."

"Do you miss Bloomington?"

"Not as much as you'd think. I like it here, like my work on the task force, like the people."

They ordered their food and some wine. Freya got the fish and chips and Clare ordered the shrimp scampi, thinking she could push the food around to make it look like she was eating. She had no appetite. Freya busied herself with her napkin and she wondered what was going on in her head. Was she thinking of this as two friends getting together or was it more like a date? It felt more like a date to her. She didn't have many female friends. Ever since law school she'd hung out mostly with men, for no rhyme or reason. They seemed to be there and girlfriends were not. This tended to be the case when taverns were your primary source of society.

"What have you been doing with your time since you moved?" Freya said.

"I don't want to admit how boring I am."

"You're not boring. I know boring, and I'm not looking at it."

Clare's instinct was to be self-deprecating and to wave away the compliment. She said a simple thank you instead. "I don't spend my time that much differently than I did when I was in Chicago. Except I'm learning to cook because there's no Grubhub here, no nearby corner restaurant. I'm left to my own devices."

"Good for you. I'm a microwave dinner gal, sad as that is."

Clare took a sip of the mediocre wine. A basket of biscuits appeared on the table. "As soon as I can cook a whole dinner, I'll have you over." It just popped out of her mouth. The idea of cooking for someone cowed her.

Freya beamed. "I'd love that."

Their dinner arrived almost immediately. She was grateful for the distraction of the food. They were close to having an awkward silence and she filled it in the least appropriate way she could. "You must spend a fair amount of your time with Jo."

"What makes you say that?" She didn't seem thrilled with the question.

"Jo's said a few things while we were working. She made it sound like it's serious."

"It's not serious," she said quickly, as if to dislodge the notion before it could take hold. "I mean, we've been seeing each other for a few months, but I don't think it's anything serious. Maybe I need to have a talk with Jo."

Clare cringed on the inside. "I'm sorry if I stepped in it. It's none of my business."

Freya stopped a server and ordered more wine. Her hair fell loose to her shoulders, the first time she'd seen it worn that way. It relaxed her face, made her seem more accessible. The sleeves of her dark blue shirt were rolled up to her elbows, leaving the long muscle of her forearms visible. Clare found herself staring at them.

"It's fine," Freya said. "It's the kind of thing friends talk about." She looked more relaxed as she drank more wine.

Crap. Now it seemed it was friendship Freya was looking for. Why was this so confusing? "Of course, I'll keep anything we say between us."

"I wouldn't think anything else. You're a lawyer, after all."

Clare laughed. "For that kind of confidentiality you'll have to pay me a dollar." She pushed her food around her plate. "Why do you think it's not serious with Jo?"

Freya hesitated. "I don't want to seem like I'm judging her, especially behind her back."

"Of course not."

Freya put her napkin on her plate, the fish and chips gone. She'd eaten very fast. Nerves? Or the appetite of a normal person?

"She seems a little possessive. She wants to spend more time together than I do, and she plans things for way in the future, with the presumption we're a long-term couple. I feel like I don't know her well enough for that."

Clare sipped her wine. She could feel the Valium relaxing her. It didn't sound like Freya was much into Jo. She wondered if Jo knew that. Maybe that's what made her so territorial. "I hope it works out however it's supposed to."

"It will. It helps to have another person to talk with."

"Are we going to be friends?" Clare said, raising her eyes to Freya's. She kept her tone light.

"Why not? I like you, we both need someone to hang out with, and let's face it—the options are not that plentiful."

That stung. "Friends by default, in other words."

Freya laughed again. "That came out wrong. Let's see how it goes."

Clare nodded. "Okay. What kinds of things do friends do around here?"

"The usual. Drink, hang out at home watching a movie or chatting, shopping. You have to go into Bloomington for that. But I have something a little more exciting. There's supposed to be a big storm coming in tomorrow. If it does, do you want to go snowmobiling?"

The thought of screaming through the frigid air on a snowmobile didn't seem nearly as enticing as lying on the couch. But with Freya driving and Clare hanging on for dear life, it had some appeal. "You have a snowmobile?"

"I don't. But we busted a meth lab that was hidden in a corner of a farmer's property. He was so grateful he offered me his snowmobiles whenever I want them."

Clare drained her wine. "Sure, I'll go snowmobiling. I don't know if I have the right clothes for it."

"Don't worry. I'll fix you up," Freya said, looking pleased. They finished up their meal and left the restaurant. Freya offered a hug as they said good night. It lasted two beats longer than a hug would between new friends. "I really enjoyed this."

Clare was flushed in the cold night air. The offer of friendship, the snowmobiling, the hug. Life in Money Creek was getting better. If Freya were only a friend, it would still be an improvement. It would mean less isolating at home, maybe less consumption of drugs. A positive influence wouldn't kill her. She watched Freya drive away in her Jeep and got into her car. The air was too cold for a snowstorm, but she hoped there'd be one, her first in Money Creek. She pictured clinging to Freya from the back of a snowmobile, racing across the flat cornfields.

She turned toward home, passing by the fast food franchises and automobile dealerships. She'd recently learned to use a shortcut to get to the downtown area, an angled road that cut through the residential neighborhoods and dumped her out in the town square, two blocks from her house. It occurred to her that a nightcap at Abe's would be a fun thing to do. Maybe she'd make some more new friends. She turned right instead of left at the end of the angled street and pulled into Abe's parking lot. The lot was half full, two cars and three pickup trucks. It was only eight thirty, and if drinkers were the same everywhere, the patrons still had hours of drinking time ahead of them. She zipped her coat and trotted from her car to the tavern door. Inside it was warm and smelled like Buffalo chicken wings. There were more people than she expected—about five at the bar, with a number of tables occupied by young people drinking pitchers of beer. She climbed onto a barstool toward the far end, her feet slipping onto the footrest like a gun into a holster. She was comfortable in that position. The back bar was well lit, and she could clearly see her reflection in the mirror. Why did taverns have mirrors there? It wasn't great customer service to allow patrons to see their own bleary faces staring back at them. For the moment, she was young, pretty, and had her act completely together. No bleariness. She'd stay for one or two drinks and then go home. There was work tomorrow.

Three hours later, she found herself sitting next to Ben, like he'd been beamed down onto the barstool next to her. She'd just snapped out of a blackout and had no idea what he was talking about. She didn't remember him coming into the tavern. When she looked in front of her, she saw a couple of empty shot glasses on the bar. She pushed them to the back of the bar for Danny to pick up and ordered another as soon as he came back down their way. It was unusual that she'd pop out of a blackout, but she was glad she'd not gotten in trouble while she was in it.

Ben stopped talking and looked at her thoughtfully. "You must have some kind of hollow wooden leg. I've never seen a woman pack so much down without showing the damage."

How dare he? He was practically a teetotaler. "How much I drink is none of your business." She wasn't slurring her words, but her body was slumping, as if her bones had softened.

"Hey, I wasn't judging. I kind of admire your capacity. It's why I'm such a lightweight. I get loaded after about two drinks."

Clare laughed. That struck her as hilarious. "That's like a disability or something. I insist you have another drink with me so we can test the theory."

He smiled. "Not a chance. I have a big day tomorrow and the last thing I want is a hangover."

She ordered two more drinks and drank them both while Ben still refused to drink one. She had a dim awareness the next day was a big one for her as well. She was scheduled to argue a motion in court. She fished in her right-hand pocket and slowly extracted another Valium. As soon as he was distracted by someone saying hello, she popped the pill in her mouth and drank it down with the glass of beer Danny had been refilling all night. Ben turned back to her. It was getting toward the end of the evening, the time she asked herself whether she wanted any company for the night. Ben's good looks and straitlaced demeanor were kind of sexy. She wished she knew what they'd been talking about. Had he been flirting with her? Had she with him? The way his stool was drawn close to hers suggested as much. When she looked up at him he was staring at her intently, not in a soulful way but more like he was watching for signs of delirium. She knocked back one more shot and turned fully toward him. She wanted to get him into bed. She had a fleeting thought it would be better if Freya were standing in front of her, but she wasn't.

"What do you say we get out of here?" Clare said, moving her hands onto the top of his thighs. It helped hold her up.

Ben stood and gently took Clare's hands away. She frowned. Was he going to be difficult?

"I'd be happy to take you home, Clare. Should we leave now?" That was more like it. She tried to put her jacket on and her arm got caught up in a sleeve. Ben reached over and got things straightened out for her. "Ready?"

She followed him out of the bar, walking slowly to keep one foot in front of the other. She remembered him snapping her seat belt on in the passenger seat of his car. After that there was nothing.

## CHAPTER TWELVE

She knew it was bad before she opened her eyes. The lids were glued together, and it took effort to pry them apart. Her bedroom wallpaper popped into view. What a relief to wake up in her own home. She rolled onto her back, which sent her insides roiling like the wake of a ship. She was poisoned, as if a Russian had jabbed her with a tipped umbrella. A few tears leaked out of her squinting eyes. In Chicago there was a certain anonymity— when she screwed up like this it was as often as not in front of strangers. But she was in Money Creek, and if she'd done anything spectacularly bad, the whole town would soon know of it.

She took a breath and turned to her other side, half expecting to find a man lying there. She blew out the breath when she found the bed empty. The linen was messed up like someone had slept in it. Who'd been lying there? Where was he? She glanced at her phone and saw it was eight o'clock. Her heart seemed to stop a beat. She had a court appearance in two hours, an important one where she was arguing a motion to extend discovery in order to take the extra depositions down in Carbondale. She hadn't set her alarm.

She pushed herself up from her bed and instantly knew she wouldn't make it to the bathroom in time. She grabbed her bedroom trash can and hurled into it, a noisy, smelly operation that left her lying on the floor. Jesus. How was she ever going to make it to court? She forced herself to get up and go to the kitchen. She needed about five gallons of water to start flushing the toxins out of her system. As she got to the bedroom door, Ben stuck his head in and scared the hell out of her. She was about to ask what he was doing in her house when she thought better of it. It was obvious what he'd been doing. Why call attention to it? She pressed a hand against the wall to hold herself up.

"I heard you making noises," he said. He had an awful grin on his face. "I wanted to make sure you were okay."

Ben didn't seem the least bit awkward or embarrassed about whatever it was that happened, while she was mortified. Why couldn't she at least have picked a stranger to go home with? With a stranger there was some hope she'd never have to think about it again. Now every time she saw Ben she knew he'd be thinking about their night together. Oh, God.

She grabbed her robe behind the door and pushed past him into the hallway. "To be honest, I've been better. I hope you won't hold this against me." She turned to look at him.

"Don't worry about a thing. I was glad to do it."

She nodded along, not really understanding what he was saying.

"I've got to go to work, but I'll see you around." He briefly put a hand on her shoulder and turned to leave.

Clare wondered if that meant he wanted to see her again. She couldn't think about it. All she could think about was whether he'd get out the door before she threw up again. She managed to hold it together as he said good-bye, and she ran for the bathroom as soon as he slipped out the front door. When she was done retching, she tried to drink a glass of water, but even that stimulated her gag reflex. She threw it up as soon as it was down. She tried to remember a hangover this bad but couldn't. If a normal person was this sick, they'd call 911. She looked at it as punishment for fucking up so badly. By all rights, she should feel worse.

In the kitchen, she grabbed a Diet Coke and drank it down in one. The sharp sweetness cut through the fur on her tongue and spread throughout her body. Her stomach didn't rebel. She was caught between wanting and not wanting to know what had happened with Ben. Was she sloppy and outrageous? She was surprised Ben would sleep with her when she was that drunk—he seemed too upstanding for that. She would have been as attractive as a dead rat in that condition. Why would he want to? Or perhaps she was fairly well behaved and accepted Ben's invitation to sleep together without him knowing she was in a complete blackout. The fact was he'd slept with her. She didn't know how much to be ashamed about, but assumed it was a lot.

She took another Coke with her into the living room and flopped on her couch. Now that she wasn't vomiting, she had a chance to start panicking about her court appearance. Her thinking was fuzzy; she was unable to process more than what was right in front of her. The motion she was to present wasn't particularly complex, but she had to be prepared to argue against the other side and answer the judge's questions. It seemed impossible.

An hour later, she was in her office, putting her notes together. Everything she did felt like it was being done underwater, slow and deliberate. Jo poked her head in the office.

"I hear you and Freya had dinner together last night," she said in a clipped tone of voice. Clare looked at her briefly before turning back to her file. "That's right."

She felt Jo staring at her. She was not in the mood to talk. The dinner with Freya was a hundred years ago and any complications with Jo didn't interest her at the moment.

"I don't know that there's anything to say about it," she finally said. "It was dinner." She picked up her file and tried to leave the office, but Jo remained at the door, blocking her way.

"As long as it was only dinner."

Clare laughed. "Really? Are you in high school? Now if you'll excuse me." She brushed by her and headed down the hall to Elizabeth's office. At least she looked presentable. She'd taken a long shower to try to steam out the smell of booze coming from her pores. Her dark gray suit was fresh from the dry cleaners and she'd even accessorized. She knocked at Elizabeth's door and saw her sitting behind her desk. As usual, she looked casually elegant, like she was French. Maybe it was the way she wore her scarf.

"Good morning. I thought I'd stop by before heading to court for the discovery motion."

Elizabeth turned from her computer and smiled. "Wonderful. I'm going with."

She blanched. "You are? Do you feel you need to supervise?"

Elizabeth looked at her with a reassuring smile. "Not supervise. Observe. I like to see all our lawyers in action from time to time."

She hesitated but couldn't come up with a reason Elizabeth shouldn't come with her. This was the worst possible scenario— she would see Clare at her worst. She tried to sound enthusiastic. "Great. Are you ready to leave?"

At the courthouse, Clare got winded going up the marble stairs to the third floor. She was woozy. Elizabeth looked at her curiously. She followed Elizabeth into Judge Carruthers's courtroom. It looked as old and stately as the rest of the building; she could easily see Abraham Lincoln trying cases here. A large gallery for witnesses and onlookers was in the rear of the courtroom. Tall windows lined the east wall, a couple of them cracked open to counteract the radiators overheating the room. A wooden bar crossed the front of the room and on the other side were the jury box, the counsel tables, and the judge's grand desk and witness stand. They took a seat in the gallery and waited for their case to be called. Clare popped some Tic Tacs into her mouth and pulled the file from her briefcase. The woozy feeling was still with her, and now she could add nervousness to the mix. She said a quick prayer, something she hadn't done since grade school.

The court clerk called their case. Clare stood and tried to walk confidently through the bar. She placed her briefcase on the floor and her thin file on the counsel table. Elizabeth stayed behind in the gallery. Sitting at the opposite counsel table was Luther Woolfe, the chief plaintiff's attorney and leading ambulance chaser in Timson County. She wondered why he hadn't sent an associate to handle the motion. The judge looked down at them.

"Good morning, Ms. Lehane. I understand you're presenting an expedited motion this morning?"

"Yes, Your Honor. Clare Lehane representing Peterson Agriculture. I'm sure you have before you our motion to extend discovery."

"I do. This is the third time your firm has requested an extension. I'm going to need a good reason to grant yet another."

"We have one, Judge." Clare gazed at her notes, looking for a prompt of what to say next. She was listing from side to side as she stood at the table. She gripped it for stability. "Yesterday I took the deposition of a witness from Ogden Lagoon's quality control and safety department. We called you in the middle of that deposition when counsel disagreed whether the witness should continue to testify about a matter not previously revealed during discovery— that members of that department were aware of previous incidents of people falling through the gate. We had not been made aware that the reason for the product recall was an actual incident of someone falling through the gate."

Woolfe broke in. "Your Honor, the defendants' attorneys have had months to take the depositions of these witnesses. Extending discovery would come at a great cost to my client and is unfair to her." His client was Oleg's widow.

Clare held tightly to the table and again stared at her notes. They seemed to be swimming along the page. She suddenly had no idea what to say in response to the plaintiff's attorney. It was just beyond her, but she couldn't reach it. Her stomach burst into rebellion and bile climbed up her throat. She started to panic.

"Ms. Lehane? Do you have a response?" the judge said.

Clare's anguish fell away as the need to get to a bathroom became paramount. She had no choice but to make a dash for it. She burst through the bar, holding her hand to her mouth as she ran through the gallery and out the door of the courtroom. The women's room was across the hall and she made it there just in time. Standing at one of the sinks was her neighbor Sally, the recorder of deeds, who got an earful of her vomiting. The room was tiled in marble, amplifying the sound. When she staggered out of the stall a few minutes later, Sally was still there. Clare ignored her and ran water in the other sink, slurping it up and spitting it out.

"Are you pregnant?" Sally said. She looked at Clare impassively.

She hardly heard her. Her head was roaring. What had she done? What must Elizabeth think? Should she go back in? She looked at herself in the mirror and knew no one would have a hard time believing she was sick. She looked like she was on her death bed.

"I said, are you pregnant?"

Clare looked at Sally. "No, not pregnant."

"Can I help in any way?"

"I'm fine. It must have been something I ate."

"I saw your light on late into the night. You must not have gotten much sleep."

Clare frowned. "I guess you didn't either if you were looking through my windows."

"I don't sleep well," Sally said, unembarrassed.

"I have to go," Clare said abruptly. She needed to be brave enough to see how things were. She walked across the hall and peered through the window of the courtroom door. Elizabeth was standing at counsel table, putting Clare's file into her briefcase. She must have finished arguing the motion. She walked through the gallery carrying both briefcases, pushed open the courtroom door, and found Clare on the other side. She handed her briefcase over, her eyes cool and appraising.

"I'm so, so sorry, Elizabeth. I didn't realize how sick I was."

"You must be very sick for that to happen. I don't think I've ever seen a lawyer leave the courtroom in the middle of an argument."

Clare had been hoping for immediate concern and forgiveness from Elizabeth, not the slight tone of censure in her voice. She was surprised. "I'm afraid I had no choice. I figured it was better than vomiting in front of the judge."

Elizabeth started walking briskly down the hall to the staircase. "No real harm done."

"Thank you so much." Clare walked faster to keep up with her.

"Aren't you curious who won the motion?"

God, she could not stop doing the wrong thing. "Of course."

"We lost, essentially. The judge gave us one week. That means you have a very short time to get as many depositions as you can lined up. Should I get Thomas to step in for you?"

Was she being replaced? "No, I can handle it. I feel a little better now." Maybe a little speed would bring her up to floor level.

Elizabeth trotted down the staircase and into the rotunda. "I have an errand to run before I go back. I'll see you at the office."

She stood still as Elizabeth strode toward the exit and out the door. This was bad. Disappointing Elizabeth was crushing. So far, she'd done such a good job of playing the role of competent associate attorney and now Elizabeth had seen her true colors—a person who ultimately could not be trusted.

By the end of the day she'd managed to schedule several depositions for the following week, which meant an overnight in Carbondale. She sat in her office chair trying to summon the energy to go home. It was pitch-black outside her window, the short days of winter seemed endless. Her hangover had resolved into sheer exhaustion. She looked at her phone for the first time in hours and saw that Freya had texted to see how she was doing. What could that mean? Had Ben told her how drunk she'd been last night, or worse, that they'd slept together? She shoved herself out of her chair and out the door of the building. The sharpness of the cold air was refreshing. Her car was parked in front and she opened the unlocked door. No one in Money Creek locked their doors. She yelped when she saw Henry sitting in the passenger seat. She put a hand on her chest where she could feel her heart galloping.

He was grinning at her. He smelled like patchouli oil, which she found surprising, more banal than she thought him to be.

"What the hell are you doing?" she said.

"Simply dropping by for a visit."

"In front of your mother's office?"

Henry waved a hand in front of him. "No worries. I just left her house where she's peeling potatoes for dinner."

Clare tried to imagine Elizabeth tending to the quotidian parts of life, the cooking and cleaning and handling of life's annoyances. It was hard. She saw Elizabeth as always operating on a higher plane. She stared blankly at Henry. She wasn't sure how much more she could handle in this soul sucking bitch of a day.

"It feels like an unnecessary surprise. Couldn't you have called?"

"The idea struck me when Mom said you were still at the office. I was leaving there anyway and thought I'd swing by. I haven't seen you since last week when you bought from me."

Clare relaxed a smidgen. "No offense, but I didn't think we were meant to see each other more than that."

Henry shifted in his seat. "You have to admit, we have a special circumstance here. I thought it'd be good for us to have a conversation."

"Can we do it another time? I'm not feeling well today."

Henry smiled. "Yeah, I heard you were knocking them back last night."

"How the hell do you know that?"

"Evan was at Abe's last night. He said he tried to talk to you but you acted like you'd never seen him before. Said you were throwing down shots the whole time he was there."

Clare didn't say anything. This was her worst fear, that news of her bad behavior would race through town and eventually land in front of Elizabeth. She was already under suspicion for the way she acted in court that morning, but at least Elizabeth didn't know it was because she had the world's worst hangover. Who else was at Abe's other than Ben and Evan?

"The reason for the visit," Henry said, "is to invite you to meet some people out at my country place."

"You have a country place?" Clare hadn't thought Henry was dealing drugs on a scale that would allow him to buy property.

"It's small, but it's private. Pretty hard to find."

"I don't understand," Clare said. "Why do you want me to meet these people?"

"You're young, smart, and professional. You'll fit in well with my crowd. It would mean something to me if you came."

Clare regarded him. There had to be something behind the request, something she didn't want to get involved in. "I think I'll pass. I'm not looking to make more friends."

He laughed. "More friends? How about some friends? You haven't had time yet to make any."

"I have. Let's just say I like to keep my circle very small."

He paused. "This is a handful of people who are close to me. Will you reconsider?"

"I think not. I hope this won't affect our business relationship." She'd do a lot to maintain that connection.

"I'm afraid it will. I was hoping you'd freely join us, but if I must stoop to coercion I will."

She narrowed her eyes. It was too bad Henry was a bastard. She'd hoped they'd be on good terms. Blackmailing her wasn't winning him her affection, but she couldn't risk him telling Elizabeth.

"If that's the way you're going to play it, I have no choice. This has to be about something other than simply meeting your friends."

"Actually, it is. I'm headed to the house at four o'clock on Saturday afternoon. We'll drive together in your car." He seemed satisfied and opened the car door.

"Where should we meet?"

"You can pick me up at my apartment. See you then, Clare."

She cranked up the heater and pulled her car out onto the quiet town square. A turn around the square pointed her toward home and she drove quickly there. The last thing she wanted was to go to a party of strangers. Would this day ever be over?

Henry was the first student out the door at the end of his senior seminar on twentieth century American literature. The other students hung back to talk to the professor about the theses due in the spring. Henry had yet to identify his subject, but it wasn't even March yet. He had plenty of time. He shrugged into his wool coat and took his phone out of the pocket. There was a notification on the screen that his business partner, Ray, had called back. He hit the return call button as he left the building and walked to the parking lot. It was picked up on the first ring.

"It's Henry. Thanks for calling me back."

"Of course. What's going on?"

It was freezing out. Henry half trotted toward his car. "I wanted to give you a heads up I'm bringing someone to the house on Saturday."

ANNE LAUGHLIN

"Like a date?" Ray's tone was mocking.

"No, not really. I'd like it to be, but I just met her."

"So why are you bringing her?"

"I think she may be of use to us. She's a customer of mine. Speed's her thing. She's also a lawyer in my parents' firm."

"Interesting." He seemed more focused. "Definitely bring her."

Henry was relieved. Even though the scope of their business was distributed equally among himself, Ray, and Bobby Hughes, Ray was the leader of the alliance. He was more decisive, more inventive than the other two and the role fell to him naturally. If he'd told Henry to not bring her, he wouldn't have pushed back.

"Sounds like you haven't heard the news," Ray said.

"What news?" Henry was always nervous about news since it was frequently bad.

"Stingy called me. One of the guys who cooks for him got busted. We don't know what he's telling the cops."

He was right. It was bad news. "There's not much he can tell them, right? I mean, the cooker shouldn't know anything about us."

"That's the business model. But if he gives up Stingy we have a problem. He won't turn on us, but it would be very hard to replace him if he's scooped up."

"I don't see what we can do other than be proactive and replace Stingy now, have him go to ground. I'm not convinced he wouldn't testify against us."

"Relax. This Morgan guy who got arrested doesn't know Stingy's real name, where he lives, who he associates with. Even if the cops tripped over him, they wouldn't know what they were looking at."

"They have sketch artists, you know." Henry's voice was tight.

"Jesus. I told you to relax. I'm monitoring the situation. Until we get our own manufacturing sites up and running, they're going to be arrests like this. You have to stand up under pressure, man."

The only time he'd been under serious pressure was when he'd been kicked out of Princeton and he'd weathered that. Now the stakes were much higher. Stingy was one degree of separation between him and the cops. If they ever got busted, he'd be middle-aged before he got out of prison. "I think we need to make sure Morgan can't testify about Stingy. If Stingy gets picked up, we don't want Morgan to identify him as his exclusive buyer. It's too dangerous."

"What are you suggesting exactly?" Ray sounded surprised.

"You know what I mean. We need to silence him." His anxiety seemed to lessen as he warmed to the idea.

"Permanently?"

"Yes, permanently. Don't you agree?"

"I see it as an option, but I'm surprised you do."

"There's a lot at stake." Henry tried to sound business like.

"Let me talk to Bobby. If he agrees, we'll take care of it."

As simply as that a man's fate was sealed, and he'd put it in motion. That was power he never thought he'd have. Their business was standing on a house of cards. The foundation would not hold if one witness could topple everything they'd worked so hard to establish. Why take the chance? Morgan was low on the totem pole and totally expendable.

## CHAPTER THIRTEEN

Freya led three deputies and Ben through the undergrowth to a crumbling hunter's shack deep in the woods, about seven miles outside Money Creek. They'd been tipped off to yet another meth lab by the new confidential informant they were breaking in. He told them a buyer had been to a lab that looked like a cleaning crew had just got done with it. Another in the series of labs being taken over by the drug organization they were trying to find.

She raised her hand and the group stopped behind her. Bright light poured from the windows of the shack. No one bothered to cover them. Motioning with her hand, she sent two deputies to the back and approached with Ben and one other deputy. Their cruisers and an ambulance sat idling a hundred yards away on a pitted dirt road. She and Ben stood on each side of the door and when Freya nodded, Ben kicked it open and she burst into the room first, swinging her weapon to the right. Ben was right behind her and aimed left. Her gun was trained on a group of three sitting around a tiny table on one side of the shack, two men and a woman. On the table was a bag of white powder and paraphernalia scattered about. Freya yelled out to identify herself.

"Illinois State Police. Hands on top of your heads. Now."

One of the men, greasy-haired and skeletal, dipped his hand below the table and she shot him in the shoulder. The other man, a twin of the first, brought a gun up while her eyes were still on the first and fired, missing her but hitting Ben in the arm. She moved her gun a few inches and shot him in the chest.

"Fuck," she said in the eerie silence. She retrieved the two guns. The first man moaned and gripped his shoulder while the woman, dressed in almost nothing in the cold shack, had her hands in the air. She wore a murderous expression. Freya checked the pulse of the second man. He was dead.

Ben stood by the door, holding his wounded arm. She looked at the deputy who had followed them in. "Are we clear?"

"All clear inside."

She grabbed her radio. "Are we clear outside?"

"All clear."

"Bring up the bus. We have an officer and suspect wounded and one suspect dead."

"Roger that."

The woman threw herself over the dead man. "You killed him. You killed my Edmund," she screeched. As a deputy approached to remove her, she swung her arms wildly, fending him off, protecting her man. The deputies grabbed her and the wounded man and muscled them out of the trailer. Freya turned to Ben.

"What a fucking mess," he said.

Freya tried not to feel responsible for the fucking mess. She should have cut down the shooter before he had a chance to fire and wound her partner. Either way, she'd killed him. They were the first shots she'd ever fired in the line of duty. She'd always wondered how she'd feel if she took a life. Adrenaline coursed through her system. Now she'd have to go to a mandated shrink to monitor her reaction to the fatal shooting. As far as she could tell, her reaction was principally one of annoyance. It was a lot of hassle, all of it pointless. The man shot at them. Her training was clear on what to do.

"How's your arm?"

"It's fine. A flesh wound." Ben looked toward the dead body. "You did what you had to. It was a good shoot." She didn't answer as two paramedics entered and took him out the door.

On the other side of the trailer was a very neat and compact meth lab, almost identical to the one they'd busted a few days before. Deputies and technicians started pouring in. She eased her way outside. The cold air hit the fine sheen of sweat on her face. Standing next to a cruiser was the senior deputy on the scene, Bill Hogstead. He was about forty, his jacket bulged in front from his belly, he wore thick glasses and a dull look on his face. Freya knew he was one of the most competent officers she'd ever met, despite his appearance. "How do you think things went?" he said.

"Considering I had to shoot a man to death, I'd say pretty well."

Hogstead looked at her sympathetically. "Are you okay?"

"I'm good." This was the first in what would be a long line of people asking how she was doing. She didn't know what it said about her that she was doing fine.

"Well, you still have two perps left. Maybe you'll get some good information out of them."

"Let's hope. Do you have things covered here?"

"Yeah. We have to wait for a forensics unit from Bloomington to take the lab apart and process the scene. I'll be here when they arrive."

"Good. I'm headed out." Freya waited in her car until the ambulance pulled onto the road and followed it to the hospital.

Three hours later, she was in a waiting room in the hospital while her suspect was in surgery. Sheriff Phillips walked in with two cups of Dunkin' Donuts coffee and sat next to her. It was the first she'd seen of him since the shooting.

"How's Ben?" he asked. He handed her a coffee.

"Heading home. They bandaged him up and cleared him to leave. He's on pain meds so he's going to sleep those off. He wanted to be here with me."

"No doubt. What can you tell me about the lab?"

Freya drank some of the coffee, which was much better than the vending machine coffee in the hospital. "It was well organized, very neat, labeled, safe. Or safe-ish, anyway. My feeling is that wasn't the work of the threesome we found in the trailer."

"You think what, that there's an organization of some sort overseeing the lab?"

"Something like that. If there is a banding together of the larger drug dealers, it seems to me they could be pooling resources to improve their whole production system. I hope to find out when I question the guy. The woman was no help. She swore she didn't know anything other than her boyfriend cooked meth."

He was quiet as he drank his coffee. "Aren't you going to ask me about the shooting? Two shootings, actually," she said.

"I got an account of it. I don't have anything to ask."

A woman in surgical scrubs walked into the waiting room. She took a sterile cap off her head and stuffed it in a pocket. They stood as she approached. "I'm Dr. Bouchard. I've just finished up surgery on Andrew Dunning."

Freya wanted to interview the witness immediately. "How is he?" she asked. The doctor was tall and willowy, with blond hair haphazardly tied into a bun on the top of her head, strands springing loose all over. Freya had eyes in her head—the woman was magazine cover beautiful.

The doctor addressed Freya. "The bullet went through the upper lung but missed all the nerves and vessels. He's lucky. He'll have a chest tube and the recovery will take a while, but he should be fine."

"Is he awake?"

"He isn't, and I don't expect him to be for several hours. I'd recommend you talk to him first thing in the morning."

Freya shook her head. "No, I'll wait here until he wakes up. I need to ask him some questions as soon as I can."

Bouchard looked relaxed, but her voice was firm. "That's not possible tonight. Even if he were awake he'd be barely coherent."

Freya was about to argue further when the sheriff put his hand on her arm. "Thank you, Doctor. What's the earliest time we can see him tomorrow?"

"I'd say eight o'clock. I'll leave word at the nurses' station in SICU." She nodded slightly and left. They walked toward the exit and agreed to meet outside Dunning's room in the morning. She got in her car and pointed toward her downtown apartment, but found herself taking a slight detour to drive by Clare's house. It was a bit stalker-ish, not something she'd normally do. But after her conversation that afternoon with Ben, she was curious about her.

They'd been sitting in their cramped office, waiting to hear back from the sheriff on the raid planned for later. Ben went out and came back with a cup of coffee.

"That's like your twelfth cup today," Freya said. "Didn't you sleep?"

"Not much." She looked up from her phone and waited for more. "It's a little delicate, but I had to help out a friend."

"What's delicate about it?"

Ben looked around, as if a pack of reporters might be behind him. "It was Clare."

"Clare? What about her?" Now he had her full attention.

"I ran into her at Abe's last night. She was already fairly lit up when I sat next to her. She downed a lot of shots. Her capacity is amazing. But by the end of the night she was showing it. Her eyes wouldn't focus. Her body was all floppy, like someone had stolen her bones."

Freya frowned. "Why didn't you stop her from drinking so much?" She was having a hard time imagining Clare flat-out drunk. She didn't like to picture it, it clashed so much with the controlled woman she was starting to get to know.

"Have you ever tried to stop a drunk from drinking? That wasn't going to happen unless I physically removed her from the place, and I didn't think it was my place to do that."

"She's not a drunk. She can't be."

"All I know is she was a drunk last night. It wasn't pretty."

Freya was silent for a moment. She was afraid of the answer to her question. "Did she ask you to come home with her?"

Ben drank down his coffee and looked at her. "She did. It was the worst invitation I've ever gotten. But I was worried about her. I drove her to her house and went in with her. She passed out right away. After she sang a rousing version of 'If You Believe.'"

Her heart sank at the news. "Did you leave then?"

"No way. I didn't want her to aspirate in her sleep. I got her into bed and lay next to her to make sure she was okay. Not much sleep, as I said."

The phone rang. Freya talked to the sheriff for a brief while and hung up. "We're a go for tonight. He's giving us three deputies."

"Great. How about six o'clock? It'll be dark by then."

"Fine." Freya couldn't let go of the story Ben just told her. "Did you see Clare this morning?"

Ben nodded. "I did. And did she ever look rough. Puked her guts out. But she was awake so I didn't need to babysit her anymore."

"I wonder if she remembered what happened."

"I'm pretty certain she was in a blackout. She looked shocked to see me, as if I was a home invader. Then she looked embarrassed."

"Who wouldn't be?" She turned the conversation back to the details of that night's raid, but she had a hard time focusing. Should she be interested in someone with an alcohol problem? That was asking for trouble. Maybe this was rare and she was really a social drinker. Whatever the case, Clare had just become more of a mystery.

## Chapter Fourteen

By Saturday morning Clare's physical hangover was gone, but the emotional one clung like a barnacle. She made a grocery list and ran out to the Kroger, glad for something to do. While she shopped she thought more about how spectacularly bad Thursday night and Friday morning had been. The self-flagellation went on and on. This bad shit didn't simply happen to her—she was responsible for getting drunk and sleeping with Ben and then screwing up the motion the next morning. She couldn't trust herself, and now that she knew booze was her nemesis, she swore off the stuff. Pills hadn't gotten her into trouble. She'd stick with those.

For all her disappointment at the dullness of living in Money Creek, she didn't want to leave it. She was sick at the thought of losing her job, which she surely would if she screwed up a second time. She loved working with Elizabeth and she was getting good work to do, work that challenged her and gave her real responsibility. She loved her little house and cooking dinners and even cleaning the dishes and putting everything away in its proper place. She was getting to know Freya, who seemed way more interesting than anyone she'd met in a while. Then it occurred to her for the first time that Freya might have heard about her sleeping with Ben. They were partners, and partners told each other everything, didn't they? What if she pulled away from her, repulsed by a sloppy drunk who dragged men home with her?

As she got back in her car her phone pinged and she saw a text from Freya. *Checking in to see how you're feeling.* Christ. Ben obviously told her. Why would she ask how she was feeling? How awkward would it be the next time they ran into each other, which was as sure a thing as any in a town as small as Money Creek? She didn't reply to the text.

She pulled into her driveway and saw her neighbor Sally in her front yard, bundled up and bent over, picking at some dead plants that were poking through the fresh snow. She hoped to avoid a conversation. Sally stood straight and watched her with her hands on her hips. She wore a bulky parka, a hat with flaps over the ears, and an enormous hand knit scarf. As soon as she was out of the car, Sally said, "You feeling okay? You were pretty sick the other day."

"I'm fine, thank you."

"Because I saw you on Thursday night. Happened to look out my window when I saw a man helping you into the house."

"So, you've said."

Sally came closer to her and lowered her voice. "It looked like you were feeling pretty good, what with the singing and everything."

Clare was cringing on the inside but tried to appear unconcerned. "As I said, I'm feeling fine. I have to get these groceries in." She turned her back on Sally and pulled a couple of paper bags out of the car. When she turned back, she was still there watching her. What a fucking busybody. How many people did she tell about Clare coming home with a man and singing her heart out at one in the morning? She unloaded the car and shut the front door of the house behind her. She could still feel Sally's critical gaze upon her. How dare she judge her? She wanted to open the door and yell at her to mind her own business. This was the real drawback to small town life. No one in Chicago would tell a virtual stranger what they thought of their behavior. Here she was fair game. She put her groceries away and got ready to pick up Henry for the get-together with his friends. The good times kept on coming.

She parked her car in front of Henry's apartment and rang the buzzer. Evan appeared and opened the door for her. "Hi, Clare.

Come on in." He sounded like they were best friends, which was odd given they'd met only once. "Your date isn't quite ready yet."

"He's not my date. Why would you say that?"

"Because I'm teasing you." He dropped onto the couch and pointed to an adjacent chair. "Have a seat. He'll be out in a sec."

She sat on the edge of the chair and looked at her hands. The apartment smelled sweet, as if someone had just made a batch of chocolate chip cookies.

"Henry likes you, you know," Evan said. "I tried to call dibs, but he ignored me. He doesn't like many girls."

Terrific. The last thing she wanted was to be Henry Nelson's girlfriend. Or Evan's for that matter. She was absorbing this news when Henry appeared in the living room, impeccably dressed as an East Coast preppie. He had on a camel colored wool sweater over a crisp, white button-down shirt. He wore corduroy trousers instead of jeans and his shoes were a British tan, like they'd come from Brooks Brothers. He stood in front of them with a smile.

"I'm so glad you're here, Clare. I've been looking forward to this."

Evan looked at Henry. "Remind me why I wasn't invited to this party?"

Henry frowned. "You're too low-level."

Evan's face was a mask. "That's what I thought you said." He stood and walked out of the room.

"That seemed a little harsh," Clare said.

He dropped into Evan's vacant spot. "Don't worry about him."

She looked at him closely. "You made it clear when we last met, or should I say when you ambushed me in my car, that I didn't have much choice about going."

Henry had one arm stretched along the top of the couch. He looked thoroughly relaxed. "No, no. I'd never do that. The only thing I have on you is the same thing you have on me. I thought we both had acknowledged that."

Now he was gaslighting her. She hadn't been that hungover she couldn't remember their previous conversation. "Okay. I'll play along with you," she said.

"Great." Henry jumped to his feet and offered Clare a hand. "Let's take off. We need to get there before my friends." She ignored his hand and stood, following him to the foyer where he got his black wool coat from the closet and opened the door for her. He gave her directions out of town and settled in to talk, which he did a lot of. He talked about Chicago and the Cubs, his college courses, Money Creek, and whether spring would arrive early this year. He chattered like a speed freak, which she should know. She turned the conversation toward something she was more interested in.

"What was it like being raised by your parents?"

He looked at her curiously. "What was it like?"

"Yeah. Were they strict, did they come to your ball games, that sort of thing."

"First of all, there were no ball games. I'm about as athletic as…Winston Churchill."

Clare laughed. "Winston Churchill?"

"I was more math and chess club. My parents wanted me to do whatever I was interested in. They were very supportive that way. But they were strict. Mom would have a fit if I came home with less than stellar grades, and my homework time was very regimented. Dad pretty much left me alone."

She turned onto a third gravel road. The countryside was a monochrome gray. Leafless trees bent with the wind, which she could feel pushing against the side of the car.

"I don't understand how you got into dealing drugs. You make it sound like you were such a good boy."

Henry rested his head against the back of the seat and stared in front of him. "That has to do with Bobby Hughes, one of the guys you're about to meet. For a glorious year and a half there was a comic book shop in Money Creek, right where the used bookstore is now. Along with chess and math, I was also a comics nerd, as was Bobby. We'd see each other on Wednesdays, when the new books came out. It was about the only thing we had in common. He's older than me, a high school dropout, but a very nice guy. We started hanging out a bit to talk comics. This was last year, when I started at Money Creek. He asked whether I knew of anyone selling drugs on campus."

Clare turned to look at him. "I thought you were a senior. Where were you before Money Creek?"

Henry moved about in his seat. "I was at Princeton."

"Princeton? And now you're at Money Creek? What happened?"

Henry pursed his lips. "Let's say that's where my experience in the drug business began. Princeton and I decided to part ways. Anyway, I told Bobby I didn't know of any drug dealers on campus, but I was pretty new. Bobby explained that he was a businessman and his business was selling drugs. He saw an untapped market on campus and asked me if I'd like to step in. He said the money would be excellent and that's something I am interested in—making money."

"He supplied you?"

"Right. Pot and cocaine mostly. Then he added ecstasy and mushrooms and finally, crystal meth. There wasn't much of a demand for that at the school, but there is in town."

"How about speed? There's always a demand for that on campus."

Henry smiled at her. "Your favorite. He didn't have any connections for speed at first, but when I explained to him how huge the demand was at midterms and finals, he found one. That's how I had some inventory for you."

She was thankful for that. "It seems a stretch to go from nerd to campus drug dealer."

"What can I say? I'm entrepreneurial. After doing this for a couple years, I have a solid business established."

"Aren't you afraid of being caught?"

"I'm very careful. You're one of the few I sell directly to. I have Evan and a couple other guys act as go-betweens."

He seemed overly confident about not being caught, but she hoped he was right. He told her to slow the car and look for a small road on the left. It was barely discernible, mostly hidden by overgrowth on either side of it. She drove up the narrow dirt road until she reached a clearing of an acre or so. A small ranch house stood in the middle and it looked like something condemned by the county. The yellow brick was sallow and sickly, the front door was pitted and dented, the gutters sagged off the roof. There was no grass or garden, only bare earth dusted with snow. She pulled up to the side of the house, and Henry popped out of the car and unlocked the front door.

The inside was equally bedraggled. He took her on a tour of the rest of the depressing house and then gestured toward a chair in the living room. She perched on the edge. He sat on the lumpy gold couch. "Can I get you a drink? Anything you like, I have a full bar." He seemed unembarrassed by the house.

She shifted in her chair. She wanted a drink. It'd been two days since she had one and her hangover had been replaced with nerves. Valium was helping somewhat, but this was breakthrough anxiety. A drink would be good.

"No, thanks." She could hardly believe it. She was not one to turn down anything on offer. The doorbell rang as Henry was walking to the kitchen for a glass of water for her. He detoured to open the door. Two men walked into the foyer and there was much slapping of hands and man-hugging. Henry led them to the living room and introduced them to her.

"This is Bobby Hughes, who I was telling you about earlier, and the other guy is Ray Barnes."

She stood to shake hands. Bobby gripped her hand firmly while Ray did that thing men do when shaking hands with a woman, a limp grip that she could barely feel. They must think women's bones were made of papier-mâché. Henry got drinks and everyone arrayed themselves around the seating area. Ray made himself comfortable on a grubby chaise lounge. He was a tall man with an athletic build, prematurely gray hair, and an intelligent face. He was still young, the flesh tight around the face. His eyes were an icy blue and they rested on Clare until she turned her gaze away. She didn't get a warm feeling from him, in contrast to Bobby, who started chattering as soon as he took a seat. He was a big man and wore an old hoodie and jeans on his well-padded body. His smile was bright.

"It's awesome to meet you, Clare. Henry's mentioned you several times, so I knew you had to be special. Not much impresses Henry." She wondered what about herself could possibly have impressed Henry. Bobby had a wide, cheery face and a bowl haircut that made him look like a little Dutch boy. He had even, white teeth. "I'm really psyched you made time for us today."

"It's not like I have a blinding schedule," she said. "I left that behind in Chicago."

"For sure. But still, it's great we get to spend some time with you." This was the mark of an extrovert, a person who always wanted to spend time with others, whether they knew them or not. It was almost impossible for Clare to understand. "Is that water you're drinking?"

Clare gripped her glass a little tighter. "Let's say today's a day I choose to not drink."

"Isn't that what they say in AA—one day at a time?" Henry said. He said this as if he were trying to support an alcoholic, which she wasn't. She tried for a relaxed grin.

"It's not a big deal. I'm simply not drinking today."

"Fair enough," Bobby said. He reached into his jacket and pulled out a couple of joints. "How about getting high? Is this a day you'll do that?"

"Absolutely," she said. She wasn't a big fan of pot, but she'd take anything at the moment. She felt on display in front of the men, as if she was auditioning for a play but didn't know which role was hers.

Bobby lit a joint and passed it. As she inhaled, Ray said, "I think the most interesting thing Henry told us is you're a lawyer."

Clare blew the smoke out and tried not to cough. "I hate to think that's the most interesting thing about me, but it probably is."

"I think it's super awesome you're a lawyer," Bobby said. "That's a lot of school to get through."

"Henry also said you like your pills and bought quite a quantity from him recently," Ray said. He hadn't changed his relaxed posture and he spoke in an unhurried but deliberate way. She was pinned to her seat.

"Is that a problem?" Clare said.

"No, it's the opposite. It makes you all the more useful to us." Ray took a long drink of his beer and lit a cigarette. Dread crept down her chest and into her gut.

Henry leaned toward Clare. "It's not so much that you're useful to us as it is how we're useful for each other." Ray and Bobby looked at each other.

"I don't know what the hell you guys are talking about," she said.

"Let me explain. There are things Henry hasn't told you," said Ray.

"Henry hasn't told me anything."

Ray swung his legs around and sat up. "Bobby, Henry, and I work together. We've joined up to control all the drug activity in the surrounding counties, which has been a pretty big job. We've converted most of the small meth labs into our system. We've centralized our source of supply and we control the distribution network."

Clare looked from one to the other. She could see Ray would determine what role Clare was to play, because, clearly, she was meant to be involved somehow.

Ray continued. "When you start making the kind of money we have, the number one problem is how to launder it so we can actually use it. And that's where you come in."

"I'm sorry. I must have missed where I agreed to being a part of your operation, because I certainly don't."

Ray smiled, tight-lipped. "We know how much you have to lose if Henry were to let his mother know her new star attorney is a drug addict. We're also the only source of your supply you'll find in the area. I'm sure you don't want that cut off. I don't like to place this kind of pressure on a person. I'd rather you join us willingly. But it's your choice, of course."

"I don't understand what you want from me." Her sense of dread grew as she saw them putting her in a stranglehold.

"It's straightforward and shouldn't be at all risky for you. We have a number of legitimate businesses through which we funnel money, and we're buying up more. The guy we used as an attorney before developed quite a meth problem and ended up in rehab. We need a new lawyer to close the deals we've made to buy a Laundromat and tavern in Money Creek. We're working on a few other places in Bloomington, where it's less noticeable when one person is buying a lot of places."

Clare breathed out. "This feels like blackmail."

"That's such an ugly word. This is a business proposition." Ray gazed at her steadily.

"That's not going to work. I'm a litigator. I don't know the first thing about commercial law." She looked at Henry, who sat still and quiet in one corner of the couch, avoiding her eyes.

"The dude lawyer didn't either. He was my criminal defense lawyer and a customer of ours. He figured out how to close deals," Bobby said. "You're a smart lady. I'm sure you can figure it out too."

She was sure that wasn't true. "Is that the limit of what you expect of me? Because I will not have anything to do with moving money to offshore accounts."

"In fact, we do expect you to manage the offshore accounts," Ray said. "That's not really a problem for you, is it?"

She left Ray's question hanging in the air. Henry looked worried.

"It's a deal breaker for me. That's a whole other world of trouble. Find a crooked accountant."

The room was silent. She passed the joint to Ray as if they were passing the peace pipe at a tribal council. It was a little longer than a roach and Ray stubbed it out impatiently. "Everything's a negotiation. We can accept your terms, at least for now, but we need you to start work immediately on these deals. The sellers' attorneys are sending us documents that should be handled by a lawyer."

At least she had that minor victory. "Agreed, under protest."

"No one wants to expose you, Clare, or cut off your supply. I think we understand each other."

She understood. She couldn't find a way around doing what they asked. Not yet, anyway. Bobby and Henry looked pleased and turned their attention to the packet of cocaine Bobby had placed on the coffee table. Henry took out a mirror, straw, and razor blade stashed in a drawer of the table and Bobby started cutting up lines. How bizarre to be partying with her blackmailers. Bobby and Henry acted like they wanted to be her friend. Ray was more of a puzzle. Henry pointed her to the long line of coke on the mirror and she bent over and snorted it up. At least the drugs were good.

## CHAPTER FIFTEEN

Freya and Ben were at the nurses' station by eight o'clock Saturday morning to see the man she'd shot the night before. Ben started talking with one of the nurses behind the desk, showing off the sling on his arm. She lit up like a bulb, her attraction to Ben about as subtle as a thunderstorm. Another nurse looked at her computer and then at Freya.

"It looks like Dr. Bouchard has given you permission to see the patient. Room 302." She pointed down the hall.

"Come on, Ben. See if you can focus."

He laughed as he joined her in the hall. "There are days when you're no fun at all."

"Yes, and this is definitely one of them. How much does your arm hurt?"

"Some. I'm okay."

"We need something from this guy. This investigation has gone nowhere since Jason's cover got blown."

"Do you want to take lead here?" Ben stopped outside room 302. A deputy sheriff sat in a chair in the hallway and nodded to them.

"Of course, I do," she said. She looked at him. "If you're okay with that."

"Sure. I'll pick up anything you may miss."

They walked into the room and saw Andrew Dunning asleep in a bed, connected to an IV and with bandages wrapped around his bare chest. He was alone in the room. The hospital was rarely full enough to make doubling up in the rooms a necessity. They took a position on either side of him and Clare called his name several times until he woke up.

"Mr. Dunning, I'm Detective Freya Saucedo and this is Detective Ben Collins from the state police. Time to wake up."

He looked confused. "Again? They don't let you sleep in this fucking place."

"You need to stay awake now." She waited while he raised his bed.

"What do you want?"

"What do I want? Let's see, last night we busted your meth lab. You reached for a gun. Your partner was quicker than you and managed to wound Detective Collins before I shot him. We have a few questions." Freya's sarcasm was evident. "First of all, who owns the lab?"

"What makes you think I don't own it?" Dunning sounded insulted.

"You're saying you're the owner?"

He hesitated. "I guess."

"Who do you sell your product to?"

He was silent as he stared at the remote control in his hands. He lowered the bed a smidgen. "Even if I wanted to tell you, I couldn't."

"Couldn't as in you refuse to or couldn't as in you don't know?"

"I'm not telling you anything until I have a lawyer with me."

"You could go that route," Ben said, "but you'll earn more leniency if you talk to us now."

"That's bullshit," Dunning said. "Get me a lawyer and a deal and I'll tell you what I know."

"You're not getting a deal. You tried to shoot a police officer."

"Then I'm not talking."

She sighed the sigh of the exhausted. Every step in the investigation had been a battle, and they were far from winning the war. Three hours later, Freya and Ben were back in the hospital room. Karl Jenkins was there to represent Dunning, a lawyer from the only other multiple lawyer law firm in Money Creek.

Freya stood next to the bed and tried to catch Dunning's eye. He was staring at his lap. "Tell us what you know and we'll push for a deal, depending on what you say. She rapped the side bar of the bed to get his attention. "What's the chain of command for your operation?"

Dunning looked resigned. "I sell all my product to a guy named Stingy."

Stingy. The same name Morgan gave them after his arrest. They'd made no headway finding him. Jason had heard of Stingy while he was undercover, but no one seemed to know who he worked for or where he could be found. It reminded Freya of World War II resistance cells—everyone knew only what was necessary to do their jobs.

"And where can we find Stingy?"

"Hell if I know. I've never seen him other than at my lab."

"Then how do you communicate? Do you have his phone number?" Claire said.

"By now I have about twenty-five numbers for him. He gives me a new one every few days."

"Burner phones," Ben said.

"Does Stingy work for someone higher up?"

"I don't know. That's about the last thing he'd tell me. I don't even know who else sells to him. All I do know is he pays me a good price for the product and doesn't allow me to sell to anyone else."

Ben and Freya stepped outside the room.

"What do you think?" Ben said.

"I think he's telling the truth, but it doesn't tell us anything we don't already know. If there's a top-down organization run by a few players, they're going to keep their identities as hidden as possible from the people most likely to get busted."

"Agreed. But we need to find this Stingy guy. What kind of name is that?" Ben said.

"I guess he's cheap."

"I guess he's pretty smart."

"We're going to have to go through every one of the contacts Jason made while undercover and press them for information. We don't have anything we can use as leverage, so it's probably a low percentage move."

"And it's going to let Stingy know he's in the crosshairs," Ben said. "Let's talk to the boss about it."

Freya walked out of the hospital frustrated and cranky. She didn't have to work the rest of the day since it was the weekend and immediacy wasn't an issue. But she headed to their office anyway. She'd compile the list from the reports Jason had turned in during his time undercover, hoping someone would give them more information. If they continued to make little or no progress, the powers that be in Bloomington would replace them with some fresh eyes. The idea of leaving Money Creek made her even more irritated. It was starting to feel like home, and now there was Clare. She didn't know what would happen with her, but she wanted to stick around to find out.

❖

Clare worked in the office all Sunday morning preparing for the depositions she was taking in Carbondale later in the week. Maybe Elizabeth would forgive and forget her courtroom catastrophe on Friday if she did a great job. Clare couldn't. She was ashamed every time she thought of it, which was frequently.

When she walked home for lunch, she felt like stretching her legs a bit. She went past her house, glad that Sally wasn't out front, to the end of the block, then turning right and left in a random path around her neighborhood. It was snowing and twenty degrees out, but she barely noticed the cold. The snow started to fall heavier, and she could smell the wood fires burning in some of the homes she passed. It was so different from a stroll around her Chicago neighborhood where she was dodging pedestrians, waiting at crosswalks for the traffic signals, bombarded by the noise of cars stopping and starting and honking. Money Creek suited her.

Just as she turned around, wondering if she could find her way back, an old Volvo pulled up beside her. She kept walking, thinking it was someone parking. Then she heard her name called. She looked back and saw Henry getting out of the car.

"What are you doing?" he asked.

"I'm walking."

You're not walking to somewhere?" He stood in front of her, dressed in his wool coat, with wool trousers tucked into Timberland boots. He was several inches taller than her five eleven.

"No, I felt like walking."

"Can I give you a lift home? Maybe come in for a cup of coffee?"

She raised her eyebrows. "I'm not looking for any company today."

He shrugged. "A lift home, then?"

"I'm out walking to get some exercise. Quite a coincidence you seeing me out here."

Henry smiled. "That's what I thought. There's something I need to tell you. Ray has cleared his schedule and can meet you at your office at one o'clock tomorrow."

"So soon?" She hadn't yet thought of how she was going to explain her new client to Elizabeth. "I can see him at the end of the week."

"Nope. It's got to be tomorrow at one. I'm sure you can find a way to fit him into your schedule."

She shivered, but not only from the cold. She was losing control of her life and didn't know how to gain it back. "Let me ask this. How's your Adderall supply? I'm going to need some before too long."

"Already? Didn't I just sell to you?"

She remembered Casey saying something similar and she was equally as pissed. "I don't need your editorial on how I use my stash."

"Okay. You're sensitive and I can appreciate that. The fact is I don't know what's happening on the Adderall front. Midterms are coming up so I need to get supplied. I'll keep you posted."

This sounded too iffy. What if he didn't have any by the time she ran out? Fear gripped her.

"Do that. I'm freezing so I'm going to push off." She turned to resume her walk.

"No good-bye? You're a tough nut, Clare. But we'll become friends. You'll see."

She picked up her pace to gain some distance from him. She didn't think the gooseflesh on her arms was because of the cold. It wasn't a coincidence he'd seen her on a street blocks from her own house, in the opposite direction of his parents' house, and far from any main road. Had he been following her? Why was he so keen to be friends with her? Couldn't he simply be her blackmailer? She walked briskly home and slammed the door behind her. The rest of the day stretched bleakly in front of her. She gathered her iPad, books, and a beer and stretched out for a long afternoon on the couch. This had been one of her favorite ways to spend time, but now a knot of fear had taken up residence in her chest. Maybe the beer would help her feel at ease, and if not, she'd try something harder. Today was a day she did choose to drink.

## CHAPTER SIXTEEN

Jo lived in one of the few apartment complexes in Money Creek. It was a relatively new neocolonial building, two stories high with a center entrance and a parking lot in front. Freya stood at the door, raising the courage to press the buzzer. The last time she'd seen her had been over a week ago, and then only briefly for coffee. Since then she'd been getting increasingly desperate texts from Jo asking, and then demanding, that they get together to talk. She couldn't put if off any longer.

As soon as she pressed the intercom she was buzzed in. She could hear the door opening to the second-floor apartment as she climbed the stairs. Jo stood at the door, one hip jutted out and her arms crossed over her chest. It was like walking to the principal's office.

"Hello, stranger. I was wondering if I'd ever see you again." Jo's tone of voice was ominous.

Freya walked through the door. "Don't be like that, Jo. I've been busy on this case."

"What else is new?" She closed the door and followed Freya into the living room.

"There's a lot going on."

Jo flopped onto her leatherette sofa. One end of it had an attached La-Z-Boy chair. Freya sat on the edge of it. Last night's takeout was on the coffee table, and there was a sickening sweet smell from an air freshener.

"There's being busy and there's being absent. I can feel the difference," Jo said. Her voice was firm, but her eyes looked frightened. "You never answer my texts anymore. Are you so busy you can't type a few words?"

Freya was silent. The situation seemed so obvious to her, but Jo was going to need to have it spelled out for her. It had been a couple of weeks since they made love and practically no communication on Freya's part since then. She didn't like being a cad, but she knew Jo was not the woman she wanted.

Jo carried on. "It seems to me you can't say you're dating someone if you never hear from them, never see them."

"I agree with that. I think we should quit pretending we're dating."

Jo sprang up from the sofa. "I knew it. It's Clare Lehane, isn't it? This all started when she arrived in town."

"Clare is straight. There's nothing going on with her."

"Wake up. She's about as straight as I am."

"You think she's queer?" Freya barely managed to keep the hopefulness out of her voice.

"I know you think so," Jo said. "Otherwise why have you been sniffing around her?"

Freya nearly laughed. "Sniffing around? In your imagination maybe."

"The dinners, the running into each other, who knows what else."

Freya wondered if Clare thought her interest was as obvious as Jo did. She hoped not. She didn't want to seem like she was pursuing her. She still wasn't sure what she thought of Clare after her drunken night with Ben. She should be cautious, but something about Clare made her want to be reckless.

"There is no *what else*. As I said, Clare's straight and I have no reason to believe she's thinking of joining our team. That's not what's going on here."

Jo sat down again, subdued. "Then what is?"

Freya took a breath. "It's nothing, really. Nothing more than realizing after spending time with you the relationship isn't right for me."

"What isn't right?"

Christ, she had to say more? Was she a masochist? "I don't see the relationship going anywhere, at least from my perspective. I'm sorry."

Jo closed her eyes and leaned against the back of the sofa. Freya went into the kitchen and grabbed a bourbon bottle and two glasses. When she got back she saw a few tears sliding down Jo's cheeks. Was there a good way to break up with someone? "Here, Jo. Have a drink."

"It's not even noon yet." She sniffled. Freya poured herself a short drink and swallowed it.

"I hope you know this has nothing to do with you. The chemistry wasn't right, and none of us can control that. It's there or it isn't."

Jo was still plastered against the rear of the sofa. She gave Freya a sour look. "Don't say more. You're making it worse."

At least they could agree on that. She put the bottle back in the kitchen and stood in front of Jo. "I'll see you around. Maybe one day we can be friends, because I really like you."

"Get out." She pointed toward the door, her face held tight to keep from crying. Freya left and trotted down the stairs, relieved when she pushed open the door and was able to breathe in the cold, fresh air.

Clare opened another beer and started reading the final chapter of her book, Thomas Hardy's *Far From the Madding Crowd*. She liked to challenge herself by reading the classics, interspersed with mystery novels. Her phone rang and she reluctantly picked it up. It was Freya.

"Put your long johns on," she said. "We're going snowmobiling."

She sat up from the couch and looked out the front window. Snow was coming down in thick, lazy flakes. A couple of inches had already accumulated on the porch railing.

"I don't have long johns." She was smiling, though Freya probably couldn't hear it in her voice.

"Layer up as much as you can. You don't want to miss this."

She didn't, but some incorrigible part of her played hard to get. "I don't? It's awfully cold out."

"It's all arranged. I've spoken to the farmer and he's pulling the machine out of the barn now." Freya paused for a moment. "You'll love it."

"It's snowing pretty hard."

"That makes it perfect. I'll pick you up in half an hour." She hung up.

Clare tossed the phone down and headed to her bedroom. This was what life was supposed to be like—a friend calls out of the blue and suggests something fun to do and you go do it. Don't fret about whether you'll enjoy it or not. And definitely don't fret about how it will interfere with your drug use. She pawed through her clothes and pulled out her sturdiest jeans and three layers of shirts. By the time Freya rang the doorbell, she was as ready as she could be for doing something she'd never done before. She pulled on her down coat and locked the door behind her. She was tingly all over. Anticipation, she guessed. This was what it was like to look forward to something.

"We have a forty-minute drive to the farm," Freya said, "but that should still leave us a couple of hours of snowmobiling"

"Do you know how to ride one of those things?"

"Oh, yeah. I've been out there a few times. We'll only take one out so you don't have to worry about driving. Unless you want to, of course."

"No, I'm good. I'll be the passenger today."

Freya put the Jeep in gear and headed north out of town. The snow was coming down harder now, and the roads were getting slippery. There was no brigade of salt trucks being deployed on the streets of Money Creek like there was in Chicago. Clare leaned forward and peered through the windshield. "My life is in your hands. I hope you'll be able to see where you're going on the snowmobile."

"Relax. We'll have fun.

She looked at Freya as she drove, her profile strong with a firm jaw and a slightly Roman nose. One hand lay casually on the steering wheel, the other on the gear shift. She didn't doubt her competence for a moment. "I'm glad to see you doing something other than work. No drug busts this weekend?"

"Only one. And I'm not your stereotypical workaholic detective. I find the work is always there whether I step away for some personal time or not. It doesn't seem to make a difference." She glanced at Clare before turning back to the road. "I'd rather have a life."

So sensible and well considered. She hoped Freya wouldn't catch on to how chaotic her life was, especially now that she was being blackmailed.

Freya parked in front of a picturesque farmstead. The house was a pristine white with black shutters, the barn and other outbuildings a classic red. Tractors and other equipment were John Deere green and looked freshly polished under the gathering snow. It was like a reality TV farm. A huge red snowmobile sat in front of the house with the key in the ignition. She handed Clare a balaclava and enormous leather mittens.

"Your only job is to hold on to me and lean when I do." Freya straddled the machine and brought it roaring to life.

She thought about wrapping her arms around Freya, holding on for dear life, and a frisson swept through her. She climbed on and kept her arms to herself as they drove slowly through the farmyard.

"Hold on!" Freya said. She was poised in front of an empty cornfield, a pack of snow covering the furrows. The snow was now coming down lightly. Clare tentatively put her arms around Freya's waist just before the snowmobile shot onto the field. She clung tightly as they picked up speed, racing through a great nothingness toward a stand of trees far in the distance. Clare's heart accelerated with the thrill of the ground racing by. She was flying, a grin plastered on her face.

The powerful machine ate up the mileage and soon they were approaching a copse of trees. When Freya came to a stop she looked behind her at Clare. "How're you doing?"

Clare kept her arms around her. "Fantastic. Let's do it again." Freya laughed. "I knew you'd love it." She put her hand on Clare's arm and squeezed.

They spent the next hour speeding through the fields, skirting around wooded areas, stopping occasionally to catch their breath and chat. When it started to snow harder again, Freya headed back to the barn. Clare climbed off the back of the machine and immediately missed holding her, felt it as a loss. The physical contact she had with others was virtually nil. She'd forgotten how good it could feel. Like anything that made her feel good, she wanted more of it.

## Chapter Seventeen

Clare was first in the office the following morning. By eight thirty, others had started arriving, including Elizabeth, who stuck her head in.

"Good morning, Clare. Can you stop by my office in about fifteen minutes?"

"Sure, I'll be down in a bit." She casually laid an arm over the book she'd been reading on commercial law.

"What are you reading? It looks like a law school textbook."

She wasn't quite ready to tell Elizabeth about her new client. "I'm reading some case law ahead of those depositions on Wednesday."

"How quaint to read out of an actual book. I miss it. It's hard on my eyes to read off the screen all the time."

Clare nodded. "I hear you."

Elizabeth moved on. How was she going to tell her about Ray Barnes? How had they met? Why did he hire a litigator to do commercial work? It was bound to raise suspicion, the last thing she wanted. What she wanted was for life to be simple again, though when she considered it, life in Money Creek so far had been anything but simple.

There was a knock on her door and Clare raised her eyes to see Jo standing inside her office.

"Good morning," Clare said. She was still trying to foster a working relationship with Jo, who was recalcitrant about everything.

The look on her face didn't bode well for furthering her cause. "Did you have a good weekend?"

"That's funny. How could I have had a good weekend?"

"I don't know. It was an innocent question."

Jo stood with her hands on her hips. Her saddle bag was strapped across her chest. "Do you mean Freya hasn't told you?"

She looked at Jo curiously. "Told me what?" If this concerned Freya she wanted to hear about it.

"Huh. I was sure she'd call you after she left my place to tell you the good news. Now that she's broken up with me, the way's all clear for you."

Clare was stunned. Freya and Jo weren't the love story of the century, but she had no idea they were close to breaking up. And why hadn't Freya told her when they'd been together the day before? "I'm sorry to hear that." She ignored the rest of Jo's comment.

"Right. I bet you are."

"Jo, there's nothing going on between Freya and me. We're friends."

"Keep telling yourself that, but it seems obvious to me. Thanks for ruining my life."

Jo left the room and disappeared down the hall. Clare closed her book and put it back on the shelf. She hardly knew what to make of Jo's news. She was happy for Freya. Jo seemed all wrong for her. But did it mean something more than that? What had been dancing around the periphery of her thoughts now came front and center. Did she want Freya that way? Her phone pinged and she saw a text from Freya asking if they could talk later in the day. She answered with a simple yes and anticipation bubbled up.

When Clare appeared at Elizabeth's door she waved her in while hanging up the phone. "I was just talking to Henry," she said. "We talk nearly every day, which I love. He's more like a daughter than a son in that respect."

"Thanks for the reminder to call my mother."

Elizabeth laughed. "Henry asked me to say hello to you. You must have made quite an impression on him at the party. He's mentioned you several times."

"That's nice to hear," she said. "Henry made an impression on me, too. You must be proud of him."

"Of course." Elizabeth shifted a few files around her desk and placed one before her. "We need to get started on our summary judgement motion in the Peterson case and I want you to head up both the brief and the memorandum. You're the most familiar with the documents at this point and I trust you to know the legal issues as well." She smiled at Clare.

Clare smiled back, mostly with relief. Elizabeth must have forgiven her for her botched courtroom appearance. "Thank you. I'm honored to get the assignment."

"I don't know if you'll thank me. It's a hell of a lot of work. You can have Thomas help you and I'm always here for guidance. I don't think our chance of winning is great, but we have to give it a shot. Their CEO has been all over me about this case."

"I'll get started today."

"I want this to be your number one priority. What else do you have going on?"

"Those depositions." She paused. "I also have a new client coming in at one today."

"New client? Who?"

"His name is Ray Barnes. He's a local investor who's been buying up some small businesses here in town and elsewhere. He wants me to handle the transactions."

Elizabeth raised an eyebrow. "He's not laundering money, is he?"

Clare looked quickly down to hide her surprise. Elizabeth was staring at her when she looked up. "No way. He seems ambitious to me, is all. He's continually leveraging as he acquires the businesses."

"We'll give this to my husband. He's handled lots of deals like that. I want a draft from you in two weeks and that's going to take all your efforts."

Inside, she was cringing, but she kept an impassive look on her face. "Let me meet with him first and see if that's okay. I'm sure I can handle it myself."

Elizabeth frowned. "I don't want anything pulling you away from the summary judgement."

"But it's new business," Clare said.

"Meet with him today and get back to me. We'll figure it out."

She left the office and stopped at the coffee station. She'd taken one Adderall that morning, but she needed more. Her stash was dwindling. She spent the rest of the morning getting her arms around the brief and memorandum she'd be writing. She was deep in that when Donna called from reception to say her one o'clock appointment had arrived. Clare walked out to greet Ray and was stunned to see him standing in the reception room dressed like the senior partner at an international law firm. His suit looked bespoke, it hung beautifully from his lean body. He was probably not yet thirty, too soon for a gut to start pushing out his belt and ruining the lines of his clothing. His shoes were black and shined to perfection. When he saw Clare, he smiled and took a step toward her.

"Thank you for seeing me, Clare."

"Of course. Let's go back to my office." She had the option of using the conference room, but she wanted to keep Ray as out of sight as possible. She closed the door as he settled in the chair in front of her desk. Clare sat in her chair, trying to look as confident as possible. She slid a pile of papers to the side and took out a fresh legal pad and pen. "As I said the other day, I don't know how much I can help you. Transactional law is not something I've ever practiced."

"And I'm fine with your agreement to do your best." He looked relaxed in his chair.

"There is a lawyer here who can better serve you."

"No. It has to be you. You must understand why. I'm sure you can get up to speed quickly."

She looked him in the eye. "To be clear, I'm representing you under protest. You've chosen to blackmail me into being your lawyer, which is not a good basis for a business relationship."

Ray gazed back at her. "I think we'll be fine. You're going to like working with me." He smiled and broke eye contact as he reached into his jacket and pulled out a check book. "How much of a retainer do you require?"

She had no idea what was appropriate, but she couldn't blather about it. "Ten thousand will do," she said. "Please make it out to Nelson and Nelson."

He looked up. "I'd rather make it out directly to you."

She shrugged. "Sorry. I work for this law firm and everything is funneled through it. Perhaps that won't work for you?"

"Good try. No, you're stuck with me." He wrote out the check and handed it to her. His hands were manicured and she could smell a woody cologne. She took the check and placed it in a drawer. "Here's what I want you to do first."

He explained that a sports bar out on Woodlawn was for sale and gave her the owner's contact information and the amount of his opening offer for the place. "I'd like to close on this as soon as possible. Get it done, would you?"

Clare didn't appreciate the directive and stood up to end the meeting. "I'll make a call and do my best. That's all I can promise."

Ray shot his sleeves and stood up slowly. "We're having another get-together on Saturday and I'd like you to come. It's social, a way to get to know you better."

"Do I really have to be social with you all?"

He smiled, but his eyes stayed static. "Yes, I'm afraid you do. You can come out with Henry. Four o'clock."

She led him back to reception and shook his hand so Donna could see it was all business. When he walked out the door her chest deflated, as if she'd been holding her breath for the past half an hour. She took another tablet of speed and worked until seven that evening, long past the time when everyone else went home. She managed to stay clear of Elizabeth so she wouldn't have to tell her about her meeting with Ray. She could only deal with so much in one day. He had the confidence and bearing of a CEO, but how big could his business be in Timson County? There were a ton of small towns in the county, and multiples of that if you included the surrounding counties. If Ray and the others controlled all traffic in the area, she supposed it could add up to a large network. It certainly took good business instincts to know how to set up such an operation.

She wasn't hungry when she got home. She planned on a beer and a few games on her iPhone to help her relax. Her new regimen of only drinking at home was working out well. She wanted that first one or two to take the edge off her day, but then it was fine. She didn't crave another. Her phone rang at eight and Henry's name popped onto the screen. She was tempted to not answer it, but he would persist until she did. She was getting to know that about him. She picked up.

"What do you want?" she said. She was pissed at the interruption of her quiet evening.

"Whoa. Are you in a bad mood or are you really that unfriendly?"

"Both," she said. "I keep telling you there's no point in you trying to become friends with me."

"We'll see," he said, as if inviting the challenge. "I'm calling to see how your meeting with Ray went."

"As expected. I told him I wasn't the right lawyer for him and he insisted I try anyway."

"Well, at least things are underway. I know you'll do a good job for us."

"And if I don't? Do you kill me when I fail?"

"Jeez. Will you lighten up? It's nothing like that. We want a lawyer who understands the drug business, or is at least sympathetic to it. You have to admit your own dependence on our supply will keep you motivated."

"I'm not dependent on anything."

Henry laughed. "Of course. Tell yourself whatever you'd like."

"Which reminds me, any word on that speed shipment?"

"Still haven't heard. You'll be the first to know."

Fear grabbed her by the throat. She'd do anything to avoid feeling like she did that first day without drugs. She kept the desperation out of her voice. "I have less than a week's worth left."

"Don't worry. I'll get you fixed up. Not that you need it or anything. The other reason I was calling was to ask you to come over. Evan and I are ordering a pizza and watching a movie. Thought you might want to join us."

She shifted on her couch to a more upright position. "You must have selective hearing. Didn't you hear me say I don't want to be friends?"

He laughed again. "Okay, cranky. Some other time." He hung up and Clare was left staring at her phone. Henry was a problem, one that she didn't know how to solve. She tried to put it out of her mind and think about Freya instead, which she'd been doing all afternoon. What did the breakup with Jo mean? There was no denying she was drawn to her. She hadn't yet responded to Freya's text asking if they could talk that evening so she sent a message suggesting they meet at Abe's at nine o'clock. She texted back and agreed. If she didn't drink any more she'd be fine.

Freya was sitting in the middle of the bar and turned her head to the door when Clare entered, getting down from her barstool to greet her. The tavern was quiet—a few people at the bar and one table used by the players standing around the pool table. They were all holding sticks in front of them like the staff of a sentry. Country western music was on the jukebox.

"I thought we could get a table," Freya said. "It's easier to talk."

Clare found herself smiling. "Sure. What can I get you to drink?"

"No, you don't. I've got first dibs since I arrived before you."

"Is that some sort of Money Creek rule?"

"It's a Freya rule. I didn't know what to get you so I waited to order."

"I'll have a Diet Coke, please."

They sat at a table on the opposite side of the room from the pool players. There was no one else in the bar that Clare recognized. She prayed no one would come up to her to remind her of her blackout on Thursday night. When Freya returned from the bar, she took a sip of her Coke, so sweet after the beer she'd been drinking at home. Freya took a long sip from her glass of bourbon.

"Jo made a point of telling me you broke up over the weekend."

Freya looked surprised. "It's true. I almost told you yesterday."

"I don't understand why you didn't. We had that long drive out to the farm and back. Isn't that the sort of thing friends tell each other?"

Freya hesitated. "I broke up with her about an hour before I picked you up. Somehow it was disrespectful to Jo if I started talking about it before she could really take it in. What was her mood like when she told you?

"Let's say she was clearly hurting." Clare tried to catch her eye, but Freya was staring into her drink. "Do you mind me asking why the breakup now?"

Freya took a sip before answering. "It's straightforward enough. I didn't think Jo was the right woman for me."

Clare leaned forward in her chair. "There can't be that many lesbians in Money Creek." Her voice was nearly a whisper.

Freya frowned. "Do you think I should be with someone because there's no one else? I'm not desperate."

She sensed she'd said the wrong thing. "I'm sorry, that was insensitive. I can't imagine you'd ever be desperate."

"I have my moments, but then I remember that I really live in Bloomington. There're a lot of queer folk there."

"But none that you're involved with now?" She was genuinely curious.

"Like a girl in every port? I can't work that way. I'm a serial monogamist. And now I'm officially single again."

Clare raised her glass. "Look out Bloomington."

Freya laughed. "I'm in Money Creek full-time now. I sometimes forget about my life there." She took another sip of bourbon and Clare tried not to wet her lips. It looked so good, the social lubricant that makes all conversations easier. She got up to get them a refill and came back with a bourbon of her own. Only one wouldn't do any damage.

"Now I get to ask you whether you're dating anyone," Freya said. "Any lucky Money Creek dude in your life?"

"God, no. Who has time for that?"

Freya pointed at Clare's glass. "I was wondering what was with the Coke."

"I was thirsty. Now I can relax with a drink." She was nervous, worried that Freya would be watching her consumption.

"Do you like to party, Clare?"

"Not all that much, no."

"I heard about you here last Thursday and it sounded like you were partying hard."

Clare flushed, angry that Freya was commenting on her drinking. What business was it of hers? She didn't reply.

"Ben told me he was here with you."

Clare's glass made a sharp noise as she brought it down on the table. "Why are you asking me these questions? It's none of your concern."

Freya looked at her for a while. "I don't know if you've figured this out yet, but I like you. A lot. It's important to me to know about this. I had an alcoholic girlfriend once and it was awful."

Clare scooched her chair back. "You're saying I'm alcoholic? How dare you?"

Freya raised a placating hand. "I'm not saying that at all."

"Thursday night was a one-off, a combination of overwork and a new medication I'm on. Why? What did Ben tell you?" This is what she wanted to hear and dreaded at the same time. She sat still in the chair.

"He didn't say much. He's a gentleman."

That meant he knew something he was too polite to tell.

"He let me know that you were pretty drunk and he slept at your house to make sure you were okay. That's it. But it concerned me."

Clare tried to hide the confusion and then relief flooding her body. She hadn't had sex with Ben after all. She pulled her chair up to the table. "He didn't have to do that, but I couldn't dissuade him." She made it sound as if she hadn't propositioned him.

"Is Ben someone you'd like to date?" Freya asked.

"No! I'm not looking to date anyone, thanks very much. I want a quiet life so I can do my work, probably the same as you. How is your work, by the way? Is there anything you can tell me about it?"

Clare realized she could act as a secret agent of sorts, possibly leveraging what she learned from Freya and Ben against the blackmail. Could she use Freya that way? Yes, if it meant easing the pressure from Ray Barnes and Henry.

"There isn't, I'm afraid. Only that we're investigating what we believe is a reorganization of the drug dealing channels in the area. We're not having much luck."

"You mean you don't have any evidence?"

Freya considered her for a moment. "It's not something I can discuss."

Damn. "I'm sure something will break for you. In the meantime, you get to stay in Money Creek."

Freya looked amused. "And that's a good thing?"

"That's a very good thing." That sounded suspiciously like flirting. Was she flirting?

Freya spoke softly. "That means a lot to me. You might not know how much."

That sounded like flirting also. At ten o'clock, they still had a lot to say, but Freya called it a night. "My shift starts early. I wish I could stay with you until closing time."

Clare would have been dead drunk by closing time. "No, this is good. I get up early also." They walked to the parking lot together and stopped in front of Clare's Suburu. Freya leaned in for a hug and held Clare closely, a few seconds longer than a friendly squeeze, and then got in her car without saying more. What was that? A prelude to a kiss? She realized that she hoped it was.

## CHAPTER EIGHTEEN

Henry sat at his kitchen table after dumping a plastic shopping bag of drugs onto it. A couple of pounds of marijuana took up the lion's share of the space. His pot customers came mostly from the town. The college students bought some, but generally seemed concerned they'd get busted at the school by using the smelly substance. Pills were more popular.

He thought of Clare as he separated the baggies of Valium from the ones holding Oxycontin and cocaine. She would freak out there still wasn't any Adderall. Whoever was sourcing it had hit a dry spell, and Clare wasn't the only one who'd be upset. Evan reported the students growing frantic as midterms approached.

Normally, Evan did the work of processing the drugs into individual units. Ounces of pot, grams of cocaine, small quantities of pills, but Evan was in St. Louis visiting friends. Henry didn't mind doing it. He was restless and the work calmed him. He popped one of the Valium Clare was so fond of. Maybe it would mellow him out, because he was nearly twitching with worry.

When Stingy delivered the drugs that morning, Henry had asked about Morgan. Stingy fell into a chair as if he'd just carried a mule up a mountain. He was ridiculously fat and out of shape.

"You haven't heard?"

Henry's eyes narrowed. "What?"

"He's gone, man."

"Gone as in he's left town?"

"Gone as in dead. I guess your associates didn't want to take any chances he would testify."

A clamp squeezed his heart. He was the one who'd floated the idea of killing Morgan. Was this what an executioner felt like? He wasn't as relieved as he thought he'd be to have the threat neutralized.

"No," Henry said. "I hadn't heard."

Stingy got up and handed several ziplock bags to him. "Try to relax, Henry. Now's the time to be cool. This is a business and businesses have problems all the time."

Henry led him to the door. "Thanks for dropping these off."

He locked the door, closed the blinds, and got started on processing the delivery. As he finished up the sorting and packaging, his phone rang. He saw it was his mother calling and reluctantly picked up. She always seemed to know when something was wrong with him.

"Hi, Mom." He tried to sound cheery.

"Hello, sweetheart. What's new?"

His mother regularly made these check-in calls, ostensibly to say hello, but Henry knew she was really trying to keep tabs on what he was up to. Ever since the incident at Princeton, she hadn't seemed to trust him. He was constantly under the microscope. There were things that happened at Princeton other than the drug dealing that his parents didn't know about. Like the time he was called before the student body board for what they called the relentless bullying of a sophomore named Brandon Montgomery. He was a rich little prick who'd purposefully humiliated Henry by leaving a party with the girl Henry brought. He was teased about it the next day when his club met, and then he set his sights on Montgomery. Henry physically intimidated him, slashed the tires of his Audi, accused him of cheating in a math class, and turned as many people against him as possible. The board issued him a warning and that proved the end of it. Montgomery transferred to Dartmouth halfway through the school year. It was no big deal, but he was glad his parents hadn't heard about it.

"Nothing's new. I'm getting ready for midterms."

"How's that going?" His mother's tone was light.

"Same as last time you asked. It's going fine."

"I'm sorry if I'm repeating myself. I'm only making conversation."

Even if she was too much in his business, he knew she did it out of love. She'd never made Henry feel anything but loved.

"Listen, I'm having a small dinner party I want you to come to," she said.

"Oh?"

"Sunday supper. If you come at five, we'll serve at six."

"Who all is coming?"

"You're the first I've invited. I was thinking of asking Clare and Freya Saucedo and her partner."

"You mean Jo from your office?"

"That's over already. She was moping around the office today and told me they'd broken up. I meant Freya's detective partner, Ben."

Great. Dinner with the drug task force. But Clare would be there so there was no question about going. "I'll be there."

"Wonderful. I hope Clare can make it. I think she's been lonely since moving to town."

He'd love to make her feel less lonely, if only he could find a way through to her that didn't involve blackmail.

❖

Clare was the first into the office again, a few hours short on sleep but anxious to continue work on the outline she was preparing for her brief. Freya was equally on her mind. She was like a kid waiting to open Christmas presents. She knew something good was going to happen and she was alive with the possibilities. The attraction was now impossible to deny, and she didn't want to.

Elizabeth poked her head in the door. "How was your meeting with your new client?"

Clare kept her voice casual. "Great. I got a ten-thousand-dollar retainer from him. I gave it to Donna to deposit."

"Good work. Did he agree to have Hank handle the transactions?"

"I'm afraid he insists it be me." It was painful to mislead Elizabeth.

"How did you say you came to meet this man?"

She hadn't said. And now she had to make something up. "I don't know what this says about me, but I met him in a bar. We got to talking."

"And his name again?"

"Ray Barnes."

Elizabeth shook her head. "No. Don't know him. It seems odd he's putting so much faith in you after a barroom conversation. You must have really impressed him."

Clare smiled. "What can I say. I know how to work a tavern."

Elizabeth laughed. "Ask Hank any questions you may have. Having malpractice insurance doesn't mean we want to use it."

She continued down the hall and Clare breathed out. She had a way of partially holding her breath and talking from the top of her chest. An observant person would know Clare was anxious, but Elizabeth didn't seem to be one of them. She went back to her outline and worked until eleven, when she thought it was late enough to call Henry. Her speed supply was perilously low, and she hadn't heard any more from him on when he was going to get more. She didn't want to wait for the party with Ray and Bobby if she didn't have to. She closed her office door and dialed his cell number.

"This is Evan."

Clare looked at her phone. "Why are you answering Henry's phone?"

"Who is this?"

"I think you know. It's Clare Lehane."

"Clare! Good to hear from you. I'm watching Henry's phone for a little bit."

"You are at his beck and call, aren't you?"

"I live to serve." His tone was not ironic. "Henry won't be back for another couple of hours."

"He leaves the house without his phone? How's that even possible?"

"Well, the truth is he's still sleeping. Don't tell him I told you that."

"How could that matter?"

She could hear him sigh. "Henry doesn't like me to say anything about him to anyone."

She decided not to tease him. The only thing she was interested in was the speed. "Did he say anything to you about a shipment of speed coming in?"

"That's a negative. And I have a ton of students breathing down my neck."

"Shit. Would you make sure I get a cut before it all goes to them?"

"I'll do my best, Clare."

"You don't need to tell Henry I called." She hung up. The situation was becoming serious. If he didn't get anything by Saturday she would be completely out. She pulled out the apple she'd brought for her lunch and forced it down. She had no appetite. Her stomach was sour with stress.

When she got home from work that evening she wanted to watch bad TV and not think. She settled into her couch after dinner and brought Netflix up on her screen. Her phone pinged and there was a text from Henry.

*Heard you called. No shipment yet. Party on Saturday at my country house. You'll want to come to it, trust me. Four o'clock. Henry.*

No, she didn't want to go to the party. Henry didn't know that Ray had already commanded her attendance. If she quit drugs she would be free of them, but could she do it? The thought terrified her. She didn't have the strength to get through the physical discomfort, let alone the raw feelings that would emerge. She would need to taper the Valium. She'd never once progressively taken less of a drug rather than more. If being coerced by a gang of drug dealers wasn't motivation enough to quit, she didn't know what would be. She no longer denied she was a drug addict. But that seemed as far as she could go.

## Chapter Nineteen

"We picked up a DUI last night you might be interested in," Sheriff Phillips said.

Freya and Ben were in their office, brainstorming ways to find Stingy. Without him they couldn't move forward in their investigation. It was clear that control of the drug traffic was concentrating on manufacturers funneling through a single buyer, Stingy.

"Why's that, Sheriff?" Ben said. The sheriff was standing at the door of their small office. He seemed to fill the entire space.

"We picked him up on Woodlawn, weaving through traffic and running a red light. The guy's name is Drew Lee."

They looked at him blankly.

"We ran the name, of course. He has a sheet, mostly for drug possession with intent to sell. I think it's your man. At least the artist sketch looks like him."

Freya nearly spewed her coffee. "You have Stingy in custody?" She was incredulous.

"Yeah. His arraignment is this morning. If you want to talk to him I'd do it now. Chances are he'll be released on bail for the DUI."

"Holy shit," Ben said. "How can we be this lucky?"

"Not lucky, but let's not blow this. We need to bring Morgan or Dunning to pick him out of a lineup. Dunning can leave the hospital for it. I want to make sure we're talking to the real Stingy."

She picked up the phone to have a panel assembled, which was going to take some time. Timson County Jail was not brimming with bodies to populate a lineup. It was early afternoon before Dunning looked at the lineup and reluctantly identified Stingy as the man he sold his drugs to. The deputies couldn't find Morgan.

They waited in the interview room for Stingy. When he arrived, the deputy plunked him down in a chair and handcuffed him to the table. Stingy looked indignant.

"I'm here on a drunk driving charge, not murder one. Can we get rid of the handcuffs?"

Freya looked at Stingy and then up at the deputy. "You can let him loose. We'll be fine."

The deputy looked doubtful but did as he was told. Stingy immediately crossed his arms over his chest and stared at Ben and Freya. He was a chubby man with thick, soft forearms, a double chin, and white teeth gleaming through his sardonic smile. He wasn't a user of his product from the looks of it, but he was a bit rough from his night in jail. "What's this about?"

"You go by the name of Stingy, correct?" asked Freya.

"That's what you've been told, apparently. I've never answered to the name." He was relaxed, as if it was Freya who had the problem, not him.

"This is going to go more smoothly for you if you tell the truth. You were picked out of a lineup."

He continued to stare but said nothing.

Ben leaned toward him. "You're a person of interest in an investigation of ours. If you cooperate, we can probably make this DUI disappear."

"You haven't asked me a question yet."

Ben jumped the gun with that offer. Now they looked more desperate for his cooperation. Freya sounded casual as she looked at Stingy. "Our witness, who identified you in the lineup, says he sells meth exclusively to you."

"And who might that be?"

"We'll keep that name to ourselves. Who do you work for?"

Stingy looked insulted again. "You're saying I sell meth? Please."

"What is it you do for work?" Ben said.

Stingy hesitated for the first time. "I have some family money. I'm between careers at the moment."

"You know how easy that is to check, don't you? Freya said. "What work did you do, then?"

"I was a manager at the AutoZone. I quit a few months ago."

"I believe that following your career with AutoZone you signed up with some meth manufacturers to be their middleman. That would be a lot more lucrative a career, wouldn't it?"

Stingy looked relaxed. "Undoubtedly. But I wouldn't know. As I said, I don't have any work at the moment and I don't know anything about meth manufacturers"

"We've looked at your sheet, Stingy. There're several arrests for possession of fairly substantial quantities of drugs." Freya said.

"Yes, but what kind of drugs? Marijuana is a far cry from meth."

"But you would have had contact with someone who sold you the pot," Ben said.

"True. But it was a long time ago."

"From your sheet it looks like your last arrest was two years ago and your probation ended a few months ago."

"Two years is forever in that business. I'm sure I don't know anyone who's out there now."

They spent the next half hour asking the same question in a variety of ways, and still Stingy would not admit to any association with drug dealing, despite being identified by a witness. An unreliable witness. He didn't ask to lawyer up. They decided not to charge him at the time. He would have to stay in the area to deal with the drunk driving charge. They returned to their office.

"That got us nothing," Ben said.

"One of us needs to get over to court to see what happens at his arraignment. The other should be ready to tail him when he leaves. We have an address for his current residence, but I don't think that's the first place he'll go."

"I'll take the car," Ben said.

Of course, Ben would take the fun part. Freya didn't argue and walked over to the courthouse. She couldn't hope to run into Clare because she knew she was downstate taking depositions. She'd been thinking about her a lot. There wasn't any other interpretation for how things were on Monday night at Abe's. They were flirting, they were getting to know each other on a deeper level, they were moving in one direction. It appeared Jo was right about Clare—whether she knew it or not, she was into women. Freya wasn't in the business of converting straight women, but she couldn't turn away from the energy between the two of them. It was as tangible as the gun on her belt.

When Stingy was released on bail, Freya called Ben to give him the heads up and returned to the office to ask the sheriff for a surveillance team. She could only hope he might lead them to a meeting with his employers.

"I was just going to call you," Sheriff Phillips said when she entered his office.

"Oh, yeah? What's up?"

"Some kids snowmobiling outside of town found a body. The first deputy on the scene recognized him. It was that Morgan fellow you picked up."

Freya sank into a chair. "We knew it could happen, but I didn't think it really would. How'd they find him?"

"Said they were taking a rest on the trail out at the state park. The body was lying right off the trail, uncovered."

"Whoever did it wanted the body to be found."

"Looks that way," the sheriff said. "They're taking it to the medical examiner now. The deputy said he'd been shot once in the chest and once in the face."

"The shooter was sending a message—this is what happens if you talk to the cops. It's got to be the drug cartel."

"I'd say so." He leaned back in his chair. "We're not used to any kind of murder here, let alone one involving drug cartels."

"This tells us a lot about what we're up against. We've got Dunning in lockup, which is fortunate for him. I don't like his chances once he gets into the prison system."

The sheriff gave her a rotation of deputies to keep an eye on Stingy, who might also be under threat. Freya left to contemplate the radically changed landscape of her investigation. Things had become darker, more urgent. She called her boss to request more people, but he couldn't pull anyone off any of the other local task forces. That left her Ben, Sheriff Phillips, and his deputies. It would have to do.

❖

Thomas stepped into Clare's office for their meeting on the Peterson summary judgement motion. She'd given him the task of assembling all the current evidence and writing it up in a memorandum. She concentrated on the legal issues but had overall responsibility for both projects. She'd been working long hours to get everything done by Elizabeth's deadline, but lost precious time when she spent the entire day in Carbondale taking the rest of the depositions at the lagoon company, which had corroborated what John Lyons had testified to. Now she was eager to get back to the brief.

He handed her an outline of the memorandum and she read it thoroughly while he sat there.

"Has your name come up yet in the pro bono wheel of fortune?" he said.

She looked up. "What are you talking about?"

"The county can't afford staff defense attorneys so they tag all of us in turn to represent the pro bono cases."

"Great. I hope my name doesn't come up in the next two weeks."

"It'll happen soon, I'm sure. I caught one yesterday and it was kind of interesting. This guy got picked up Tuesday night on a DUI and it turns out he's a person of interest in that drug investigation Freya and Ben are conducting."

That got her attention. "Did he give anything up?"

"I wasn't with him for the initial interview, but he told me later he didn't know anything about what they were asking him. I saw him through the DUI arraignment, and they cut him loose."

She'd have to ask Henry who this man was. If he knew anything that could bust Henry and the others it would be bad news for her. There wouldn't be any other drug connections she could hope to make.

"Did you talk to Freya about it?"

"There's nothing I could say to Freya and she's not likely to tell me what they plan to do with Stingy."

"Stingy?"

"It's his stage name."

She reached for her cold cup of coffee. "It sounds like you pulled a pretty easy case. Does that mean your name is off the wheel for a period of time?"

"Yeah. You go off for a month once you've handled a case. I'm clear for a while."

She worked the rest of the day wondering if she should call Henry or not. He and the others would like to know about Stingy being arrested, if they hadn't heard already. She knew he hadn't talked and that was valuable information. It might save a life, too. If they thought Stingy talked to the police, she guessed Stingy would be eliminated. That's how things worked in the movies, anyway. They couldn't afford to have a witness against them. When the office emptied out at five, she placed a call to Henry.

"Clare! A phone call from Clare. I'm pinching myself."

"Don't get too excited," she said dryly.

"What can I do for you? Wait, you're probably calling about the speed shipment. I'm supposed to hear something today, so why don't you plan to stop by here tomorrow. I'll fix you up."

She was relieved. She'd taken her last two speed tablets that morning. Things were at the crisis point. "I'm glad to hear it, but I called about something else."

"Lay it on me."

"Do you know a guy named Stingy?"

There was silence on the other end of the line. "Henry?"

"Why do you ask?"

"I heard he'd been picked up on a DUI and was interrogated about drug activity in the area."

"That's interesting. How do you know that?"

She chose her words carefully. "I have sources. I'm in a position to know what happens in the legal community."

"That's interesting, too. Do you know if this Stingy told the police anything?"

"I can tell you that, but I want something in exchange. If I keep you informed on what I hear on my end, I want to be released from representing Ray."

"I'm afraid that's not possible. We consider you an important part of our operation. Your counsel will be valuable." She didn't respond.

"Tell me what Stingy did or did not say," Henry said.

"If I'm a part of your organization, you can't continue to blackmail me. Threats don't make for loyal associates." She hoped he could hear the steel in her voice.

"I can't unknow what I already know about you, but I don't intend to use the information. I'll chose to believe your participation is voluntary."

That left the landscape essentially as before. The cost of crossing them was too high. She didn't want to lose everything she had in Money Creek. She loved her work. And there was Freya. She could imagine her reaction on learning Clare was a drug user. That relationship would be over before it even started.

"He didn't say anything," she said. "You should let the others know right away so Stingy doesn't get killed. I don't doubt they would off him."

"We've heard from Stingy today, as it turns out. But your corroboration is very useful."

"Why didn't you say that? And you wonder why I don't warm up to you," Clare said.

"You will, I'm sure of it. Come by here tomorrow after work. You'll like me much better then."

They hung up. An unseen hand pressed down on her shoulders, keeping her in place so she wouldn't explode from too much pressure. But there were glimmers of good news. Her work, Freya, the resupply of her stash. She'd try to concentrate on those. Freya was coming over for dinner. She should have been nervous about it, but there was no room for it at the moment. She left the office to get groceries for the meal.

❖

Clare put some chicken and vegetables in the oven to roast, trying to time it so it would be ready about half an hour after Freya arrived at seven. She changed out of her work clothes but had a hard time figuring out what to wear. Was this a date? How did you dress for a date with a woman? It seemed it should be different than with men, though she hadn't gone on dates with men so much as ended up with them at parties or a bar. That was far less stressful than a formal date. Was the excitement in her chest anxiety or anticipation? She put on jeans and her asymmetrical knit top that dressed things up a bit. Her Dansko clogs made her an inch taller.

Freya arrived on time carrying two bottles of Perrier. She could feel the message behind the choice of drink. She wanted to see if Clare was comfortable not drinking. Of course, she was. Two Valiums and she was fine with it. She took the bottles from Freya and invited her in.

"What a great place," Freya said. "It's so comfortable looking." She followed Clare into the kitchen. Smoke was starting to seep out of the oven, so Clare turned on the vent fan. It roared to life, making it harder to speak.

"Don't worry," Clare said. "It's roasting, not burning."

"I wasn't worried at all." Freya smiled at her and Clare thought it was the greatest smile she'd ever seen. She made their drinks and led her into the living room, sitting at her usual spot on one end of the couch while Freya sat on the other. It was a long couch.

"I heard about what happened to you." Thomas had told Clare about the meth lab bust and Freya's shooting of the two men there. "Is that the first time you've killed someone in the line of duty?"

"How did you hear about that?" Freya asked.

"You know how it is here. Someone in my office told me. I don't know how he heard. I'm surprised you didn't mention it the other night."

Freya looked at her hands in her lap. "It's not the sort of thing I'd bring up. I'm not proud of myself."

"How are you feeling about it?" Clare imagined it felt horrible to have killed someone, but she was a bit dazzled by the thought of Freya in a gun battle. It was beyond her comprehension. She'd always wondered how brave she'd be if put to the test. Not very brave was her guess.

"I'm mostly fine. We're trained for these situations. Two men pulled guns on me and I shot them. They were clean hits. Considering I would have been shot dead if I hadn't fired makes me okay with what happened."

Clare quit staring at Freya long enough to pick up her drink. Her eyes fell on a spot on the floor in the middle of the couch where her pillbox was poking out. She resisted the urge to shove it back under, which would only draw Freya's attention. Instead, she reached for her drink and moved a little closer to the middle of the couch.

"I'm glad you like the place," she said, meeting Freya's eyes and slowly pushing the box under the couch with her foot. "I've grown to love it."

There was a definite static in the air as they talked about banal things like the weather and the party at Elizabeth's house that Sunday and how much work they both had. Clare put dinner on, the smell of the herbs and lemon filled the kitchen.

"Would you like some wine?" Clare asked.

"No, I'm good with the water. School night and all that."

"Right. I won't bother opening a bottle. I've got a big day tomorrow too. They're all big days." Not that that had ever stopped her from opening a bottle.

After dinner they moved back to the couch, both of them sitting slightly closer to the middle than before. Clare ate her slice of cherry pie, suddenly much more nervous than before. She couldn't imagine what would happen next. Or she could imagine it, but it made her stomach clench.

Freya drank her coffee and then put the mug down. They were silent, conversation gone, air heavy. "I have to ask you something."

Clare's head snapped up from her pie plate. "You do?"

"This sort of thing isn't easy. I'm nervous as hell."

"Maybe you shouldn't ask."

Freya hesitated a moment. "I have to. I know you've told me you're straight, but I'm wondering if that's really how you identify. I feel a connection between the two of us. Am I imagining things?"

Her body suffused with some chemical—the one that made her elated and terrified at the same time. She could dodge the question, but she found she wanted to be honest. "No, I feel it too. I don't know what that makes me. All I know is what I feel now."

Freya smiled and reached for Clare's hand. "Tell me more."

She stared at the hand holding hers, the long slender fingers wrapped around her own. "I have slept with a woman before." She didn't remember a thing about that night a few weeks earlier, but there must have been some part of her that thought sleeping with a woman would be a good thing to do, even in a blackout.

"You have? That changes everything." Freya looked relieved. "Now I don't have to feel so responsible."

"Responsible for what? I'm a big girl, you know."

"You're right. Maybe it's arrogance on my part to feel responsible for your first experience."

They were silent for a minute. "Maybe we're getting ahead of ourselves," Clare said.

Freya flushed. "Good point." She let go of her hand and Clare felt the absence of it. They both reached for their coffee and stared at each other over their mugs.

Clare started to relax, the Valium working its magic. She put her coffee down. "Now what happens?"

"This is the part where I come close and kiss you, if you'll allow me."

She nodded, her eyes wide open. She watched as Freya scootched toward her and stopped when they were half an arm's length away. "Oh, God," Clare said. Freya leaned toward her and kissed her gently on the lips, pulling away to see how she reacted. Clare put her arm around Freya's back and pulled her into a more serious kiss, one that lasted a long time. They leaned against the back of the couch and made out for a while. Clare could feel arousal, unmistakable and strong. When Freya moved her mouth to her throat she gasped. Would it be slutty to ask Freya into her bedroom? Were women generally slower to jump into bed?

Freya pulled back from her. "We either have to stop or move to a bed. My body is getting out of control."

So, not slutty. Clare rose from the couch and took Freya by the hand. "Let me show you the bedroom."

She closed the door behind her, locking out everything she'd known before, anxious for what was to come. Her own drug use and her involvement with drug dealers were not insignificant things when falling in love with a cop. But caution had no chance against desire.

## CHAPTER TWENTY

It's like the speed you're used to, but more so." Henry pointed at the crystalline powder that sat on the coffee table.

"How can it be like speed?" Clare was terrified.

"What you usually take is Adderall, which is pharmaceutical amphetamine. Crystal meth is also amphetamine, but not pharmaceutical grade. Meth heads are addicts because they do too much of it. If you do the right amount, it will be business as usual."

It was crisis time. After Freya left Friday morning to go to work, Clare had pulled out her pillbox and looked at the empty compartment where the speed normally was. The afterglow of her night with Freya, so filled with sensations and feelings she'd never had before, couldn't dispel the panic that dropped on her like a sack. She had a day's worth of work ahead of her and her body cried out for her drug. She'd gotten very little sleep the night before—they'd made love until they passed out from exhaustion. How was she going to work on a brief, as well as learn a new area of law? She was sludgy, as if mud were sucking at her sides.

Henry sat down and started chopping the lines. "Personally, I like to make the powder as smooth as possible, but other people like the rocky feel. This is already pretty smooth, which means it's high quality. We're not giving you crap."

"When do you think you'll get the Adderall in? Maybe I can wait it out."

Henry patted the space next to him. "The word is a week or so from now. And that's iffy."

She knew she couldn't get the work done she needed to in that week. She sat down.

"Did you know that Hitler had his whole army running on methamphetamine? They fought a war on the stuff," he said.

She looked at him. "That's the finest endorsement of a product I've ever heard."

He laughed and handed a straw to Clare. "Don't worry, this is a beginner's dose. I wouldn't let you do anything that would harm you."

She doubted that was true, but had no choice. She snorted the two lines and almost immediately the rush cascaded down her body. It was like she'd been punched by it, different from the much slower payoff with tablets. She leaned against the back of the couch. A sense of clarity and energy began to take hold. She smiled.

"How are you?" Henry asked.

"I think I'm good. How long does it last?"

"Longer than regular speed. You probably don't want to take any more today if you want to sleep at all tonight."

At the moment she wanted to do everything. Work, make love with Freya, build a cathedral. She sat for a few more minutes enjoying the rush and then stood. "I'm going back to the office."

Henry nodded and handed her the remaining powder in the packet. "This is on the house."

She took it and shoved it into her pants pocket. "I'll see you later, I guess."

"You'll see me tomorrow. Don't forget the party we're going to. I'll meet you out there."

Clare frowned. Some form of magical thinking had allowed her to forget the party. "I'm not going to be able to make it."

"What do you mean?" Henry matched her frown.

"I'm too busy. I have to work all weekend. You'll probably have a better time without me."

"Your attendance is expected. I've got to drive on my own. Do you remember where it is?"

"Barely. It was like a labyrinth getting there."

"Here's the address. Your GPS will get you close."

She took down the address in her phone and left. As she walked to her car she looked around the quiet street. It was a warmer day and she left her coat unbuttoned. Everything around her, even her thoughts, seemed crystal clear, almost too sharp to be comfortable. Sparrows chirped loudly in the trees above her. The houses on the street nearly shimmered in the sun. She got in her car, anxious to get to her desk to concentrate on one thing. Her brain was whirring and needed settling down. This was like speed multiplied by ten. She loved it.

At work she burrowed in her office and started writing the draft of the summary judgement motion. She didn't look up until she heard people saying good night outside her door. The past four hours had seemed like a minute and she'd written like the wind. Her cell phone rang and she saw it was Freya. She struggled to pull her head out of the cave of legalese it'd been in and answered the call.

"Did that really happen last night?" Clare said.

Freya chuckled. "It was very real. Why don't we get together tonight?"

Clare hesitated. She wanted to work another few hours. She wasn't sure whether Freya would be able to tell she was on something. "Not tonight, though I'd love to. I'm working another few hours here and then crashing as soon as I get home. You wore me out last night."

"Oh. I should have realized you wouldn't want to get together so soon."

"I do want to, but I can't tonight."

"Understood."

"I've thought about you all day." That was a slight lie. She had thought of Freya, but only during bathroom breaks. Her total focus was on the brief.

"Me too," Freya said.

Clare waited for something more, but Freya was silent. She'd embarrassed her by turning her down and she didn't want that. "How about tomorrow night? My house again?"

"That would be wonderful," Freya said, her voice sounding more relaxed. "I'll call you tomorrow to see what you'd like me to bring."

"Just yourself, I think. That's more than enough."

When they disconnected, Clare was excited and slightly aroused. She wanted to see her…what? Girlfriend? How odd that sounded, and how good, too. But not tonight. She wanted to dive back into the brief and that feeling of being suspended in time she'd experienced all afternoon. When she got home that night shortly after eleven, she took a couple of Valium and tried to sleep. Three hours later, she finally did.

❖

The storm was getting worse as Clare drove out of Money Creek. Flurries were whipping around the car, making visibility difficult. Snow whirled in small cyclones in the empty cornfields. It was still daylight, with the edges of twilight closing in. She was anxious as she neared her destination. She fumbled a couple of Valium out of her pillbox and swallowed them dry.

She saw the tiny road to Henry's house when she was almost upon it and took a hard left up the drive. At the top of the drive were three cars—Henry's old Volvo, a beat-up pickup truck, and a low-slung Chevy Malibu. She would have thought drug dealers could afford better rides.

She parked behind the pickup and got out. The house and the grounds were still awful, unimproved by the beautiful snowfall. How had it come to this? She was nothing like these people.

The front door opened and Henry leaned out.

"You made it. I was afraid the snow was going to get worse." It hadn't occurred to her she might have used the weather as an excuse not to come. Stupid. She walked to the door, holding her coat closed at the collar.

"You better let me in. If I've got to be here I don't want to freeze to death."

He opened the door to let her pass. "Don't be that way, Clare. Everyone's looking forward to seeing you."

She walked past Henry and shrugged out of her coat in the tiny foyer. He hung it in the closet and took her by the elbow into the living room. A feeble lamp cast a dim light in the dark room. She would have expected them to have a nicer party house, too. This looked like a place squatters would never get thrown out of.

Bobby Hughes and Ray Barnes sat around the coffee table and a woman who must have been Bobby's girlfriend leaned against his shoulder.

"Welcome, Clare," Ray said. "Join us." He went back to chopping up lines of cocaine on the coffee table.

Bobby stood and reached out his hand. "Hi, Clare. I'm glad you could come." He made it sound like she had a choice. "This is my fiancée , Caroline."

Caroline popped up from the couch and came over to give Clare a big hug. "So nice to meet you! I was thrilled when Bobby told me another woman would be here. What can I get you to drink?"

"Is coffee possible?"

"No coffee, I'm afraid," Henry said. "Beer, wine, anything you can think of."

"Anything non-alcoholic?"

He grimaced. "Except that."

She'd resolved to not drink at the party. She didn't want to blindly agree to anything they might propose.

"I'll take the beer."

"I'll get it!" Caroline said. She turned toward the kitchen and hurried away. Clare could see the tattoo on her lower back that said "Bobby." She hoped they had a long marriage in front of them. She sat on a dining room chair across from the couch, where Henry and Ray occupied chairs on either side of it.

She took the beer from Caroline and looked from one man to the other." "Please don't take this the wrong way, but I don't understand why I'm here."

Bobby looked insulted. "Isn't hanging with us reason enough?"

"Frankly, no. I didn't know I was meant to become buddies with you all."

Henry looked uncomfortable, as if a date were making a scene. "In our business, everything is about relationships." He made it sound like they ran a client-based service business, which she supposed they did. "You're a person we definitely want a relationship with."

"But why?" She took a long drink of beer and thought about whiskey.

"I'm your client, right?" Ray said. "That's one aspect of our relationship. But we want more. We want to rely on you for legal advice and we want you to convey information to us, like you did yesterday to Henry."

She sat still, though the meth made her want to bounce her leg. "And if I refuse?"

"Same rules as before. You'll lose your drug supply and Henry will tell his mother you're an addict."

"That will expose him to Elizabeth, as well. And I'm not an addict."

"That doesn't worry me," Henry said. "I wish you'd relax, Clare. Let's just hang out and get to know each other."

"What about the speed that's supposed to come in?" she said. "One thing you can do for me is get that shipment."

Ray shrugged. "We can't control everything. There's a crackdown on Adderall and it's gotten hard to come by. Be patient. That shouldn't be hard if you're not an addict." His expression was just shy of a smirk.

Clare ignored the remark. "Do you think it's a matter of days, weeks?"

"Why so nervous about it?" Bobby asked. "It seems the meth has gone over well with you."

"That's not something I mean to repeat." She hoped that was true.

With the help of some more beers and shots of tequila, Clare made it through a couple hours of conversation about topics she couldn't care less about. Caroline pulled a chair next to her and tried for some girl talk, but she didn't want to talk about boyfriends. What she really wanted was to talk to a friend about Freya, but Caroline didn't qualify. And there was the question of letting these people know she was a...what? A lesbian? This was downstate Illinois, where each small town had eight churches and the vote was reliably Republican.

Henry stood and put his phone in his back pocket.

"I'll say good-bye, then. I have to get going." He turned to Ray. "Remember I told you I had that thing I have to be at?"

Ray nodded and Henry reached for his coat.

"I'll go with you," Clare said, rising quickly from her chair.

"No, you'll stay," Ray said, looking up at her with penetrating eyes. "We're just getting started here."

"Please, I want to go home."

Henry shifted his eyes from Clare to Ray and back again. "Not now, Clare. Just relax and enjoy yourself." He left the room quickly and she heard the front door close behind him. Clare sat down again.

Furious, she got up to excuse herself to the bathroom. Even a short break from these awful people was welcome. Freya was coming by her house at nine. She had to get home by then. She stared in the bathroom mirror a full minute, trying to figure out how she'd gotten into so much trouble. She wanted a simple life, and now it was anything but. Suddenly, an explosion of gunfire erupted and she threw herself to the floor, biting her tongue to keep from screaming. The shooting continued for what seemed an eternity but was probably less than ten seconds. When it stopped she could hear her heart beat, pulsating in her ears. There wasn't a sound from the other side of the door. She was nearly catatonic, terrified the gunman would search the house and kill her, too. There was more gunfire and footsteps pounding through the house. Then she heard the backdoor slam. She got up and peeked out the bathroom window and saw a man walking along the side of the house carrying a pistol in his hand. He wore a vigilante mask on his face, an open camouflage jacket, and a green Guns N' Roses concert T-shirt. He was tall and lanky.

She heard an engine start and the sound of gravel crunching under tires. She started shaking, making it hard to open the door. The bathroom was at the end of a hallway lined with three small bedrooms. She crept toward the living room and smelled cordite. She peeked into the room. Bobby was pressed against the back of the couch, the front of his shirt bloody. Caroline was draped over the end of the couch, still alive. By the time Clare had turned around to call an ambulance, she was dead. There was no mistaking the fixed stare from her blue eyes.

Bobby had fallen forward on the coffee table, his arm across her phone. Ray had fallen out of his chair, a bullet hole in his forehead and many more in his body.

The smell of fresh blood made her gag. She looked at the bodies with glazed eyes, seeing but not seeing the surreal sight in front of her. Then she took a breath and reached for Bobby's arm to move it off her phone, but realized she should put her gloves on. They were thick and wooly and made her hands clumsy, but it was better than leaving anything identifiable behind. Her self-preservation instinct had kicked in. She went to the closet to retrieve her things and put her coat and gloves on, then carefully lifted Bobby's arm and slipped her phone out from under it. She went into the bathroom to rub everything down that she'd touched.

Back in the living room she looked out the window to see if anyone was in front of the house, but all was empty and silent. She opened the door with her gloved hand and slid outside. No one should be able to detect she'd been there. She pointed her car down the drive and tried to slow her racing mind. What should she do? It was bad enough she was fleeing the scene of a crime, but could she leave the murders unreported? It could be months before anyone found the bodies, if at all. She found another Valium and swallowed it, trying to counter the meth, but doubting there was enough Valium in the world to make her unsee what she just saw. As she drove to Money Creek, she kept a look out for a public phone booth, praying they hadn't all been eliminated as they had in the city. There was one outside a Texaco gas station about halfway to Money Creek. She called 911 and when the dispatcher picked up she spoke with an unnaturally low voice.

"There's been a multiple murder at 15264 Lamont in Timson County."

"What is your name, ma'am?"

She hung up and drove quickly away from the station, hoping no one noticed her or her car, and pulled up to her house at eight thirty. Freya would arrive in thirty minutes. That was undoable—she'd have to cancel. She sent a text and said she'd become ill, which was certainly true. Freya would be upset, but no one was more upset at the moment than she was. She poured a healthy amount of bourbon in a glass and sought refuge on her couch, where she looked about her with unseeing eyes, thinking about something that was unimaginable.

## Chapter Twenty-one

B en looked at the scene in front of him. "Jesus Christ."
Three bodies were sprawled around the small living
room, blood everywhere. The air was sticky with it. Freya picked
up a shell casing from the floor with her gloved hands. "Nine-
millimeter. I would have though an AK-47 from the looks of
things." She looked from one body to the next. She'd never seen a
triple homicide and tried to keep a professional face on, though the
bloodshed was horrifying. "De we have their phones?"

Sheriff Phillips walked into the living room from the rear of the
house. "You two got here quick."

"What do you think, Sheriff?" Ben said. Freya picked up a
phone from the coffee table with her gloved hands. It had a pink
cover so it had to be the woman's. She patted down the pants pockets
of the two men and pulled out a phone from one of them.

The sheriff looked at the scene with his hands on his hips.
"I think we have a fucking mess, is what." He turned to Freya.
"I informed you of this as a courtesy, but you know this is our
jurisdiction."

"You can understand our interest," Freya said. "Seems logical
to me this is some kind of drug hit."

"And I'm not going to shut you out, but I am going to run the
show. Agreed?"

"That's fine," Ben said. "What else can you tell us?"

"We received an anonymous call at 2013 hours and the first
responders got here about 2045. Deputies have secured the scene but

left everything untouched. They've started a canvas of properties in the area, but as you can guess, they're far away from here and it's unlikely anyone heard anything."

"Someone may have seen a car on the road or going up the drive," Ben said. "Will you let us know what they find?"

The sheriff nodded. Freya stepped over to the adjacent dining room and fished through the jackets on the table. She found a third phone. All three had security locks on them.

"Do we have an ID on these guys?"

"Ray Barnes, Bobby Hughes, and Caroline Sommers."

She touched the numbers on one of the phones that corresponded to the word RAYB and the screen lit up. Not very sophisticated for a drug dealer. She couldn't get the other two open. As the sheriff and Ben began to go over the scene, Freya scrolled down the contacts list in Ray's phone. She got to the Ls and her heart nearly skipped a beat when she saw Clare's name. What the hell? If these were the area's main drug traffickers, as she suspected they were, why did one of them have Clare's number? She looked at Ben and the sheriff to make sure they were occupied, then deleted it from the phone before she could think better of it. Her instinct was to protect Clare, but at what cost? Tampering with evidence could end her career. She'd stop by Clare's later to find out what she could. Stingy's name appeared on the list as she scrolled farther down.

"Ben?" She found him in the kitchen where he was looking in drawers. "Ray Barnes has Stingy's name and number in his phone. That makes me pretty sure these were the guys he worked for."

"No doubt. I'm surprised there's a number there for Stingy."

Freya called the number and an automated voice directed it to voice mail. She hung up, wanting to see how long it would take for him to return a call from Ray's phone.

"If Stingy's our man for this, what was his motive?" Ben said. "Do you think he was trying to take over the business?"

"Possibly. Or he was worried they'd eliminate him after his DUI arrest. He had good reason to think so after what happened to Morgan. They wouldn't want anyone under pressure from the police to turn against them and testify."

"That seems brutal," Ben said.

She shrugged. "These aren't nice people."

They looked closely at the bodies. Rigor mortis had not set in and the blood looked fresh. There wasn't more to see. When they stepped outside they found the sheriff talking to a deputy. Freya zipped up her down jacket and took her latex gloves off in favor of her leather ones. Her breath was visible in the cold air.

"Did you find anything else?" Freya asked him.

"No. There's nothing in the house that indicates who owns it. No papers, no photographs. It's somebody's party house."

"Let us run the property title down for you," Ben said.

"Fine. We'll take all the bottles and glasses in and run the DNA against the database. I've already run the names of the victims and no one has a previous record except for the woman, who was arrested for possession of meth. It was a low quantity—she didn't serve any time."

"There was a small amount of meth in her bag, so she hasn't quit the stuff," Ben said.

"Sheriff, I'd like to keep hold of Ray Barnes's phone. I think Stingy might call him back. If he doesn't it's likely because he knows Ray's dead and the police have got his phone."

"I'd rather you hand it over," he said.

She gave it to him. "Let me know, will you? And I'd like to see the other phones when you break into them. There may be more interesting names there." God forbid Clare's was one of them.

"I'll put a couple deputies on calling all the names in their phones and let you know what we find. Do you think these are the traffickers you were looking for?"

Freya stamped her feet. Why were they talking outdoors? "Stingy's name is in Barnes's phone, so I'd say yes. We need to find where they lived. There may be computer files or notebooks in their homes that provide evidence. If Stingy doesn't return the call from Barnes's phone, he becomes more of a suspect. I think he'd get right back to his boss if he thought he was alive."

"I agree. Let's head back to the office and we can start sorting this out," Ben said.

They got into Freya's car and headed into town. She dropped Ben at the office and told him she had to run home first. She drove toward Clare's house, a knot in her stomach at the thought she was somehow involved. It was true she didn't know her well, but could she be that far off base? Getting ridiculously drunk one night was one thing. Associating with drug dealers was quite another.

The house was dark. Freya phoned her from the driveway, but there was no reply. She went to the front door and rang the bell, which seemed unusually loud, like a dinner gong. After a minute or so, Clare opened the door and stared at her, obviously sleep stunned. She didn't seem to recognize her.

"Sorry to disturb you, Clare. Can I come in?" Freya took hold of the doorknob before Clare responded. She stirred and her eyes came into focus.

"Why are you here? It's the middle of the night." She stepped aside to let her in.

"Actually, it's ten thirty."

She followed Clare into the kitchen where they sat at the table. Freya was alarmed when she took a close look at her. Her pupils were dilated—she looked high. She remembered the relationship she'd had with an alcoholic—the lies, the distance, the scenes. She wouldn't go through that again. How could she be falling in love with the type of person she loathed?

"What's up? There has to be something big for you to come by like this," Clare said.

Freya leaned forward across the table. "Do you know a man named Ray Barnes?"

Clare's eyes closed for a tick longer than a blink. "Why do you ask?"

"Answer the question."

Clare sat back in her chair. "I don't understand."

"There's been a multiple murder. One of the victims was a man named Ray Barnes. He's been identified as a drug trafficker in the area. Your name was in his phone."

Clare waved a hand in front of her. "That I can explain. I met Ray Barnes recently and he retained me to represent him in some commercial transactions. I didn't know he was a drug dealer." She said it without emphasis, as if admitting she didn't know he was an insurance salesman.

"That's good," Freya said, only partially relieved. She noticed Clare hadn't asked anything about the murders. "Where did you meet him?"

She looked embarrassed. "Abe's. It seems I'll meet everyone in this town if I go to Abe's often enough."

"Have you started working on one of these commercial transactions?"

"No, we haven't got past an initial meeting in my office. I know very little about him."

"Except that now he's dead."

Clare shifted. She was wearing a T-shirt and gym shorts, her hair piled on top of her head. Much of it had broken loose from its fastener and fallen across her face. Freya thought she looked adorable. "Yes. That's pretty shocking. Can you tell me what happened?"

"Only that Barnes and two others were murdered in a house out in the country."

Freya tried to catch Clare's eyes, which flitted around the room and refused to settle.

"I hope I cleared that up for you," she said.

"Sure. It's a small town. Why not have you as his lawyer?"

"Exactly." Clare nodded. "And I'm sorry I had to cancel last evening. But I guess you would have been called into work anyway." They both stood and Freya walked around the table to stand in front of her. She raised a tentative hand to Clare's face and touched her cheek with her palm. Her doubts about her seemed to do nothing to lessen her attraction.

"I've missed you," Freya said. "There doesn't seem to be time to spend together."

Clare drew Freya toward her and kissed her gently. "Do you have to leave?"

"I need to get back to work."

"Right away? Can't you stay for half an hour?" She smiled.

"I thought you weren't feeling well," Freya said.

"Oh, I'm much better now. I needed to lie down for a bit." She took Freya by the hand and walked toward the staircase.

She knew she had to get back to work, but what was half an hour? Her thinking compartmentalized and now it was in the quadrant that found Clare irresistible. As soon as they were in her bedroom, Clare pulled Freya down on top of her. The half hour turned into an hour before Freya peeled herself away.

"When will I see you again?" Clare said, a hand clasped on Freya's arm.

"I'm going to be pretty busy with this investigation." She saw the frown on Clare's face. "But as soon as we both have a minute. We'll find a way." She kissed her good-bye and hurried to her car. Ben was going to give her hell for being away so long. Clare seemed too present, too skilled, to be high on anything. Maybe they were solid as a couple. She was shaken by how much she wanted that.

On the way, the sheriff called to report there'd been no return call from Stingy to Ray's phone, indicating he probably knew about the murders. As far as she was concerned, he'd just moved into the role of prime suspect.

❖

Clare had woken on many a Sunday feeling much worse than she did now, but the combination of drugs she'd taken the night before left her body hazy and suppressed. She wasn't sure it would answer her commands. She slid out of bed and managed to put a robe on, but it seemed to take a long time to do. It wasn't only the physical component that made her sluggish. She was still gobsmacked by the murders, as if she'd just heard the gunfire moments before. Maybe coffee would help.

She drank her first cup standing at the sink, slurping at the hot liquid. Her mind was a blank. She became more unsettled when she moved to the kitchen table with a second cup. Her life was completely altered, as if a color film had turned into black and white. Everything looked different. Her life as a lawyer hung in the balance—if it was discovered she was at the scene, her career would be over and she'd likely be charged with withholding evidence, at the very least. Her new relationship with Freya—or whatever it was—would not only be over, but Freya would hate her for not coming forth immediately with what she knew. She'd hate her for being a drug user. Freya was already trying to ignore things like her blackout night of drinking in order to keep what they had together intact. She wouldn't overlook something as big as this. She hadn't really been in the mood to make love last night, but she succeeded in getting Freya's attention away from her association with Ray Barnes.

And Elizabeth. She couldn't stand thinking about how Elizabeth would view her if she were discovered. Her opinion meant something to Clare, but she was unsure what. That was a therapist's territory, one she would leave unexplored. She imagined the look in Elizabeth's eyes once she knew. Condemned, exiled, rejected. There'd be no comfort from anywhere.

The second cup of coffee was having no effect. It was as if she was bolted to the chair. Her brain lit up when she realized she still had some of the meth that Henry had given her. Her speed stash was completely gone, and surviving the day in her present condition seemed impossible. The meth wasn't as scary as she thought it'd be. Taking a measured dose made it seem medicinal. It made her hyper alert, filled with energy, able to focus, and decidedly more optimistic than she now was. She went into the living room and reached under her couch for her pillbox. A little packet of folded paper was wedged into one of the compartments and she carefully took it out. Then she found a credit card and a dollar bill and went to work cutting it into two lines. She rolled up the dollar bill and bent over the coffee table to snort them up, then fell back against the couch and waited to feel the impact, which was almost immediate. It sparked something in her brain and a wave swept through her body that was so good she almost immediately wanted to do more. But she wouldn't. She sat for a few more minutes enjoying the rush, then got up to get dressed and head into work. She didn't want to waste the meth on a Sunday of doing crossword puzzles and puttering. She'd apply it toward working on her brief, which would also distract her from her worries. It seemed like an elegant solution. Plus, there was Elizabeth's dinner that night where she had to be functional. Meth was not the demon drug she'd imagined.

Her cell phone rang just as she'd gotten up to take a shower. She picked up when she saw it was Henry calling.

"Have you heard?" she said.

"Yes."

"That Ray, Bobby and whoever that woman was were murdered last night?"

"I know. It's unbelievable." His voice was hushed.

She sat back down and thought about having a cigarette for the first time in five years.

"I don't understand," Henry said. "How are you still alive?"

"Because I was in the bathroom. Having to pee saved my life. The fact that you left early saved yours."

There was a pause. "Jesus. Tell me what you know."

Clare filled him in on what happened but kept to herself that she'd seen the gunman leaving the scene. She didn't want to expose herself should Henry have anything to do with it. She knew it wasn't him she saw leaving the scene. He was more solidly built than the man she saw. "I called it in anonymously from a pay phone. No one knows I was there."

"That's good, Clare. We'd both be up shit's creek if you told."

"Do you think I'd tell them you were there too?"

"Of course not. I'm more worried about them finding out who owns the home."

"Right, I hadn't thought of that. Public records should tell them pretty quickly." Clare knew enough about real estate law to know that.

"I may be okay. The property is in a private land trust. They shouldn't be able to see who the beneficiary is."

"I don't think that's right. I think they can subpoena the information."

"Fuck. I need to go. Keep your mouth shut." He hung up.

As they'd talked, Clare had become more unsure of Henry's part in the murders. Had he left the party early knowing someone was going to come in and kill everyone in the house? Did that mean he intended for her to be killed as well? He didn't seem surprised when she answered his call, but he was a cool dude. He seemed capable of playing many roles. She was equally unsure whether Henry would give up her name should the property records reveal him as the owner of the property and he was brought in for questioning. She was sick to her stomach.

She got up to shower and again the phone rang. It was Freya. Clare stared at the phone but couldn't bring herself to answer. She would sound like someone whose neck was under the guillotine. The ringing stopped and shortly afterward a text message popped up. *Clare—wanted to let you know I'll be busy with work for the foreseeable future. I've been thinking of you, missing you. At least we can see each other tonight at the Nelsons'.*

Some part of her reacted warmly to Freya's words, but it was fleeting. She couldn't imagine there was anything left to their story. There was no place in her new world for dating a cop and living in fear she'd find out Clare's true story. She didn't reply to Freya's message.

# Chapter Twenty-two

Clare walked the few blocks to the Nelsons' house for the dinner party, hoping the brisk air would break the deep funk she'd fallen into. The streets were nearly soundless, and she could see families gathered together behind brightly lit living room windows. It made her think of family and friends, love and support, things she was in short supply of. Freya's Jeep was in front of the house. Despite her state of mind, she was thrilled at seeing her again. Henry's Volvo drove down the street toward the house and she hurried to the front door. She didn't want a private conversation with him. Her nerves couldn't stand it.

Hank greeted her at the door and led her into the living room. Elizabeth, Ben, and Freya were sitting in front of the crackling fireplace. They all rose to greet her. Elizabeth leaned in for a hug and the others followed suit. Elizabeth's hug was warm, Freya's circumspect, and Ben's more enveloping. Were these her friends? The start of community? It was all false, based on a version of herself that didn't exist, like the Wizard of Oz pulling levers to create an illusion of control, when she was really desperate and alone.

Henry walked in just as Hank was offering her a drink. He threw his coat over a chair. "I'll have a beer, Dad." He joined the standing circle, a confident smile on his face, his body relaxed, hands in his pockets. He seemed entitled, as if the heir had arrived for a good fawning over. He greeted everyone with equal charm. When he turned to Clare though, he did not meet her eyes. They greeted each other politely and Elizabeth smiled as they talked, as if she especially wanted them to be friends. Hank got the drinks sorted and they sat in a semicircle and chatted about the weather and the ISU basketball team, an area passion that mystified her.

"I hate to bring up something unpleasant," Elizabeth said, "but has everyone heard about the triple homicide last night? Hank ran into the sheriff today and he told him about it."

"That's right," Hank said. "He said it was some sort of ambush involving drug dealers. It's like something out of the movies."

"Except it's here in our backyard. I find it very disturbing." She turned to Freya. "Do you know anything about it?"

Clare took a peek at Henry, who was peeling the label off his beer bottle. He looked bemused, of all things. Her stomach was lurching like a drunk at two in the morning.

Freya looked at Ben, who shrugged. "Ben and I were at the scene last night."

"That must have been intense," Henry said. She marveled at his ability to speak at all.

"It was. Sorry I can't tell you more, but we don't know much at this point."

"Of course," Elizabeth said. She turned to Clare. "Had you heard about this?"

She suddenly found it hard to swallow and she could feel Henry's eyes on her. "No, I hadn't heard a thing. I wouldn't have imagined there was such a large drug operation in the area." If only she could swallow. She felt like she was going to fly apart. She took a drink of her wine and forced it down. Everyone was looking at her.

"Drugs are a real problem around here," Hank said. "Meth is all over the place. The rural population seems particularly vulnerable to it."

Elizabeth had a serious look on her face. "It worries me. It's terrible for Money Creek's reputation. Let alone dangerous. I don't like the idea of desperate addicts coming into town to rob people."

"That hasn't happened, so far," Freya said.

Hank took a sip of his whiskey. "Here's the other thing. The sheriff told me an anonymous source called in the homicide, probably a witness who doesn't want to be identified."

"A lot of questions could be answered if we got hold of that person," Freya said.

"But we have no leads on that. We're waiting for forensics to process the bottles and glasses to see how many people were there," Ben said.

Clare felt the color drain from her face. She'd forgotten the beer bottles. What an idiot she was. There were a few with her DNA all over them and there wasn't a thing she could do about it. Luckily, and somewhat miraculously, she'd never been arrested, so her DNA wouldn't be in any database. She was standing on a cliff with her toes over the edge. She looked at Henry, who was in the same boat. His jaw was clenched.

"I hate this," Elizabeth said. She looked anguished. "I hate drugs and drug people. It's a scourge."

"I think we got that, Mom." Henry drained his beer.

"There's no need to be sarcastic, Henry." It was the first time she'd seen Hank with a dead serious expression. An awkward silence followed, with Freya, Ben, and Clare all staring into their drinks.

Elizabeth stood. "Let's move into the dining room. I'll put supper on and we can find something else to talk about."

The dinner conversation flowed easily. Clare tried to contribute, but it was as if she had lockjaw. Freya looked at her a couple of times with a question on her face, and she forced herself to smile back. She was paralyzed by the number of landmines in front of her.

Henry unlocked the apartment door and slammed it behind him. Evan popped up from the living room couch.

"What's the matter?" He looked anxious as he faced Henry. An episode of *Ice Road Truckers* was on the television.

"Nothing's the matter." Henry took off his long coat and hung it in the closet. "Why do you ask?"

"Because you slammed the door, man. Scared the shit out of me." He followed Henry into the kitchen and took two beers out of the fridge.

"Sorry. I just came from my parents' house. You know how it is with family."

Evan's face fell. "You know I don't."

Henry winced. He knew Evan had grown up in group homes and a variety of foster homes. He'd done remarkably well in school for someone with his background and had gotten a full scholarship to Money Creek College. But there was no one to be proud of him. He sat across the table from Evan.

"Mine drive me crazy. I usually feel worse leaving there than I did going in."

"Your parents are cool. Why can't you see that?"

"You're not their son. They look totally cool from the outside, but behind doors it's another matter."

"How bad can it be? At least you have parents," Evan said. He started rolling a joint.

Henry let it drop and got up from the table. "I'm beat. I'm turning in."

"It's like eight o'clock."

Henry looked at him with a steady gaze. "I'm going to relax in my room. Is there a problem with that?"

Evan raised his hands. "No problem. I'm going to smoke a joint if you want to join me."

"Good night, Evan." He grabbed another beer and walked down the hallway to his bedroom. When he closed the door, he let out a breath of relief, as if he'd just beached a small ship during a Category 4 hurricane. He was safe, for the moment. He took off his cashmere sweater and corduroys, his hundred-dollar T-shirt and brogues. He flopped on the bed in his underwear and tried not to cry. Everything he'd built was crashing down around him. His business was in a state of limbo following the death of his two partners. He didn't have all the contacts they did with meth suppliers, or with the dealers who supplied them with other drugs for resale. His job had been to operate the town/gown side of things, selling directly to townspeople and Money Creek College students. Stingy operated the rural business and reported to Ray and Bobby. Henry also contributed capital for expenditures, including the purchase of legitimate businesses. He handled the accounting. Stingy would bring him bags of money, which he and Evan would count and distribute back to the partners. He concentrated on the areas assigned to him and ignored the day to day operation of the entire enterprise. How was he going to step into the breech?

There was the very real question of whether he'd even be around to start putting things in order. It was only a matter of time before it was discovered that Henry was the owner of the house where the murders occurred. Did that give them enough to arrest him? If he said that persons unknown must have broken into his house, would they have anything else on him? What about the DNA on the glasses left in the house? He'd had several beers. But his DNA wasn't in any database. Would they make an arrest simply to get a swab from him and see if it was a match with the beer bottles? If so, he was sunk.

He thought of Clare at the dinner party that evening. She was trying to maintain composure, but he could see the tautness in her face, the rapid movement of her eyes. Freya kept looking at her in what he thought was a proprietary way, as if they had a special connection. That was worrisome. If Clare decided to confess to Freya, his life would be ruined.

He needed a plan and he needed it fast. The only one he could come up with involved running. Taking what cash he had and getting out of town. It was a pretty awful plan. The sheriff and state police would immediately know he had something to do with the murders and the manhunt would begin. Maybe he could wait. The DNA might come to nothing, and they might buy that he was ignorant of anyone using his house. He might be able to let things cool down for a while and then get the operation up and running. If he did run, however, he intended to take Clare with him. There was a good chance she'd be ready to go. She clearly was suffering under the strain of what she witnessed and withheld from the police. A life on the run would probably seem better than that.

## CHAPTER TWENTY-THREE

Freya hung up the phone just as Ben came in carrying coffee and bagels from Bean There. She smiled as she took a cup from him.

"Stingy has surfaced."

"No shit?" Ben sat in his chair and started slathering on cream cheese.

"He showed up at Olie's Ham and Egger and Deputy LeBeau spotted him there. That was him on the phone."

Ben didn't look up from his bagel. "Is he scooping him up?"

"I told him to ask Stingy to come in for questioning and if he refused, arrest him."

"We don't have enough to arrest him."

Freya uncapped her coffee and stirred in some stevia. "That's true, but I'm not going to let him slip through our fingers. We can hold him for twenty-four hours."

Ben chewed for a bit. "What do we have on him?"

"It's all circumstantial. He went to ground after his DUI arrest for fear he was going to be killed by the drug cartel, but that's an assumption. Then he emerged after the murders, which points to him thinking it was safe to be seen. That leaves a motive of killing them to ensure his own safety."

"And taking over their business"

"It's not enough to interest the prosecutor, but at least we'll get to question him."

Twenty minutes later, Stingy sat in the interview room and glared at Freya and Ben. "I don't appreciate you ruining my breakfast."

Freya grinned. "And you think we care about that?"

"You have nothing on me. I don't know anything about any murders on Saturday night."

"We have enough to question you, and the first thing I want to know is why you went into hiding after being released on your DUI charge?"

Stingy shrugged. "I wasn't hiding. I have a quiet life. Why were you following me?"

"We know from two of your meth suppliers you're trafficking drugs," Ben said. "The two men who were killed Saturday also are drug dealers and you worked for them. Do you know Bobby Hughes or Ray Barnes?"

"Are those the dudes who were killed? Never heard of them."

"You know we'll be able to place you with one or both of them. Not telling us about it now hurts your case," Freya said.

Stingy leaned back in his chair as if he were relaxing at the end of a busy day. "I don't have a case because I don't know what you're talking about."

"Really? In an area as small as this, no one in the drug community told you that Hughes and Barnes were killed in a home invasion Saturday night? I find that really hard to believe."

"That's your problem, not mine. This conversation is over. I want a lawyer."

This didn't surprise Freya, but her heart sank all the same. "Fine. Get your lawyer. We'll question you again with your attorney."

Freya and Ben stayed seated as Stingy was led out of the room. "This is bad. We'll be lucky to hold him twenty-four hours now that he's lawyered up," Ben said. They got up and walked back to their office. Freya stopped at the front desk and asked the deputy there to call her when Stingy's attorney arrived.

"I don't believe him for a second. He knows those people and he knows they were murdered. But knowing and showing are two different things," Freya said.

They waited.

❖

Clare sat at her desk with her head cradled in her arms, sick with the thought of the conversation at Elizabeth's the night before. She was to meet Elizabeth later in the morning to give her a status report on the brief and memorandum. She was prepared enough to impress, but she couldn't escape the fact that she was the sort of person Elizabeth said she hated. Thomas was due any moment to go over their progress and determine how much was left to do. She craved more meth. She'd brought some with her from home, determined to not take more but making sure she could if she decided to. She slipped the paper packet, a credit card, and a dollar bill into her pants pocket and made her way to the washroom. It was a one-seater, so she had privacy. She set out her supplies, opened the packet and sniffed up two lines, instantly feeling more alert and a little buzzy.

Thomas was waiting in her office when she returned. "What time do you see Elizabeth?"

"Ten o'clock. I want to be super prepared. How are you doing with the memo?"

"I'm close. Jo's preparing the exhibits and those are nearly done," Thomas said.

"Have you added anything since I read it yesterday?"

"About two pages." He slid them across the desk to her. Clare read them quickly and with total focus. Her phone interrupted her. She could see it was from Donna at reception and she considered letting it go to voice mail. But Donna would page her, so there was no point.

"Good morning!" Donna said. "I see you beat me into the office again this morning."

"You're slowing down, Donna." Was that an inappropriate thing to say to someone in a wheelchair? She flushed, ashamed of her insensitivity. "Sorry. I was teasing and it came out wrong."

"What came out wrong?"

God, now she'd made it into a thing. "What I said about you slowing down."

"What are you talking about?"

"Never mind," Clare said briskly. Thomas must think she was insane. "What can I do for you?"

"It's the county clerk. I'm transferring her now." Donna hung up and a cheerful voice came on the line.

"Is this Clare Lehane?"

"Yes, how can I help?"

"Well, sugar, you've got yourself your first pro bono case. I'm Sonia Bertel, the county clerk. We met at the Nelsons' party. I put your name in the rotation a week ago and here you are."

Clare sagged. She didn't have time for this. It was impossible. "This is a really bad time for me now. Is there any way you can move to the next lawyer on the list?"

Sonia laughed. "I haven't talked to a lawyer yet who hasn't said it was a really bad time for them. It won't work, I'm afraid"

"What's the case?" She looked at Thomas and shook her head.

"It's a capital case, so pull on your big girl pants. Your client is being held at the county jail in relation to a triple homicide that happened over the weekend."

Her heart took an extra beat. "I can't handle a capital case. I've never practiced criminal law."

"You can take that up with the judge. For the time being you're it. Now you need to get on over there so they can question the guy."

"But I can't. I have a meeting."

"The coin's not dropping for you, is it? Your meeting has to wait. You're obligated to represent this man. You should leave now."

Thomas was giving her a quizzical look. "Fine. I'll be there." She hung up.

"You got tagged, didn't you?" he said.

Clare didn't answer, lost in thought about what just happened. Despite how absurd it was to have her represent anyone in a murder case, especially this one, it was good news that someone was in custody. If they've arrested the killer, then a tremendous weight was off her shoulders. She grew excited. All she had to do was represent him during questioning and then get the judge to order a new defense lawyer at the arraignment. Easy.

"I have to cancel with Elizabeth because they've assigned me that triple homicide."

Thomas whistled. "Now you're talking. I've mostly gotten DUIs."

Clare came around her desk. "I'm going to see her. Wish me luck."

Elizabeth was coming out of her office when Clare arrived.

"I thought we were meeting at ten," she said.

"I have to talk to you about that. Can we go into your office?"

Elizabeth retreated to her desk and Clare took a chair. She looked at her boss and had the same feeling she always did. She wanted her approval and was barely hanging on to it.

"I've just been assigned a pro bono case by the county clerk," Clare said.

Elizabeth frowned. "That's rotten timing. You can't really afford the time to be pulled."

"That's what I told the clerk, but they were crocodile tears. I'm stuck with it."

"What's the case?"

"It's the triple homicide. It would be crazy for me to handle a capital case. That would be an instant appeal based on insufficient counsel. If they file charges I'll ask the judge to change lawyers."

Elizabeth smiled. "Excellent idea."

"But I have to leave now to be with the client during questioning and the arraignment."

"Funny you getting this case after that talk we had about it last night."

"I'm not seeing the humor, sorry." She smiled limply and left the office. As she grabbed her briefcase and legal pad, she realized Freya would probably be questioning the witness, putting them squarely across the table from each other. Things were getting more complicated at every turn.

Clare was shown into an interview room where she was to spend a few minutes alone with her client. When they led him in, she saw immediately that he couldn't be the man who committed the murders. The man she'd seen flee the scene was tall and lean, while her client was of medium height and quite chubby. This man wasn't the murderer, leaving Clare responsible for getting an innocent man released before they charged him. One complication layered over another, seeming without end. A wave of exhaustion passed through her. Everything seemed like a mountain to move and she didn't have the energy to give a nudge.

"Mr. Lee, it says here that you're being held for the triple murders Saturday night."

"They have nothing on me. I mean nothing. It's not even circumstantial."

She doubted Freya and Ben would detain anyone without some evidence against them. Still, she knew he was innocent. They couldn't have too much on him.

"Let's see how the questioning goes. Please pause before answering the detectives' questions so I can stop you if necessary. If I say don't answer, don't answer. That's very important. After the questioning the detectives will consult with the state's attorney to see if they want to file charges, after which you'll be arraigned in front of a judge. Do you understand?" She'd taken two criminal law classes and remembered precious little

"They better not charge me. I'm no angel, but I didn't do this. You've got to fix this."

Clare was about to reply when Freya and Ben walked in the room. Her body sparked, though whether from fear or desire, she couldn't tell. Freya nodded to her. Clare got up and joined her client on one side of the table, with Ben and Freya on the other.

"Now that you have your attorney present," Freya said, "we'll continue with our questioning. Where were you on Saturday night?"

Stingy looked at Clare and she nodded. "I was at my mother-in-law's. I'm there a lot. My wife always wants to be with her mother, what can I say? But that's at least two people who can vouch for me being there."

"We'd like to hear what evidence you have against my client," Clare said. "As far as I can tell, you don't have anything to hold him." She looked at Ben as she talked. She could feel Freya's eyes on her.

"We're not compelled to lay that out for you, counselor." Ben looked at her kindly and she blushed. She had no idea what she was supposed to expect during this sort of interview.

"Where is your mother-in-law's?" Freya asked. Stingy slouched in his seat.

"She lives out toward Cranston," he said.

"Is that far away from the murder scene?" Clare asked. She had no idea.

"It's the opposite direction," Ben admitted. "But Stingy's alibi could be based on his family members lying for him. It's not the best alibi in the world."

"It's rock solid, man."

Clare put her hand on Stingy's arm. "Wait for a question before you speak."

He looked at her grumpily and leaned back in his chair.

Freya seemed to be avoiding eye contact with her. "Do you have anything to corroborate your alibi?"

Stingy thought for a moment. "Yeah, I do. I stopped for gas on my way to my mother-in-law's. My wife was with me. It was the Phillips station in Cranston."

"Do your homework before charging my client," Clare said. "There should be video of him at the station."

"We'll do that," Freya said, looking at Clare for the first time.

"Good. In the meantime, I suggest you release my client. You have nothing to hold him on."

A flash of annoyance crossed Freya's face. "We've got time before we have to release him."

"That's bullshit," Stingy said. "I want out of here."

"Let's see if your alibi holds first," Ben said. "If it does, you've got nothing to worry about, right?"

Stingy gave him a sour look. Freya terminated the interview and a deputy came in to take him back to his cell. Ben and Clare got up to leave.

"I'll meet you back at the office," Freya said, looking at Ben. "I'd like to have a word with Clare."

Ben looked from one to the other and then picked up his notebook. "I'll leave you to it, then."

When they were alone Freya leaned back in her chair and sighed. "This is unbelievable. How did you get this case?" She seemed more upset than annoyed.

"I was forced to take it pro bono. It's the last thing I want."

"I don't want to be on the other side from you."

If only Freya knew how far on the other side Clare really was. "If Stingy's alibi pans out, the issue will be moot. You'll have to let him go." Please let that be the case. She couldn't let a man go to prison for something he didn't do, but it would mean disaster for her.

"If that doesn't happen, promise me you'll get off this case." Freya leaned forward. She moved to take Clare's hand and then thought better of it.

"What are you so afraid of? We're both professionals," Clare said.

"I'm afraid it'll impact our relationship."

Clare was silent. This was the first time the idea of a relationship had been mentioned. She didn't know if she was happy or frightened. It seemed impossible she could be happy, given her current circumstances, but a feeling of safety washed over her. Had she found someone who loved her for who she was? Of course, Freya didn't know who she really was, but at least she was serious about what she saw. She hadn't realized how hungry she was for someone to want her. Maybe if everything played out exactly right, she wouldn't lose Freya.

"They'll have to let me off this case. It's a capital charge and I've no experience with criminal defense."

"You seemed like you knew what you were doing," Freya said.

"I had one mock criminal trial in law school, and I barely remember that."

"I don't want to be distanced from you or arguing with you over the case." Her eyes blinked rapidly and she moved around in her seat. She waited nervously for Clare's reply.

"Nothing is going to distance me from you. I won't let that happen." Not if she could help it. "Can you come over tomorrow night?"

Freya looked relieved. "I'll be there. Whatever happens, I'll be there."

Clare returned to the office and met with Elizabeth about the summary judgement motion. Later in the day, Ben called to tell her Stingy's alibi was corroborated by gas station footage of him filling up around the time of the murders. They were letting him go, but her problems were far from over. She wished she'd brought more meth with her. She wanted the distraction of that initial buzz. It eased her worry, if only for a short time. But it was too late in the day. She didn't want to lose a night's sleep when she needed to be as sharp as possible. She left work early and went home. A drink would have to do.

## CHAPTER TWENTY-FOUR

Freya put on her sunglasses as she sped toward Bloomington. The snow on the ground made the sunny day almost blindingly bright. In the folder on the seat next to her was the subpoena obtained by the state's attorney compelling the Prairie Title Company to release the name of the beneficiary of the trust that owned the house where the murders took place. She was certain it belonged to one of the dead drug dealers. When she got to town she swung by her apartment and checked that everything was fine. The place hardly felt like home anymore. So much of her life was in Money Creek now, including a girlfriend. Was Clare her girlfriend? Her passion in bed said yes, but it was no guarantee. She hadn't responded when she'd used the word relationship in their talk yesterday in the county jail. Had she scared her away?

She pulled up to the title company's offices and fifteen minutes later returned to her car with the documentation in hand. She got in before reading the page revealing the beneficiary. Her mouth opened when she saw that it was Henry Nelson who owned the house. Christ. Her first thought was of Elizabeth and how this would break her heart. The second thought was to bring Henry in for questioning as soon as possible. She called Ben to set the wheels in motion and sped back to Money Creek. She wouldn't have thought Henry was involved with a major drug operation. Still, there was something a little sly about him. She always thought his extreme politeness masked a more sinister personality, though she could point to nothing concrete. His involvement surprised but didn't shock her.

❖

Henry tapped his pencil on the side of his computer, blankly looking at the screen. He was searching for a topic for his senior seminar thesis, but couldn't focus enough to pick one. What the hell difference did it make whether he wrote about themes of isolation in the novels of Thomas Hardy? He'd soon to be under suspicion for murder. He knew it was only a matter of time before the cops discovered who owned the house, and then he was in deep trouble. He lit a joint and started pacing the living room. He would plead ignorance, of course. The house was used without his knowledge. But how would he explain the house to his mother? She had no idea he owned it. He assumed she would know he'd been brought in for questioning. Barely a thing happened in Money Creek without his mother hearing about it.

As he calmed himself he realized how little the police actually had on him. There was nothing putting him at the house at the time of the murders. The only one who knew he'd been there at all was Clare, and she certainly wouldn't be telling anyone.

He snubbed out the joint and collapsed on the couch just as the doorbell rang. He prayed it was Evan who'd forgotten his key. It rang a second time right after the first, which probably meant it was the cops. He wondered if he'd be arrested for smoking dope. It probably wasn't smart to have stunk up his apartment with it. They wouldn't find any stash, though. He'd hidden that away in a secret hole in the backyard. At least he was smart enough to do that.

When he pulled the door open he saw Freya and Ben, standing a few feet from the door. Ben had his hand resting on his gun. Jesus. Did they expect him to shoot his way out of this? He stepped away from the door and gestured them in.

"Come in," he said, closing the door after Freya and Ben walked into the living room. Ben waved his hands in front of him.

"Christ, you must have just put that joint out. It stinks in here."

"I wasn't expecting such august company." He smiled the smile that usually worked to get him out of awkward situations. "Can I get you something to drink?"

"No," Freya said. "If we look around, are we going to find drugs here, Henry?"

He employed the smile again. "Feel free to look around. There's nothing here. I had that joint sitting around from a long time ago."

"And you decided to smoke it in the middle of day?" Ben looked confused by this.

"Sure, why not? I have the rest of the day off. No harm done."

Freya and Ben remained standing. "Henry, you may know why we're here."

"Actually, I have no idea."

"You had to know that we'd figure out sooner or later that the house where the triple homicide occurred is owned by you." Freya looked him in the eye.

He was able to act surprised at the news. "What do you mean?"

"Do you own a house at 15264 Lamont?"

"I hold it in a land trust, so I'm not sure how you got the information."

"You don't deny owning it?"

"I don't think there'd be any point in that. I own the house. Of course, I know nothing about any homicide." He thought he was doing a great job of acting. There was no reason for them not to believe him.

Ben shifted his weight. "We're going to take you to the station to ask you some questions, after the effects of the pot have passed."

"I'm perfectly clearheaded," Henry said.

"All the same, I think it's best we wait a couple hours. Do you want to grab a coat, maybe something to read?"

He could kick up a fuss and refuse to come in, but full cooperation now might keep their eyes from focusing too much on him. He grabbed his coat and phone and followed them out the door and into the back of their borrowed cruiser. Two hours later, he was in the interview room with Ben and Freya.

"Am I under arrest?"

Ben looked up from his notebook. "Let's say you're a person of interest as the owner of the house."

"That doesn't answer my question," Henry said.

"Believe me, you'll know it if we charge you. But if you have nothing to hide, then there's no danger of that, correct?" Freya said.

"I guess. It's not that I entirely trust you guys."

Freya smiled at him. "Henry, we've eaten together, been at parties together. We know each other. I'm not trying to trap you into anything."

"What do you want to ask me?"

"First of all, why did you buy the house and with what funds?" Freya said.

"I bought it because it was a good investment. I wanted a place I could fix up."

"You're a college student. How did you have the money to buy it?"

Henry relaxed in his chair. "Sports betting. I'm good at it. And the house only cost nine thousand dollars."

"Sports betting? What do you mean exactly?" Freya said.

"Online. There are sites where you can place bets. I thought it might be a good way to make some extra cash, so I studied up on it."

He was more relaxed. It had been inspired to think of sports betting as the source of his cash.

"Why do you hold title in a blind trust?" Ben said.

"I read somewhere it was the smart thing to do, so I followed that advice."

These were all plausible answers. They'd have to let him go soon. His fear started to ebb.

"Does your mother know about your house?" Freya said.

He shifted in his seat. "I don't see what possible relevance that has."

"I'm getting a picture here of a property owned by someone who didn't want to have his name associated with it, didn't want his family to know about it, and was the site of a triple murder of drug associates. Do you know a Ray Barnes or Bobby Hughes?"

"No, I do not."

"Where were you Saturday from four o'clock on?"

Henry's hesitation was slight, but he felt Freya's eyes staring at him. She would notice anything. "I was here at home. I was supposed to go on a date, but she canceled on me." This was true, but the date was supposed to start at nine o'clock, leaving room for him to have committed the murders and get back to Money Creek.

"We'll need the name and number of your date to corroborate." Henry gave it to them.

"What time was your date?"

Henry told them. Freya and Ben looked at each other.

"Unfortunately for you, that would not clear you of the time the murders took place. It's a pretty poor alibi," Ben said. "You can see that it simply adds to our belief you do know the murder victims and may have been present in the house yourself."

"You're wrong. There's nothing that points to me being there."

"We'd like to get a sample of your DNA. We can clear this up right away by checking it against any DNA we picked up at the house," Freya said.

Henry put a hand to his throat, which was suddenly constricted. "Do I have to?"

"I'd think you'd want to, Henry." She continued to stare at him, trying to catch his eyes. "If you have nothing to hide, that is."

He saw the beer bottles on the coffee table as clearly as if they were in front of him now. Of course, his DNA would be there somewhere. He'd had a number of beers before he left. He was finished if they put the two together. "I chose to not give you a DNA sample."

Freya paused. "That's very interesting. Makes me more convinced you're involved in the homicides. Is that the impression you want to strengthen?"

"Are you done with me here?" he said.

"For the moment, yes. I'm sure we'll be talking again," Freya said.

Henry sped out of the sheriff's department, hoping he wouldn't run into his mother coming to the courthouse. He hadn't been offered a ride home so he walked quickly with his hood up and his head down. He was numb to the cold. Numb, period. Somehow in all his dealings with Ray and Bobby, he never seriously contemplated what could happen to him if the police discovered he was a major drug dealer. Their organization was so business-like it almost seemed legitimate. But now the authorities were one DNA sample away from putting him at the scene of the murders, and there was no way to explain that away. If he ended up arrested and a sample taken from him against his will, he'd have no choice but to put Clare at the scene too. She was the only one who could corroborate that he wasn't there at the time of the murders. He'd throw her to the wolves in a heartbeat if it kept him from being charged with murder. But would Clare's account really help him? What if the police inferred that he'd returned with a gun after leaving the house, killing all present? No, that should be okay. If that were the case, he would have killed Clare too, not left her behind as a witness. She was his ace in the hole. He'd ruin her life before he'd ruin his own.

It was bad enough Clare's world was about to fall apart, but to run out of drugs at the same time seemed overkill. Her pillbox was nearly bare. There were a dozen or so Valium, which she relied on more heavily since the murders. The Oxycontin was gone. She was terrified that she'd have no more source now that the drug triad had been destroyed. Perhaps Henry would pick up the pieces, but he was smart enough to lay low while the murders were being investigated. She was nearly through the packet of meth she'd been given. She wondered if Evan had any more. It turned out there wasn't anything about the stuff that was particularly scary, after all. She took it, she worked with the strength of ten, and she let it wear off for the night. It made the Adderall seem like boxed wine compared to vintage. Still, she'd go back to regular speed if it was available. She didn't want to tempt fate and become addicted to meth.

It was early evening. She went home, threw her bag on the kitchen table, and grabbed a beer. Freya was coming over in an hour for dinner and she considered having a pizza delivered. Her nerves were jangled enough to make cooking an obstacle course she wouldn't be able to manage. She slumped on her couch and took a long drink of the beer. Then her phone rang. Henry, of course, the person she least wanted to talk to. But she had to know what was happening on all fronts.

"What's new, Henry?" She drank more beer.

"I got called in for questioning, that's what's new."

Clare's drinking arm stopped halfway to her mouth. "What for?"

"They found out I own the house. I'm fucked."

He sounded furious with her. "Why are you mad at me?"

"I'm not. I'm mad at everyone. I told them I had no idea anyone had broken into my house and used it on the day of the murders, but I don't think they believed me. They said there was no sign of forced entry. My alibi sucks. They asked for a DNA sample."

Clare walked to the kitchen and pulled out a bottle of bourbon. "The beer bottles at the house. They want to see if you match any of that DNA."

"That's obvious. But I didn't give them a sample, which puts me under even greater suspicion."

She quickly calculated the position she'd be in should Henry be arrested for the murders. She didn't doubt for a moment that he'd tell the cops she'd also been at the house in order to confirm he left before the shooting occurred.

"They can't force you to give one," she said.

"I'm not so sure. I'm thinking of running."

She wished he would disappear. "That's a pretty drastic step. But I can see the logic." She heard him sniffle. Was he crying? How long would he stand up during questioning if he was already crying?

"I want you to come with me," he said. "I've got plenty of money. We can find a safe place and live well."

"There is no safe place. Once you run, you'll always be running. That's not for me."

"Are you going to tell the cops about me instead? You'll be sorry, if you do."

"Is that a threat? Are you going to tell the cops about me in turn?"

They were both silent. Was his finger hovering over the button, ready to drop the bomb? They both had the nuclear option available. Would it be better for her to confess everything?

"It's best for us both if we swear to silence," he said. "We have to trust each other."

Trust was not a possibility. They both knew the other would turn as soon as it was expedient to do so. She was probably living on borrowed time. "I'd give more thought to your escape plan. You can hide out more easily on your own. Dye your hair and get it cut differently, grow a beard, wear glasses. You can live in St. Barts and no one will know you from Adam."

He hung up on her. She threw her phone on the table and drank back two fingers of Maker's Mark. It would have to be her last one. She had to be sharp around Freya. What if she got drunk and told Freya everything? It could happen. No previous blackout would be as catastrophic as that would be.

The doorbell rang at exactly seven. Clare opened the door to find Freya on her front stoop, holding a box of pizza. The hard edge she presented when she was wearing her gun and belt had given way to something more feminine. She wore a V-neck sweater that showed a little cleavage, skinny jeans, and boots with a two-inch heel. Clare looked down at her own worn jeans and sweatshirt and was embarrassed. Freya had dressed for Clare, while Clare had dressed for herself.

"You read my mind. Literally," Clare said.

Freya handed over the box before taking off her parka. She seemed shy. "I thought if you'd already started dinner we could have some of this as an appetizer, or dessert for that matter." She followed Clare into the kitchen.

"I really was going to order pizza," Clare said. "You get big points for this." She opened the fridge and grabbed two bottles of Budweiser. Craft beer was not a thing in Money Creek. "Beer?"

Freya took one. They stood facing each other a few feet apart. She didn't know how wide a chasm there really was between them. Funny to think if she knew the truth Freya would want to arrest her, not make love to her.

"Let's sit in the living room," Clare said, leading the way with pizza and plates. They sat on the couch as they had the first time

Freya visited her, the first time they'd made love. "Have you run into Jo since you broke up with her?"

Freya cocked her head, as if the question was the last she'd expected. "I saw her at the coffee shop a couple days ago. It was awkward but inevitable. We're going to be running into each other repeatedly. I smiled at her and she ignored me."

"I feel some compassion for her. I wouldn't want you to break up with me." Clare looked at her steadily.

"That surprises me," Freya said.

"That I wouldn't want you to dump me?"

"More that you feel we have a relationship from which one can be dumped. I mean, I'm glad you do." She put her hand out to Clare, who touched her fingers with her own.

"We haven't seen each other that much, but this seems like something, doesn't it?" Clare said.

"Oh, yes."

"I mean, it's not like I'm looking to date anyone else. You're it."

Freya laughed. "As I said, I'm a serial monogamist. There's no one else for me, either."

Clare tried to imagine them as a couple, constantly worried the truth would come out about her role in the murders. The only thing more unimaginable was a future without Freya in it.

Freya scooted along the couch and gave Clare a soft kiss. "You were my choice as soon as I saw you." She kissed her again.

"Let's have some pizza while it's hot, but I'm looking forward to what comes afterward."

Freya backed away and opened the box of pizza with a frown. "Stupid pizza."

Clare's desire broke through a sea of worries. She put a couple pieces of pizza on a plate and handed it to Freya. "What's new in your world? You must be working all the time."

"We're helping the sheriff out with the investigation. It's not like I'm leading the case."

"But still, it's a big deal. There can't have been three people murdered around here in the last decade."

Freya chewed and seemed to consider her response. "It's a very big deal. It's not only homicide. We think the victims were part of the big drug operation we've been trying to uncover."

"Do you have any suspects?"

Freya paused. "You can understand I can't really talk about this, especially with you being a suspect's attorney."

She raised her hands in the air. "Of course. I didn't mean to pry. I'm curious what you're up to, what you're up against. And frankly, the whole thing is kind of sexy. I mean, not that there were murders, but that my girlfriend is in hot in pursuit of justice."

"I like the girlfriend part, but the truth is we don't know much. We have some DNA, but no bodies to match it with. It does no good on its own."

"That must be frustrating."

"It goes with the territory."

They finished eating and Clare quickly cleaned up and brought back two more beers. That would be her third of the evening, but she didn't think of beer as an intoxicant. It took quite a few to make her feel anything but normal, and she wouldn't be drinking that many. All she had to do was keep the bourbon in the cabinet. She looked at Freya sitting next to her and put her arm around her waist. "I think it's time to practice."

"Practice?" She turned inside Clare's arm, their faces inches away.

"The ways of lesbian love. I'm still a beginner, as you know."

Freya smiled. "You'd never know it." She leaned in to kiss her. "But I'm happy to practice as much as you want."

Clare returned the kiss, wondering how long she could operate from this swamp of deception. She pushed her down on the couch and leaned over her, determined to pretend that everything was normal and they were simply two lovers doing what lovers do. It was a wonderful fantasy.

## CHAPTER TWENTY-FIVE

Freya parked her car to the side of Henry's street. It was just past dawn and no one was about. She had on the clothes she wore the night before, gathered from the floor of the bedroom while Clare slept soundly on. She closed the car door gently and walked to the end of the block, looking for the alley that ran behind Henry's apartment house. The air was crisp and cold and fresh snow was on the ground. It was completely silent. She sneezed and it sounded like an explosion.

She walked to the garage behind the house and saw three metal garbage cans lined up, each with an apartment number on it. They couldn't have made it any easier for her. She lifted the lid of the can marked Apartment One and saw a plastic bag on top. She untied it and peered inside to find at least a dozen beer bottles. She opened the canvas shopping bag she'd taken from her car and carefully put all of the bottles inside. Then she retied the plastic bag and placed it back in the garbage can. When she started to walk back up the alley, the bottles clinked and she was sure everyone, including Henry, would hear it. She held the bag to her chest and quickly returned to her Jeep.

She wanted to deliver the bottles directly to forensics in Bloomington. Ben and the sheriff would point out the DNA from the bottles was worthless without a chain of custody, but this got her closer. Any DNA match she found between one of the bottles from Henry's garbage and one from the scene of the murders would have to be established some other way. But if there was a match, she'd be able to talk the DA into an arrest warrant. As soon as Henry was in custody, his DNA could be obtained and matched in a way admissible in court. She found it hard to believe Henry had anything to do with the murders. How could that happen with Elizabeth and Hank as parents? But ever since Henry refused to supply his DNA, Freya was certain he was hiding something.

She stopped by Bean There to pick up coffee and then drove toward Bloomington. She had plenty of time during the long drive to reflect on her night with Clare—exciting, sexy, and somehow disturbing. As they'd lain in post-orgasmic bliss, Freya had tried to start a conversation.

"I feel really close to you," she said, holding Clare against her shoulder. There was no response. She couldn't see her face. Maybe she'd fallen asleep? "Clare?"

"I'm here." Her voice was flat. She didn't snuggle up to Freya. Her body was as still as a corpse.

"Are you okay?"

"I'm fine."

"It's just you seem a little distant."

Silence. After a few moments, Clare turned over so she was facing Freya. "Really, I'm fine. I have a lot on my mind. It's hard to relax and just be."

Freya touched her cheek with the palm of her hand. "Okay. As long as it doesn't have anything to do with us."

"I'm still getting used to there being an us. Seems strange."

What did that mean? Was she pulling away from her? You'd think she'd do so before they made love, not after. "There's only an us if both of us want there to be."

Clare looked Freya in the eye. "I want there to be. But I'm so tired. Let's talk about this later." She turned away and settled herself into her pillow. Freya was scared. Which Clare would show up when they next talked? The warm and inviting one or the cool and distant one? It was a guess to say either way. She watched Clare sleep as she lay in bed, wide awake.

❖

Freya was gone by the time Clare woke the following morning. Her side of the bed was still warm. After their conversation last night, you'd think she'd hang around a bit to say good morning, but she'd not even left a note. Clare felt bad she'd been so off-putting. She was overwhelmed, unable to entertain the idea of a relationship. She wondered how Freya was feeling but chose not to speculate about it. She had other business at hand. Today was the summary judgement motion and she was out of speed. She referred to it as speed because that sounded innocuous compared to meth, which brought to mind all kinds of terrible things. She called Evan.

"Hello," he croaked, his voice phlegmy and muted.

"Evan, it's Clare. I hope I didn't wake you." Like she cared.

"It's seven in the morning. Of course, you woke me."

"I'm sorry, but now that you're up I wonder if I can get some speed from you. I ran out of what you and Henry gave me. I'll pay."

Evan coughed. "If you mean meth, I have a little. Not much. I should be getting more tomorrow."

She wondered who he was getting supply from. "How about I buy you a coffee at Bean There?" She was cheery, as if they were old friends grabbing some time together.

"What time?"

"Can you make eight o'clock?"

"See you then."

She made some coffee and sat at her kitchen table, taking her time eating breakfast and staring out the window. A thrum of fear seemed to have parked in her midsection, reminding her constantly she was a thin line away from being found out. She had to start considering her options. If Henry was arrested, she probably should go to the police with what she knew. She put her head in her hands at the thought of losing her life in Money Creek. It didn't help that she was a little strung out. There were no drugs in her system, a state as rare as an early spring in central Illinois. She wouldn't be able to think straight until she took something. She got dressed and walked to Bean There, her down coat zipped to the throat. She grabbed the last table open and waited for Evan. He sat down five minutes later.

"Let me get you a coffee," Clare said.

He still looked sleepy. His shirt buttons were in the wrong holes. "I don't know why I'm doing this. It's like the middle of the night for me."

"Well, I appreciate it." She went to the front and returned with two coffees and a wad of napkins. He took a couple of the napkins and through some sleight of hand passed them back to her with the drugs underneath. Clare crumpled the napkins and stuffed them in her suit jacket pocket.

"That was smooth," she said.

"I've done this a time or two." He slurped at his coffee and watched her. "That's just a small amount. Call me if you need more."

"I don't need it at all. It's a placeholder while I look for more Adderall. Do you think you'll ever get some?"

"The murders took out two-thirds of the drug suppliers in the area, so my guess is it's going to be a while before those kinds of connections are set up again. It's up to Henry."

"I heard. How is Henry doing? I haven't seen him."

"He's wigging out over his partners being killed. I know he's not sleeping because I can hear him pace around at night. I haven't seen him eat in days, and he's smoking a ton of weed."

She didn't tell Evan she had been at the house, too. The fewer who knew, the better. It didn't sound like Henry had told him either. "I'm sure it was a shock for him. He just missed being killed himself."

Evan pushed his chair back and picked up his coffee cup. "Okay. My work here is done. But there's one more thing."

Clare raised an eyebrow. "What would that be?"

He smiled and his face changed entirely. He was handsome and sexy and she could tell he knew it. "I want you to go out with me."

She stifled a laugh. "Is that an invitation or are you stating a fact."

"It's an invitation. I'd like you to go out to dinner with me, say this weekend. What do you say?"

"I say no." She didn't want to put her drug connection in jeopardy, but she wasn't dating Evan. It would feel like dating a younger brother. And then there was Freya. "I'm sorry, Evan. I don't think of you that way."

The smile had faded and she saw the disappointment in his face. "You could learn to think that way. You have to give me a chance to show you what a wonderful guy I am."

"I'm sure someone your own age would love to go out with you." Her voice was gentle but not patronizing. She appreciated how hard it was to get turned down.

"Girls my own age aren't the problem," he said. "But a sophisticated woman like you is a prize. Please change your mind."

"I can't do that. It will never be what you're looking for."

He stood and pushed his chair back under the table. "You're making a mistake, you know." He seemed upset.

"I'm sorry, Evan. Thanks for bringing this to me this morning. I owe you for it."

She left for the office. Her primary job for the day was to support Elizabeth during her oral argument for the summary judgement, which was scheduled for one o'clock. Most of her nerves were focused on that. A little meth would focus her attention on the task at hand.

Elizabeth was parking her car when Clare came around the corner carrying her coffee. She waited as she gathered her briefcase and bag and got out of the car. She looked completely at ease and had a broad smile on her face. If Clare had a huge motion to argue that day she'd be whimpering. They walked into the office together. Apparently, Elizabeth had not heard that her son owned the house where the murders occurred and had been questioned by the police. Surely that would throw even the composed Elizabeth off her stride a bit.

"Why don't you come by my office in a little while and we'll go over the outline one more time?" Elizabeth said. "Your help has been invaluable, Clare. You could argue the motion yourself."

A shudder raced through her body at the thought. "I enjoyed working on the brief."

Elizabeth paused at the entrance to Clare's office. "It's excellent work. I'm really pleased." She put her hand on Clare's shoulder. "See you in a bit."

She flushed with pleasure as she watched Elizabeth stride down the hallway. A crack was about to appear in Elizabeth's world, but it was only a crack. Clare envied the solidness of her life—the pleasure of being a great lawyer able to practice interesting law, the steady marriage, beautiful home, multiple friends, and the high regard of everyone in town. In comparison, the crack in Clare's life was like the San Andreas Fault. An earthquake was likely to ensue.

She tossed her briefcase onto her desk, hung her coat up behind the door, and left her office for the bathroom. The door was locked. The small packet of meth was burning a hole in her pocket. Now that it was there, she was anxious to take some of it. She went to the coffee station to pour a cup, hoping the bathroom would be free by the time she got back. As she stepped back into the hall she saw Henry walking toward her. She blocked his way.

"What are you doing here?" she hissed. She pulled him into her office and shut the door.

Henry looked unlike his usual urbane self. His hair was uncombed, he wore a Money Creek College T-shirt and sweatpants under his open jacket, as if he'd rolled out of bed and come straight here. His eyes looked tired. "I've got to tell my folks about the house. They're sure to find out anyway, and I want to get in front of it."

"You can't do that. Not today."

"Why not? Putting it off doesn't do any good."

"Your mom is arguing a major motion today. You'll ruin it for her." Henry probably didn't think of his parents' daily lives, their work, their need to make a living. He thought of them only in relation to himself and how they could serve him. Like a child.

"I don't see why that makes a difference. She must have important things going on every day."

"You're wrong. This is a very big deal. If she thinks you're in trouble she won't be able to concentrate. You can't do this now."

This was all true, but she also wanted to push back the inevitable as long as possible. Once he told his mother he owned the house, it was entirely possible he'd tell her the whole thing, including Clare's presence at the house when the murders happened. She could practically hear the fissure crack beneath her.

"Okay. What time will the court appearance be over?"

"It could go all afternoon. I'd forget it today."

"No way. I could get picked up again and I want my parents on my side. I'll talk to them tonight and hope no one tells them before that." He brushed by her on the way out of her office and turned toward the exit.

She hurried to the bathroom and locked the door behind her. She was quite adept now at emptying a small amount of the meth onto the metal shelf over the sink, cutting it into lines, and snorting it through a rolled-up dollar bill. A punch hit her bloodstream and the worries of a moment before vanished. She returned to her office and gave herself five minutes to feel the drug in her system before walking down to Elizabeth's.

❖

There was a smattering of observers in the courtroom, mostly older men who made court watching their retirement hobby. There were no criminal proceedings taking place, so they were stuck watching a summary judgement motion in Courtroom Two, Judge Carruthers presiding. Clare recognized a few of them from the times she'd been in court to present minor motions. A couple nodded to her as she turned around at the counsel table and looked toward the door. She'd gotten to the courtroom early with a few boxes of exhibits. The motion was scheduled to start in five minutes and Elizabeth hadn't arrived.

Several minutes later, she breezed in and walked confidently through the bar, plunking her briefcase on the table and smiling at Clare. She took out her notepad and a pen and put the briefcase on the floor behind the counsel table. "All set to go?"

Clare nodded. "If you are, I am." She wanted to shrug out of her suit jacket. The room was overheated, the old radiator clanking away. Someone had opened a window a crack, but it wasn't cooling the room down. She was clammy.

The bailiff walked in from the chambers area behind the courtroom. "All rise."

She glanced at Elizabeth as they got to their feet. She seemed unflappable. Clare was very flappable. Judge Carruthers sat and everyone else followed suit.

"Ms. Nelson, would you like to begin?"

"Yes, Your Honor. Elizabeth Nelson for the defendant Peterson Agricultural." She smiled up at Judge Carruthers, a good friend of hers and Hank's. Today he was all business.

"Good afternoon, counsel. You're here to present a motion for summary judgment. I have read both briefs and am ready to rule today."

"Thank you, Judge."

"Luther Woolfe for the plaintiff, Your Honor." He turned toward Elizabeth and smiled as if he pitied her.

Clare sat at the counsel table next to Elizabeth, ready with a list of case law in the event she needed help remembering a name. She also had the boxes of tabbed exhibits on the floor behind her, ready to grab whatever was necessary. She could smell Elizabeth's delicate perfume and she admired the suit she wore. It was a beautiful gray wool that draped perfectly, the skirt showing off the right amount of her very good legs. She waited for the argument to begin and tried to stop her left leg from vibrating underneath the table.

"The defendant, Peterson Agricultural, moves for summary judgment on the grounds that the plaintiff has failed to produce any evidence Peterson had knowledge that the gate through which Mr. Oleg fell was faulty or damaged. The undisputed facts, taken in a light most favorable to the plaintiff, do not support a negligence claim against Peterson as a matter of law."

Clare gazed at Elizabeth, losing focus on her role as assistant as she watched her work. She thought about her a lot. She realized with a shudder it could be sort of a mother thing. Maybe a therapist wasn't a bad idea.

Elizabeth continued speaking without notes. "In order to go forward on a claim of negligence, the plaintiff must submit evidence that the defendant, either by action or omission, failed to exercise that degree of care, vigilance, and forethought which a person of ordinary caution and prudence ought to exercise in the present circumstance. Peterson exercised that degree of caution, and there's no evidence to the contrary."

She now dove into the case law supporting these assertions and the argument got into the weeds. Clare tried to focus on every word. She knew the case law by heart. But her mind kept wandering to what Henry was going to tell Elizabeth later in the day. Would Elizabeth be as calm and confident then?

After the arguments, Judge Carruthers retired to his chambers for half an hour before returning. The courtroom rose again as he entered. When they sat back in their seats, Elizabeth put her hand on Clare's arm and winked. The judge looked at both lawyers. "I'm ready to rule." He then cited the evidence presented, the case law, and the arguments from both sides. "I'm denying the motion on the grounds the question of whether Peterson Agricultural received a recall notice is a disputable fact and therefore properly left for a jury to decide."

Elizabeth closed her eyes briefly before moving for a continuance on the current trial date, which was granted. Trial was set for two months. The judge left the courtroom and Elizabeth and Clare started packing up their things.

"I feel like I've been kicked in the stomach," Clare said. "I can't believe we lost."

"That's because you're so thoroughly in our point of view. It's hard for you to give any credence to the plaintiff's argument. But we both knew this was a possible, if not probable, outcome. Now we prepare for trial."

Elizabeth left Clare to deal with the boxes of documents. She wanted to kick something. All those weeks of work down the drain. And the work she put in preparing for the motion would pale in comparison to preparing for trial. The idea of a trial, though, began to feel exciting. She'd never been in one before and as a litigator, she needed to get that experience. Maybe Elizabeth would let her question some of the witnesses. Depending on how she looked at things, the future was not entirely bleak.

## CHAPTER TWENTY-SIX

E van came home at six in the morning. Henry expected him to be drunk or high or both, but he bounced into the kitchen with clear eyes, full of energy. Henry sighed. He'd spent a sleepless night agonizing over when to tell his parents about his trouble with the police, finally getting out of bed at five. He'd chickened out the night before. He made a pot of coffee and looked out the window at the gray wintery day. He was sick to death of winter. He was sick to death with worry. Something had to give. He handed Evan a mug.

"Why are you up so early?" Evan said.

Henry sat at the kitchen table. "Never fell asleep."

"Did you do some meth or something? That's not like you." Evan sat opposite Henry and appeared to be completely focused on him.

"No, I've got something on my mind."

"Well, spit it out, man. I'm here to help."

He didn't treat Evan very well, but he got nothing but loyalty and support from him. He resolved to do better. "You know the little house I have out in the country?"

"Yeah, of course."

"That's where Ray and Bobby got killed and the cops know I own the house."

Evan leaned back in his chair. "Holy shit." He didn't let on Clare had said as much.

He told Evan of being questioned, about the beer bottles at the murder scene with his DNA on them, his refusal to give a sample, his certainty Freya and Ben still suspected him.

"It's not really a big problem, is it?" Evan said. "I mean, you left before the shooting started."

"I'd like it better if they didn't even know I was at the scene. Leaving the party doesn't mean I couldn't come back and ambush them. Plus, it exposes my association with known drug dealers"

"But why would you ambush them?" Evan said.

"I'm sure the cops can provide theories as to that. Clare's the only one who can confirm that I left at all."

Evan stopped before taking another sip of coffee. "Clare?"

"Yeah, she was there. No one else knows, so don't say a word."

"Of course not. What do you take me for? But why wasn't she killed with the others?"

He smiled. "Because she had to go to the bathroom. Luck of the Irish I'd say." He looked at Evan. "Where have you been? You look like you're ready to go to class."

He ran his hand through his thick hair. "I was with a nice girl last night. Doesn't drink or smoke. It was kind of sexy."

"And you lasted a whole night with her?" Henry got up to pour more coffee.

"I like her. I'm only here now because she had to get up for a six o'clock shift at the hospital." He paused. "Did Clare tell you whether she saw the shooter while she was there?"

"If she did, she didn't tell me and I'm sure she would have."

Henry was at his parents' office by nine thirty. Donna pointed him in and he walked the fifty feet to his mother's office as if it were a gangplank. The light was on in Clare's office, but she wasn't there. Thank God for small favors. He saw his mother with her head bent over some papers on her desk. He knocked softly on the door. She raised her head and a smile spread across her face.

"Henry! What a nice surprise. What are you doing here?" She came around her desk and gave him a hug. It was getting harder by the minute to tell her.

"Can't a son come visit his mother?" His smile felt thin and stiff.

"Of course, you can. Anytime. Have a seat. Do you want some coffee?"

"No, thanks." He was silent for a moment.

"What is it, Henry?" Her brow furrowed with concern.

He sat up in his chair and crossed his leg over his knee. "I've got something to tell you, and you're not going to like it."

She frowned. "You haven't been kicked out of school again, have you?"

He wished. "No, school is fine. I wanted to tell you that the police have called me in for questioning."

Before he could get another word out, she was halfway out of chair. "What about? You didn't talk to them, did you?" She sat back down, as if surprised she had risen at all.

"Try to stay calm while I explain. This is going to come as a big surprise." He shifted in his chair, put both feet on the ground. "I own the house where the triple murders took place." Her face betrayed nothing. She hadn't taken in what he'd said. "You tend to know everything that happens in this town, so I thought I'd tell you before you found out from someone else."

Her hand went to her forehead. "I don't at all understand what you're saying."

"I own a small house out in the country. I use it as a retreat. Some people broke into the house and however it happened, the shootings occurred there. I don't understand that part any more than you do."

"But how can you own a house that we're not aware of? Where would you get the money?"

He waved a hand dismissively. "It cost less than ten grand."

She leaned into her big leather chair as if blown back. "You're dealing drugs again, aren't you? There's no way for you to get that kind of money anyway else."

He told her about the sports betting. She looked skeptical.

"The police tracked down who owned the house and brought you in for questioning?"

"That's right. I didn't have anything to do with those people. For some reason they chose my house to break into. I don't know anything beyond that."

"I don't understand why you didn't want us to know about the house."

"I didn't want you to know about the gambling."

She looked more like her lawyer self, calm and focused. "And what did you tell the police?"

"Only what I've told you. They asked for a DNA sample and I refused to give one."

"Why?"

"Why? Wouldn't you advise against giving a DNA sample if you were acting as my lawyer."

"From now on I am acting as your lawyer. But, no, if a DNA sample can help exonerate my client, I advise him or her to give it. Is that not the case with you?" He saw the fear in her eyes.

"I didn't think of it that way. I thought it was the best thing to not offer the authorities anything they don't already have. You know how many times they get the wrong man in these cases." It sounded weak even to himself. He rose and stood before his mother. "I've told you. My duty is done. Now I have to go."

"Your father is going to be upset."

"I'll go tell him now, if you'd like." He wasn't as concerned about his father's reaction. It was his mother who was the emotional center and moral compass of the family.

"He's out at a meeting. I don't think he'll be back for a while. I'll tell him."

"Thanks, Mom."

"And if the sheriff or the Illinois cops want you to answer any more questions, call me. That's an order."

Henry gave her a mock salute and left, grateful she hadn't blown a gasket. The sports betting line was genius. If she found out he was dealing again she'd be off her head. He was no longer beholden to his parents—he was almost twenty-one and not dependent on them financially. He took the lousy allowance they gave him every month to make them think he was. He'd have to brush up on the world of online sports gambling and set up some accounts; he knew his father would question him about it, half curious himself.

"You're sure about this?" Freya held her phone to one ear as she drove into work.

"The testing is solid. You've got a match." The technician sounded annoyed. They'd rushed the test

"Can you send me the report ASAP?"

"Of course. We're here only for you, Saucedo." He hung up and Freya threw her phone onto the passenger seat of her Jeep and stepped on the gas. Now they had evidence someone drinking beer in his Money Creek home had been on the scene when the murders took place, most likely Henry. It was time to bring him in. He probably had a roommate. She'd send a sheriff's deputy to pick them both up, put some fear into Henry's arrogant demeanor.

Ben was getting out of his car when she pulled into the sheriff's department lot. She told him about the forensics hit.

"Wow. It's got to be Henry, don't you think?"

"I'm keeping my mind open and so should you. But I have to admit, it's not looking good for him. We have to get an official sample from him."

They went to the sheriff's office and found him reading the *Chicago Tribune*. His feet were on his desk. The industrial green room was festooned with ISU swag—pennants, a mug, a bobblehead of the football coach. He pointed to the two seats in front of him. "Every time I read this rag I thank my lucky stars I live here instead of the city. There were nine shooting deaths in Chicago yesterday. Nine." He shook his head and put the paper away. "Of course, we had three in one day here, so I shouldn't be smug. What can I do for you?" Despite his assertion of jurisdiction at the time the murders occurred, Sheriff Phillips seemed content to let Ben and Freya take the lead.

Ben brought him up to speed on the DNA. "We'd like a couple of deputies to pick them up. Put the fear of God into them. Can we borrow them?"

"Sure. More than two if it raises the intimidation level."

"It would, actually," Freya said. "We'll take three."

"Fine. When do you need them?"

"Right now, if we can."

Phillips picked up the phone. "I'll have them meet you in the lobby."

They left the office. Freya walked quickly, excited at the break in the case. When the deputies arrived, she said, "There should be two men at the apartment, and I want them both brought in. Read them their rights. One is named Henry Nelson, the other is his roommate, if he has one. Put them in the interview room and give us a call when you do." The deputies left, one looking a little sour at doing Freya's bidding. No doubt the order would have been received better coming from Ben. They headed back to their office to wait. She poured a couple of cups of coffee for them and settled behind her cramped desk. The room was particularly claustrophobic. Ben seemed to be sitting on top of her instead of across their desks.

Thirty minutes later, they were back at the jail, facing Henry and his roommate, Evan Bishop. She had a deputy take Henry into a holding area while they talked to Evan. As soon as he left the room Evan said, "I have no idea why I'm here. I don't know shit about these murders, other than Henry owns the house where they happened."

"Did Henry tell you that?" Ben said.

"Who else? He told me after you guys pulled him in for questioning. I don't understand why I'm here."

"What else did Henry tell you?" Freya said. She took note of his bouncing leg and clasped hands. He was clearly nervous, but many people were when they found themselves being interrogated by police.

"That's all he said. He doesn't know who broke into his house. Neither do I."

"We have a problem, Evan, and we're hoping you'll help us sort it out." Ben said.

"Sure, anything."

"We found DNA on some beer bottles from your garbage that matched DNA from bottles found at the murder scene. We have to make sure that DNA doesn't belong to you."

"Is that even legal? Looking in someone's garbage, I mean," Evan said. His head was cocked to one side.

"It's not illegal," Freya said. "But it doesn't get us anywhere without an official sample from you. Will you let us take a swab?"

"Of course! Please take as many swabs as you want. I have nothing to hide."

He relaxed visibly and she knew he wasn't at the murder scene. "Have you ever been out to Henry's house in the country?"

"Sure. We go out there to party once in a while. Mainly it's an investment for him."

Ben leaned forward, as if in confidence. "A house costs a lot of money. Where do you think he got the funds to buy it? I mean, you're college students."

Evan hesitated for the first time. "I'm not sure. I never asked. I know his parents are pretty well off, being lawyers and all. I thought it was them that bought it for him."

"Do you participate in online sports betting with Henry?"

Evan's was a malleable face. His eyes narrowed as he tried to figure out what trap was being set for him. "No. I don't care about sports."

"But you're aware that he gambles to earn money?" Ben pressed on.

"He spends a lot of time in his room. I don't know what goes on in there." He sat back in his chair as if exhausted.

"Henry's never talked to you about sports betting?" Freya said. She could see his uncertainty.

"I think he's mentioned it a time or two. He mostly keeps to himself."

"How about drugs, Evan? Do you or Henry deal drugs, on campus for instance?" Ben said.

Freya saw his Adam's apple bob up and down. "We have reason to believe Henry was involved with the drug dealers who were shot to death last week."

"I don't know anything about that."

"That's a lot of stuff happening in your house that you're unaware of. It's not that big of a place, is it, Evan?" Freya's tone was conversational.

"We live separate lives. We're only roommates. Why don't you take that DNA sample and we can clear all this up."

For half an hour they tried to get more out of him, but he stuck with his plea of ignorance. They left the room and conferred in the hallway.

"He knows what Henry's been up to. That was all bullshit," Ben said.

"I agree. Henry made up the sports betting as a decoy and didn't let Evan in on it. If there was drug dealing going on in the apartment, Evan knew about that. But we don't have anything to leverage against him. Let's get the sample and then cut him loose. We can always bring him in again."

"Okay. I'll take care of it. What do you think we should do with Henry?"

"Let's let him stew for a bit longer, then we'll question him. He'll be worried about what Evan may have said."

Freya left Ben and made her way across the jail complex to the main sheriff's reception area. As she looked toward the door she saw Elizabeth burst through and make a beeline straight to her.

"What the hell is going on?" she said. "I want to see my client immediately."

"You're acting as your son's attorney?"

"Of course, I am," she said impatiently. "Now please, bring me to where I can see him. I don't know what's gotten into you, Freya. I wouldn't have pegged you as a witch hunt kind of cop."

Freya bit her lip as she looked up at Elizabeth. She could see she was as fearful as she was angry. "I'll have Henry brought into the interview room where you can talk. I'll join you when you're ready." A deputy led them back to the interview room and then left to fetch Henry.

"This is my son, Freya. How can you think he had anything to do with a triple homicide?"

"There were DNA samples found at the murder scene that did not match the victims. I believe you son's DNA is a match for one of those."

"How could you possibly know that? He refused to give you a sample last time he got hauled in here." Elizabeth took a seat and ran her fingers through her hair.

"Because I took some beer bottles from Henry's garbage and DNA found on them matches DNA found at the murder scene." She could see the flash of alarm in Elizabeth's eyes.

"Are you kidding me? That means nothing. You can't hold him."

"I didn't say I was going to arrest him. I'm going to ask him for a sample. I'd suggest you advise him to give us one."

Henry was brought into the room and Freya left, but not before Henry gave her a scornful look. She met up with Ben and they walked over to Bean There for a decent cup of coffee. When they returned the desk sergeant pointed toward the jail and said the witness was ready for them. They walked in to find Henry and Elizabeth both playing with their phones, apparently having nothing further to say to each other. Freya and Ben sat and Elizabeth put her phone down. Henry continued to stare at his.

"You've kept us waiting," Elizabeth said. "I'd have expected better of you both."

Freya ignored her and looked at Henry. He lifted his head and looked back with a dull expression. "Henry, will you give us a sample of your DNA to help with our investigation?"

"What happens if I don't?" Elizabeth put her hand on his arm.

"We'll arrest you for the murders of Bobby Hughes, Ray Barnes, and Caroline Sommers."

"That's outrageous," Elizabeth said. "You have nothing on him other than the ownership of the house."

"Add that to the lack of an alibi and the refusal to provide DNA and we have enough to file charges. We're ready to do that right now, Henry," Ben said.

Freya looked at Elizabeth before turning to Henry. "Will you give a sample?"

"I will not." Henry looked sullen but determined. She glanced back at Elizabeth and saw a flash of shock on her face.

"I'd like to confer with my client."

Freya and Ben left the room again and stood out in the hall. "Elizabeth freaked out in there. Did you see her face?" Freya said.

"Yeah. Now she knows Henry's guilty of something."

After five minutes they walked back into the interview room. Elizabeth looked shaken, though she was clearly trying to maintain a neutral exterior. In the war between the mother and the attorney, the mother was winning. She should get someone in to replace her. With Freya's luck it would be Clare and they'd have to be on opposite sides again. She didn't need new reasons why they shouldn't be together.

"What's your decision?" Ben asked.

"My client will decline giving a DNA sample." Henry looked satisfied, though he must know what would come next.

"You give me no choice but to place him under arrest." She nodded at Ben, who read him his rights for a second time. "We'll be holding Henry here; you can visit anytime. But the first thing we'll do is take a DNA sample while processing him. There's no way around it now."

Henry gave her a maleficent look as he was led away by the deputy. Elizabeth reached for her briefcase and wiped at her eyes.

"I'm sorry, Elizabeth. You can see that we had to do this, can't you?"

She stood from the table and brushed by her. "I'll be filing an emergency habeas corpus motion."

They watched Elizabeth walk out of the room. "She's desperate," Freya said. "There are no grounds for a habeas corpus ruling."

"Can't blame her for trying, though. I'll get the deputies to start processing, including getting a sample from him right away," Ben said.

"Good. Send the sample to forensics, of course, but let's get a second sample and use the portable device on it. That'll give us a pretty good idea if we've got a match or not. I'll go up to see Lorena and get the okay to file charges." She left the department and walked over to the courthouse, praying she wouldn't run into Clare or Elizabeth. The social structure of Money Creek was about to be caved in by Henry's arrest. She didn't know how Elizabeth would recover from whatever he was hiding. That he'd done something seriously bad was clear to everyone.

## Chapter Twenty-seven

Clare tried to keep her jaw from falling open as Freya told her that Henry had been arrested for the murders. Her stomach lurched and she resisted the urge to go to the bathroom. Freya took a seat on the couch, with a concerned look on her face.

"Are you okay?" she said.

"My stomach's been a little dodgy today, but I'm fine. Can I get you a drink?"

She pulled two beers out of the fridge and grabbed the bottle of bourbon. At the moment she didn't care what Freya though of her drinking. She needed to feel the liquor hit her system and slide down to her toes. It was the only way she could continue acting as if she were calm. She collapsed on the adjacent chair.

"What do you have on Henry?" she asked nonchalantly.

"This has to remain between ourselves."

"Of course."

"We have a fair amount. Today a preliminary DNA test showed he's a match with DNA found at the murder scene. That will have to be confirmed, but it's a pretty safe bet he was there, which means he's already been lying to us."

"But isn't that all circumstantial? What if Henry had been there some other time and left beer bottles behind. It's his house, after all."

Freya paused. They'd considered Henry's beer bottles as coming from another time, but the way they were all grouped together on the coffee table made that seem like a real stretch. "A witness would help, but the witnesses are all dead. Except for Henry and the anonymous woman who called in the shooting. I'd give a lot to be able to talk to her."

"No luck tracing her?" She assumed there weren't enough clues to track her down as the person making the call. She could only pray that was true, or certainly she would have heard by now.

"We traced the call to the Texaco station on Lincoln Avenue and scoured the security footage that was available. We can see a figure in a parka go into the booth, but the hood was up and the face turned away from the camera. The car was not in view. The coat is like a hundred other parkas, and the video is in black and white, so we don't know the color. It's like your parka, as a matter of fact."

Clare blanched. "Are you going to arrest me? Because it's kind of sexy."

Freya laughed. "When I do, I'll wear my uniform."

Clare drank more bourbon and followed it up with some beer. She was speeding, having taken some meth that afternoon, which was stupid. Her life was surreal. If the police had evidence putting Henry at the scene, he would have only her testimony that he left the house before the shootings. That might be the reasonable doubt he would need to avoid a conviction for triple murder. She was fucked. Freya might be arresting her for real at any time.

"Let's not talk about that anymore," Freya said. "I'm pretty sick of Henry Nelson right now."

"Sure. Anything else going on in your life?" Her posture was stiff and she tried to unclench herself.

"I have zero going on, except for you. Why don't you join me over here?"

Clare felt about as sexy as a dish rag, but she moved over to the couch. She remained a foot away from Freya, hoping she wouldn't want to make love. But why wouldn't she? That's what they did when they saw each other, and normally Clare would be filled with desire simply being next to her. Their relationship was about to implode, and that was the least of her problems.

Freya picked up her hand, which lay limply on her lap. She stared into space. "You still seem a million miles away."

She smiled as brightly as she could. "Do I? I guess I'm a little tired."

"And the news about Henry can't be easy."

"I worry about Elizabeth. What must she be feeling now? Her treasured son may be a murderer. What can be harder than that?"

"I was thinking the same thing," Freya said. She moved a little closer to Clare and put her hand on her thigh. "It's going to be impossible for her if it turns out Henry committed the murders. Hank, too. She was pretty angry today when we arrested him. I think she hates me now."

"That's the mama bear thing. I'm sure she was fierce. I'm glad she didn't send me in to represent him. She'd want the best counsel for him and that's certainly not me."

Freya reached over and touched her face. "You have a bad habit of denigrating yourself."

"I do?" No one had ever told her that.

"You do it all the time. You see a completely different person than I do."

She was afraid to ask but did anyway. "What do you see?"

Freya dropped her hand and looked into Clare's eyes. "A beautiful woman in every way. You're sweet, kind, funny, smart, hardworking, compassionate, filled with integrity, and did I say smart?"

She blushed as the list went on, though surely Freya was talking about somebody else. That her view of Clare was about to be shattered seemed sad. "You're making that up," she said, looking down at her lap.

"There you go again. You can't take a compliment. Why are you so hard on yourself?"

"That might take years of therapy to find out."

"It's never too late to start, though I don't know how many good therapists are in Money Creek."

She smiled, trying to stay present in the conversation. "Maybe I'll think about it."

Freya laughed. "That's so noncommittal. You're not even agreeing to think about it."

"I have a problem with commitment." She knew as soon as she said it that it was the wrong this to say. "I mean, not with relationships, for example, but with more personal stuff."

Freya cocked her head. "What could be more personal than a relationship?"

She was getting annoyed. She may as well be under interrogation. She reached for the bourbon. "Would you like another?"

"No, I'm good." They were silent for a minute. "You don't want to go too deep in this conversation, do you?" Freya said.

She sipped some whiskey. "I'll go deep. Maybe not tonight though. I'm not feeling so great."

Freya looked like she was going to say something, but then held her tongue. They were quiet a few more moments before she looked at Clare again. "Should I leave, do you think? I don't want to outstay my welcome."

"You couldn't do that. Why don't we go to sleep. Do you mind if we keep it at that?"

Freya looked relieved. "Of course not. I'd love to spend the night with you."

Twenty minutes later, they lay in each other's arms. Clare stared at the ceiling, as wide awake as she'd ever been, wired and wondering why she hadn't let Freya leave. This was going to be a long, long night, and her thoughts were filled with dread. She knew there was only one thing she could do and that was tell Freya everything in the morning. She could no longer keep up the charade, hiding her drug use, and hiding her role in the murders. Her life seemed completely out of her control. And it was better to tell her before Henry could say she was there at the house. It was the right thing to do, had been for some time, but she'd clung to the illusion that she could maintain her Money Creek lifestyle while a wild fire formed a ring around her. Now the illusion was destroyed. And with that, she fell asleep.

❖

When Clare woke at eight, Freya was gone from the bed. She slowly swung her legs to the floor and stood. She was dizzy, as if her blood pressure had sunk to a perilous level. Her hangover was mild, but her stomach was still in turmoil. The morning had not changed her mind about confessing to Freya.

She slipped her feet into her moccasins and made her way to the living room. No sign of Freya except for a note. *Feeling very close to you. Call me later. XO.* She sank onto the couch. There was no way she would stay with her after learning Clare was a drug addict and unreported witness to a murder. She was emotionally exhausted. Morally bankrupt. She couldn't take it anymore. It was her addiction ruining her life. She wasn't sure she was ready to quit, but didn't see much choice. She couldn't imagine a life without drugs, but she no longer could imagine a life with them.

She picked up the phone and called Freya.

"Good morning," Freya said. Her voice sounded warm, perhaps for the last time.

"You left here early."

"I needed to get home to get ready for work. Thought I'd tiptoe out so you wouldn't wake."

Clare took a deep breath. "I need to talk to you about something. I should have done so last night, but I didn't have the guts."

"That's mysterious. Can you tell me now?"

"It has to be in person. Can you come over before work? It's important."

"Sure. I'll be there in fifteen minutes."

The time dragged, each minute an eternity in which she tried to talk herself out of the confession. There were so many reasons to come forward, not the least of which was to prevent Henry from being convicted of a murder he didn't commit. She didn't like Henry, but she couldn't live with herself if she let him be put away for life. She went into the kitchen to make coffee for them both. When the door rang she opened it to find Freya dressed in her tactical gear, concern written on her face. She was sick at what she was about to do.

"Should I be nervous?" Freya said as she walked into the house.

"No. There's no point. I'm nervous enough for both of us. Come into the kitchen and we'll have some coffee."

Freya sat at the kitchen table and watched Clare carefully as she poured a mug of coffee and set it down in front of her. "What is it? I can't stand the wait."

Clare sat down with her own cup and dove in headfirst. "I was at the scene of the murders."

"Pardon me?"

"I was at the scene while the murders happened. I'm the one who called it in from the Texaco station." She watched Freya closely, saw her face change from one of openness to one of confusion, as if she'd just stepped into a bear trap but the pain hadn't yet registered.

"I don't understand." Her voice was strained.

Clare told her the whole story from her drug use to why she was at the party with the drug dealers and making the anonymous 911 call. Freya grew pale.

"Please tell me you're making this all up," she said.

"You know I'm not. That would be insane."

"What you've just told me is pretty insane." The sadness in her eyes was unmissable. "I'll have to take you in for questioning. You'll need to call into work. We're going to be a while."

Freya didn't bring up the state of their relationship and how the news affected it. Who could blame her?

"Of course, but I'd like to tell Elizabeth before she hears it from anyone else. Can I stop by there before coming to talk to you?"

"Meet me at the sheriff's department at ten. That should give you time to talk to Elizabeth." She scooched her chair back from the table and stood. "You're a Jekyll and Hyde, Clare. I never would have guessed this from you. Apparently, I don't know you at all." She walked out of the kitchen, slamming the door behind her.

She cringed at Freya's anger but was primarily relieved. She was about to lose her job, possibly her law license, her relationship with Freya. She might also be facing a jail term, but she still was better than she had been the day before. Telling Elizabeth was going to be much harder, her disappointment more painful to bear than

Freya's. And as quick as a thought, she latched on to the idea that it would be the perfect time to do one last hit of meth. She would have to quit, but today was not the day to do it.

She called Evan, despite the early hour. He picked up on the first ring.

"Hey, Clare. What's up?"

"You sound wide awake."

"I have class at nine. How are you?" He sounded cheery, almost unnaturally so.

"I'm all right, but I need a little of your product."

"You finished what you got the other day?"

She flushed. Another arrow piercing the fiction she had her drug use under control. "It wasn't that much."

"I'm not the one to discourage business. Do you want to come over?"

"Do we have time before your class?"

"Sure. I'll see you in a bit."

She hung up and hurried into her bedroom to throw on some clothes. She'd get ready for work when she got back and go in a little late for once. Ten minutes later, she was in Evan's apartment, sitting at the kitchen table. He wore a camouflage hoodie and khaki cargo pants and smiled at Clare as she got settled.

"How much do you want?"

"Can you sell a single serving size? I don't want to do more than the one hit."

He cocked his head. "Are you thinking of quitting?"

"Not thinking of it. Doing it. Right after this."

He pulled a small packet from his hoodie and opened it. Then he took the razor on the kitchen table and cut the amount into halves, wrapped the two in paper and pushed one half toward her. "That's one healthy dose."

"How much do I owe you?"

"That's on the house. Consider it a farewell present, though I'm not entirely convinced you won't be back."

"Thanks for the confidence." She put the packet into her jacket pocket and started to rise.

"Wait. I wanted to talk to you about something," he said.

She sat down and tried to tamp down fear. There were few conversations lately that didn't bear bad news.

"Have you heard that Henry was arrested for the murders?"

She decided to pretend ignorance in all things. "What?"

"They know he owns the house, and there are some other things as well."

"Shit. That's terrible for Henry. And Elizabeth. She's got to be hurting."

"I imagine." He was gazing at her steadily.

"Do you think he did it?" How much had Henry told Evan? Did he know she was at the property? It was hard to gauge the proper amount of ignorance to show.

"They have a pretty good case against him. I know he resented Bobby and Ray. He thought they were starting to squeeze him out of the business. That was probably the motive. I don't know what he's capable of. I think the only thing that could exonerate him would be a witness at the scene."

He had to know she'd been there, but why not simply tell her that? Henry must have told him. He leaned back in his chair and unzipped his hoodie, revealing a dark green Guns N' Roses T-shirt. She gasped. The image of the masked man leaving the scene came to her, his jacket open, revealing the exact same concert T-shirt. That man was tall and lanky like Evan. When she raised her eyes, she saw him with a half-smile on his face.

"You'd be a lousy poker player. It's obvious from your face you saw me at the house. Good thing for you I didn't know it at the time. I would have taken care of things then."

"I don't know what you're talking about," she said, trying to keep the panic from her voice.

"You don't need to lie. Henry told me you were there."

She remained silent.

"You didn't see a man wearing this T-shirt?"

"No! I didn't see anything. I was on the floor of the bathroom."

He had a lopsided smile on his face. "The bathroom has a window."

"I didn't see you. I only heard the shooting."

"I don't believe you," he said. He reached into the cargo pocket of his pants and pulled out a nine-millimeter pistol. Her heart took up residence in her throat.

"You don't want to kill me, Evan."

"Not right now. I've got to figure out the pros and cons here. You're the only piece of evidence against me. It makes sense to kill you."

A chill settled in her bones. "I can think of some cons, like how much worse killing me would make things for you."

"Worse than a triple murder? I don't think that's possible. No, the only con I can see is that I like you. I've had a thing for you from the day we met at the college."

That day was like a hundred years ago. She'd aged a lifetime since then. "I'm flattered. More than you know. Doesn't it make sense to let me go with my promise to not tell anyone? We can see how things go between us."

"Your promise isn't worth shit. I've got to think about this."

"What if you knew how much I care for you? Would you want to murder your lover?" She didn't like taking this tack, but what choice did she have? She saw a hopeful look in his eyes before they shuttered and became cold and suspicious.

"I don't believe you. I should kill you right now for playing with my feelings. He pointed his gun at her and reached into his other cargo pocket for a pair of handcuffs. He stood and walked around her, his gun resting on her back. "Put your hands behind you." She hesitated and felt the gun push hard against her. "Now."

"Handcuffs? Do you have a taser in your pocket as well?"

He brought her wrists together behind the chair and snapped the cuffs on. "I got them at a gun show. I think they're pretty."

"Apparently, we have different aesthetics." Her brain had taken on a second existence, leaving her petrified body in order to banter with him. She couldn't understand how she was functioning at all.

He pulled out a couple of long plastic ties and secured her ankles to the chair. "Are those from the gun show too?"

"Home Depot." He stood and looked at her admiringly, as if he'd just gift wrapped a present. Then he sat and drank more of his coffee.

She glanced at the clock on the microwave and saw it was quarter past nine. She'd never been late to work at Nelson & Nelson. They'd wonder about her soon. It didn't look like she'd make her ten o'clock appointment with Freya either, and she could only imagine what she'd think of her then.

"Why did you kill those people? You might as well tell me, since you're not letting me go."

He got up to grab a beer from the fridge. "It was Henry I was after, but taking the entire organization out was a business opportunity. My plan had been to pick up the pieces and start where they left off. Henry told me a lot about how they're organized. It wouldn't be a problem to get up and running. Stingy and I are already working together."

She remained silent, stunned at his cavalier way of explaining three murders. Her hopes for her own survival plunged further. "Why Henry? I thought you were best pals."

"Henry's a stuck-up, entitled bastard who basically treated me like a lackey. I made a lot of money through him or I would have left long ago. But recently he crossed a line."

"Which was?"

He lit a joint and leaned back in his chair. "He didn't invite me to that party of his, after all the work I've done for their organization. I was sick of not being respected. And there was something else, too."

"I'm listening." The more she got him to talk, the better she'd be.

"He wanted you, and he talked about it all the time. I found it unbearable."

"So, you decided you'd wipe them all out."

He looked at the ceiling, as if daydreaming. "It wasn't so much a decision as an impulse. When he left for the party I realized I could get rid of him, increase my chances with you, and move in on an established drug business all at the same time. It seemed brilliant."

She could tell it didn't seem so brilliant to him now. "What do we do now? Are you going to keep me here *ad infinitum*?"

"Is that lawyer talk or something?"

"I mean you can't keep me here indefinitely. I think I have a right to know what you plan to do."

His face hardened as he stood. "You have no rights. You're merely an obstacle. You're staying here for now."

He grabbed his beer and walked toward the bedrooms in the rear of the apartment. She looked around for anything that might liberate her, but there was nothing. The blinds were all drawn, so no passerby was going to see her tied up like something from Abu Ghraib. Her phone was in her jacket pocket, but she couldn't get to it with her hands cuffed behind her. Her head dropped forward and her eyes stung with tears. She didn't want him to see her cry. But she was scared. And she had to pee.

## CHAPTER TWENTY-EIGHT

Freya debated whether to tell Ben about Clare's confession, but she knew she had to. She'd been stunned while driving from Clare's home into work, but even with all the revelations she'd made, she didn't hate her. Apparently couldn't hate her, despite her drug use and everything else. Her thoughts raced through the ways the situation could be salvaged, that somehow things could return to where they'd been with each other only ten hours before, when they'd innocently fallen asleep together. There must be a way.

She pulled into the sheriff's parking lot at nine thirty, hoping Ben had picked up some coffee on his way in. She entered their office and saw he'd not disappointed. A large cup and a bagel sat on her desk. He was huddled over his, looking over the sports section of the *Chicago Tribune* as if it were a case file.

"I have news," she said.

He looked up, his eyes bleary from reading hockey box scores. "What?"

She told him every detail of Clare's confession, except for how it'd blown a hole in their relationship. He wasn't a genius, but he'd figure that much out.

"Holy Christ," he said. "That makes her not only a witness but a possible suspect, too."

"You can't seriously believe Clare murdered three people in cold blood."

"How do we know? Could you have guessed the things she just told you? We have to treat her as a suspect." He gentled his voice. "I know she means something to you. You must feel awful."

She looked at him with an eyebrow raised. "You think?"

He ignored her sarcasm. "Why didn't you bring her in with you?"

"She's coming in at ten. She wanted to take care of a couple of things first."

"You let a murder suspect walk away from you? You're not thinking straight."

"She's a witness, not a suspect. And she'll be here. I could tell she was relieved to finally tell someone about it."

Freya's phone rang and she picked up.

"Freya, it's Elizabeth Nelson."

"Hello, Elizabeth. What can I do for you?" She expected an earful about Henry.

"I'm wondering if you know where Clare is. She hasn't come into work yet, which has never happened before. She's not answering her phone."

Freya felt a tug of concern. "Maybe she's out running errands?"

"Well, that would be strange on a weekday. I know you two have a relationship and thought you might know where she is."

She wasn't about to talk about their relationship "I don't know. I haven't seen her lately."

"It's very odd. Clare is always on time, if not early. While I have you on the phone, I wanted to let you know I'm arguing the habeas corpus motion in federal court this morning. I'm leaving for Bloomington in a few minutes."

"Good luck with that. You know we have a clean arrest."

"We'll see," she said before hanging up.

Where was Clare? She was supposed to be talking to Elizabeth right now. Ben looked at her curiously and she told him what Elizabeth had said.

"Let's hope she hasn't flown the coop," he said. "Should we put out an APB?"

"No, let's give her some time." She left it at that. "What we need to do right away is track down the man Clare said she saw leaving the scene."

Ben's phone rang and it was a deputy telling him the prisoner Henry Nelson wanted to speak to them both immediately. They crossed over to the jail and met him in the interview room. Henry looked sallow and his eyes were darting all over the place. "I have something to tell you both."

"You've requested to see us without your attorney present?" Ben said.

"That's correct. I want to get you this information. You'll probably let me go after you hear it."

"We're all ears," Freya said.

"There was someone else at the murder scene, and she can corroborate that I left the house before the murders took place."

"You're admitting you were there?"

"I feel I don't have any choice. The DNA says I am. But I can show you I wasn't there when the murders happened."

"If you're talking about Clare, we already know about it."

His face sagged like a fallen soufflé. "She told you?"

"Yep. She told us everything, including your association with the victims."

"But I wasn't there, not when the shootings happened. Didn't Clare also tell you she saw someone leaving the scene after the shootings? That wasn't me."

Henry's eyes started darting around again. They knew it was unlikely Henry murdered his associates and the unfortunate woman who was with them. The man Clare said she saw was tall and lanky, while Henry was of average height and more solidly built.

"Thank you for telling us this, Henry. You did the right thing."

"You'll let me out now, won't you? I mean, isn't there reasonable doubt that I was the killer?"

Freya almost smiled. For a young man with seemingly endless confidence, he was remarkable naive. "I'm afraid it's the jury's job to determine reasonable doubt. We provide the likely candidate, and that's still you."

Henry slapped his open hand on the table. "You can't keep me here! I didn't do this."

Ben leaned back in his chair. "That's something you might want to talk to your attorney about. For now, we're sending you back." He got up and went to the door to call a deputy.

Freya looked at her phone. It was nearly ten o'clock. A deputy came in to remove Henry, who had tears in his eyes. She didn't feel sorry for him. They stayed behind at the table.

"He probably didn't do it," Ben said.

"That may be true, but I'm sure as hell not releasing him until we've formally interviewed Clare and she's signed a statement. It makes sense Henry didn't do it—he knew Clare was in the house and would have finished her off before leaving." Cavalier words for an idea that made her shudder.

"Do you think we should arrest her for withholding evidence?"

She'd been hoping Ben wouldn't bring that up. "Let's see if she'll be a fully cooperating witness. I'm not inclined to make the arrest if she is. If she clams up, we will."

"Fair enough. I'm going to get more coffee. You coming?"

They got up and left the room. Freya reminded the desk sergeant to call her as soon as Clare came in and they returned to their office. By ten thirty Clare had still not shown up and Freya called her for the third time. She didn't know whether to be mad or alarmed. It didn't make sense that she wouldn't come in as she said she would, but what if she'd changed her mind? Left town? She called Clare's office and spoke with the receptionist, who said she hadn't come in yet. She drove by her house and saw her car was gone. She was growing sick with worry something had happened to her. The people she'd been involved with were unforgiving, revengeful. What if the killer got wind that Clare had been at the scene and decided to eliminate her? She put a BOLO out on Clare's car and prayed she was right about her.

Clare was in agony. Her arms ached from being bound behind her. She longed to change position, every part of her body stiff. But the worst was she had to pee. Badly. She'd been strapped in the chair for hours and was ready to burst.

"You're going to have to let me out of this chair so I can go to the bathroom," she said, not for the first time. Evan was lounging on the living room couch and looked like he'd ignore this request as well. "Honestly, I'm going to pee all over if you don't."

A look of distaste flashed on his face. "You're going to have to hold it."

"What planet are you from? There's no holding it, you idiot." She didn't care if she antagonized him. This was an emergency.

He threw down the video game controller he was holding, having been occupied for the past two hours with his Xbox. "Christ. What a pain you are." He walked over to her and put his hands on his hips. "Are you going to try to run as soon as I untie you? Because I don't want to have to shoot you. Not yet anyway."

She was too occupied with holding her bladder to feel any alarm at his words. "All I want to do is get to the bathroom. Pronto."

He put his gun in the pocket of his hoodie and pulled a knife out of his cargo pants. "I'm coming in with you," he said as he cut open the ties at her ankles.

"Suit yourself. I don't even care." He held her by the elbow as they walked to the bathroom in the rear of the apartment. "But you'll have to uncuff me. Unless you want to take my pants off and wipe me."

"I wouldn't mind getting your pants off, but this isn't the scenario I had in mind." He took off the handcuffs when they got to the bathroom and watched her as she went. It took a long time. She was embarrassed to wipe herself in front of him, but really what did it matter? He was probably going to kill her. The thought sank into her core, now that she could think straight. He put the cuffs back on and grabbed her elbow again.

"I have to wash my hands, you philistine."

Evan pulled her out of the bathroom. "Shut up. You're starting to piss me off."

"Where do you see this going, Evan? How long do you think we can stay here like this?"

He pushed her back into the chair, cuffed her wrists, and put new plastic ties around her ankles. "It depends. I haven't decided. The cops don't have any reason to think I'm involved, so I can keep you here as long as Henry's in jail. Or we might get in the car and go. It might be a better idea to kill you when we're far away."

Now that she'd relieved herself she could feel the full complement of not only her fear, but also the withdrawal symptoms that were growing stronger as the day went on. She'd not had any drug in her system for nearly twenty-four hours and craved something. Anything. She wouldn't be picky about the drug.

"What can you give me?" she said. "I need some meth, or whatever you've got."

"Really? It didn't take long to turn you into a meth head."

She flushed, even now feeling shame at her dependence. "If you're going to keep me in this chair you've got to give me something. I'll lose my mind if you don't."

"No, I don't imagine you'd be any fun to be around in full withdrawal. Let's see what I have." He disappeared down the hall and came back with an odd smile on his face. "This'll fix you up."

Clare watched as he placed a packet of meth, a spoon, a lighter, a rubber tourniquet, and a syringe on the table. "Oh, no. I snort the stuff. You can put it right to my nose and I don't have to be uncuffed."

"I think you'll like this. Ups the intensity." He uncuffed her and brought her hands to the front, cuffing them again. He reached for her shirt sleeve and pushed it above her elbow. Then he held her forearm and scrutinized it, looking for the best vein. "This'll do. Now relax, I'm not going to kill you."

Bile rose in her throat. Shooting up was the one line she swore she'd never cross. It put you irredeemably into the category of lost cause. It meant you were dirty, broke, desperate, criminal, disgusting. She was none of those things. She watched with horror as he melted the crystals in the spoon and then pulled the liquid up into the syringe. With her bound hands, she hit him below the jaw with enough force to snap his head back and he instantly swung his hand and slapped her full on the cheek. Why did slapping people in the movies look more like insult than injury? This hurt like hell. He'd managed to split her lip on a tooth and blood started to roll down her chin, dripping onto her lap. Her cheekbone felt broken.

"What the hell was that?" he said. He cradled his jaw in one hand while holding her arms down with the other. He tied one arm off above the elbow and tapped on her vein. As he reached for the syringe, she hit him again. She knew it was stupid, that he'd do something in retaliation, but she didn't care. She was desperate to avoid the needle. He shot up from the table and cocked his arm as if he were going to slug her, but hesitated before lowering it.

"I should kill you now. You're nothing but a giant pain in my ass."

"I never claimed to be anything but." She put her hands to her mouth and wiped the blood away. She could feel it continue to swell and flow.

He grabbed her right arm in his strong hand and plunged the needle in. Almost instantly, her head exploded with sensation, like a race car was coursing through her system at two hundred miles an hour. Her body twitched and her head dropped forward, leaving her staring at her lap. It was the most intense high ever and she hated it. It was one thing to slowly kill herself using drugs voluntarily. It was something else to have them forced upon her. She raised her head and looked at Evan, who was sitting in a chair next to her, enjoying himself.

She opened her mouth to say something, but it was unintelligible, the frustrated cry of someone who couldn't get their tongue to work. She dropped her head again. All she could think through the static in her brain was he was probably going to kill her and how sorry she was Freya would be left thinking so little of her.

## CHAPTER TWENTY-NINE

"If we assume Clare is being held against her will, who would we look to?" Freya said. She was hunched over her desk, glaring at Ben.

"That's a large assumption. She could be on the run all by herself." Ben popped two pieces of gum in his mouth and stared back at her.

"Fine. We're looking for her either way. But we have no clues where she would have gone. We only have the names of people we already know about. I say we go check out what Stingy's up to."

"What motive would Stingy have for grabbing Clare? He's not a suspect—he has a different body type from the man Clare described and he has an alibi. He has nothing to cover up."

Freya pushed away from her desk and stood, too anxious to stay still. "What if Stingy's alibi isn't as strong as we think? What if there were more than one man at the scene after the murders and Clare saw only one of them? We can't not talk to him."

Ben looked resigned and stood as well. "Fine. Let's take a ride."

She led the way out of the building, feeling strangely at odds with Ben. She knew he suspected her of giving Clare the benefit of the doubt without much cause to do so. What if he was right? But even when she took a cool look at the situation, she couldn't see Clare as a murderer. She couldn't see her on the run. No, someone had her and her life was in jeopardy.

They drove her Jeep the twenty-five miles to Stingy's rural property. There were no cars in the front drive when they arrived, no lights shining from the simple farmhouse. The paint had peeled down to the raw wood. The front yard was dirt and gravel. They approached the front door with their weapons drawn and then Ben made his way to the rear. She rapped on the door three times, pausing in between, but there was no response. She was about to knock a fourth time when Ben opened the front door from the inside.

"The back door was unlocked," he said. "It doesn't look like he's here."

Freya entered and immediately went into one of the bedrooms and looked in the closet. It was empty. The other bedroom closet was the same. There were no clothes in the dressers, no toiletries in the bathroom. The milk in the fridge was sour.

"Shit. He's run." Ben holstered his weapon and looked at Freya.

"I don't like this. He could have taken Clare and have fifty miles on us by now. But in what direction?" Freya said.

"I think we should head over to his mother-in-law's. The family could have moved there."

Freya flipped through her notebook to get the name and address of Stingy's mother-in-law and they pulled back onto the rural highway. They were silent as she drove. She didn't expect to find Stingy there. She was convinced he had a gun on Clare right now, who would not have gone with him voluntarily. Unless Stingy was offering her drugs and she couldn't resist them. She realized she didn't really know how bad Clare's drug use was, but it was bad enough to get her into the colossal amount of trouble she was in now.

Mona Fisher's double-wide was about fifteen minutes away from Stingy's property. It stood in a small subdivision of other manufactured homes, with straggly trees growing in small patches of lawn separating the trailers. The neighborhood was ringed by cornfields, billboards on the highway the only sign they weren't literally in the middle of nowhere. Number fifty-nine Myrtle Street had two cars parked in front. They could hear the sound of a television as they approached the door. Freya knocked loudly and the television went silent. The door opened.

Mona's figure took up much of the width of the doorframe, her hips flaring out to the sides. She wore a floral short sleeve blouse and gray sweatpants that were stretched to capacity. Her face was pretty and nicely made up, but the look of suspicion was clear in her eye.

"What do you want?" she asked.

Freya identified herself and Ben and they held up their IDs. Mona scrutinized them, wrinkles appearing everywhere as she scrunched up her face to peer at their badges. She looked much younger with a bland expression, the plumpness of her face hiding the wrinkles for the most part.

"Ms. Fisher, we're looking for your son-in-law. Is he at home with you?"

A young woman appeared behind Mona, peering around her shoulder to see who was outside. "What's going on, Mama?"

"These police are looking for Drew." She turned to her daughter, whose face crumpled. "Go on back, now. I'll take care of this."

Freya could see the daughter's damp face and red eyes as she continued to gaze past her mother. "We don't know where he is. He's gone. If you find him, you can kill him for me."

"May we come in?" Ben said. He reached a hand toward the doorknob.

"You cannot come in here without a warrant. I know that much."

"Ma'am, we're trying to find your son-in-law, not arrest him. You might be able to help us."

"Let them in, Mama."

Mona reluctantly opened the door and stepped back so Ben and Freya could enter. They all stood in the small kitchen, uncomfortably close, but Mona didn't invite them farther in. The trailer smelled like bacon. Ben turned to the daughter and explained about finding Stingy's house deserted.

"I'm Kirsten, by the way," she said. "Drew's wife, at least for now. Yesterday he wanted us to move all our things to Mama's house and I was excited about staying here for a while."

"I wasn't," Mona said. She reached into her breast pocket for cigarettes and lit up.

Freya peered at the living room area and saw twin toddlers, their faces smeared with banana. They stared back at her.

"How do you know he's gone?" Ben asked.

"All the stuff of his that he moved last night is gone, his clothes, his toiletries, his favorite yo-yos. He has a huge collection of them and you can see some were pulled out of the display case. I can show you."

"No, that's okay." Freya tried to swallow the moan in her throat. She was convinced Stingy had Clare. The timing was too perfect. "It's very important that we find him," Freya said. "Can you think of anywhere he might have gone? A favorite campsite or vacation spot? Anywhere that has special meaning to him?"

Mona and Kirsten looked at each other blankly and shook their heads.

"Did he leave you any note or hint as to when he'd return?"

"Nothing, that bastard. I don't know if he's gone for good or not. Do I have to wait seven years for a divorce if he's abandoned me?"

"We wouldn't know about that," Ben said. "What was the make and model of his car? License plate would be great if you have that."

"He drove a dumpy old Honda Civic," Mona said.

"Don't know the license number, but it was silver," Kirsten added.

He looked at Freya. "Do you have anything else?"

Freya took a business card out of her wallet and handed it to Kirsten. "Please contact me if he surfaces."

They made their way back to the Jeep and drove toward Money Creek.

"Shit," Freya said. "I'm sure he has her now."

"You might be right." He called the sheriff to get an APB put out on Stingy. "I doubt he's still in the county."

"Roger that. They're long gone." Fear began to take hold. She didn't think Stingy would be one to prolong doing what he meant to do. Clare might already be dead. Her throat tightened as she tried to hold back tears. She would not let Ben see her crying.

❖

Freya called Henry back into the interview room. She was grasping at straws. She hadn't yet asked him about Clare's drug use. Hadn't wanted to know and still didn't, but there might be something there that would lead to her location. He waived having an attorney present. Elizabeth wasn't available and she was glad they wouldn't have to wait for her.

"Henry, I want you to tell me about selling drugs to Clare. When did that start?"

He looked hopeful, as if there was still a chance he could talk his way out of jail. "Soon after she arrived in town, I think. I know she was looking for a connection. We weren't the first to sell her drugs, that's for sure."

"We?"

"It was Evan she made contact with first. She found him on campus and he brought her to me."

Evan had lied about selling drugs from the apartment. "What was she looking for?"

"Speed, mainly. That was her drug of choice. Valium and Oxycontin to manage the speed. I was able to fix her up."

"How much did she buy?" Things became worse with every answer. Clare had told her about using drugs, but it was different hearing it from Henry. More real and more sordid. She didn't know the real Clare. Hadn't even been introduced.

"She bought whatever I would sell her. I had to wait for shipments from my associates, so a lot of times she couldn't get nearly what she wanted. Then we stopped getting speed altogether and she started using meth."

Clare hadn't told her that part. Freya felt the bottom drop out, as if any hope of salvaging something of their relationship had just fallen out of sight. "You sold her meth?"

Henry shrugged. "I'm in business. Was in business. We supply what the customer wants."

"And your business included Evan?" She wondered why he was admitting to drug trafficking. Elizabeth would be upset.

"He's sort of my right-hand man. He wasn't a principal in my association with Ray and Bobby."

She turned to Ben, anxious now to wrap up the interview. She hadn't thought of Evan, had only met him to get DNA from him, which had been clean. But the killer was unlikely to have drunk any beer while he was there. "Do you have anything else to ask Henry?"

"Not if you don't," Ben said.

They left the interview room and stood in the reception area. "We need to find Evan. He might have Clare."

"Agreed." Ben nodded.

"Will you assemble a team? I'm going to run over to Clare's one more time. Maybe she's home and we can avoid a raid. I'll call her office, too."

Ben left for the sheriff's office while she moved quickly out the door to her car. Clare wasn't home, she knew that. She could be at Henry and Evan's and she wasn't going to waste a moment getting there. She drove at speed and parked across the street from the apartment house. She knew theirs was on the first floor. The blinds were drawn in front, but she could see there was a lamp on in the living room. Her heart beat a little faster.

The house sat on a lot with a long front yard. On either side were single family homes. Gangways on both sides led to the rear of the property. She got out and closed the car door as silently as possible and then walked to the north side gangway. The bottoms of the side windows were forehead height and the blinds were all drawn here as well. The second living room window had a broken slat that gave a ruler sized view into the room. She grabbed the cement window ledge and pulled herself up, her feet dangling above the ground. She had a partial view of the living room and kitchen and could see the bottom half of a chair with legs tied to it. Clare. She let herself down and crept toward the back of the building where a rear exit led to the small backyard and garage. The door was unlocked and led her into an enclosed area with stairs going up one side and the entrance to the first-floor apartment in front of her. She slowly turned the knob and exhaled as the door opened with only the slightest noise. One of the advantages to law enforcement in Money Creek was that doors were seldom locked. Evan might not have even thought of it.

Before she entered the apartment, she took her boots off and left them outside the door. She pushed it open as slowly as she could, praying there wouldn't be any creaking sounds that would travel to the front. It opened silently. She drew her weapon and crept down the hallway, adrenaline pumping through her system. At the end of the hallway she flattened herself against the wall and listened.

"How could you have to piss again?" Evan said. "It's not like you've had much to drink." He sounded annoyed, maybe at the end of his rope.

"What can I say? Nature calls." Clare's voice sounded strained. She must be terrified. Freya risked a peek into the living room where she saw Evan removing the ties around her ankles. There was a gun on the floor beside him. She waited for him to free Clare's legs before stepping into the room with her gun trained on his midsection.

Clare didn't really have to pee again. But she couldn't stand one more minute in that chair and this was the only method she could think of to get out of it, at least for a little while. Evan put his gun on the floor beside him as he went down on a knee to cut the plastic ties from her ankles. When he was finished she stretched her legs with a groan as he rose, gun back in hand. She felt wonderful after having her legs tied to the chair legs for hours. Happiness was circumstantial and wouldn't last long, but for the moment she was grateful.

She caught movement from the hallway and nearly choked when she saw Freya standing there with her gun drawn. Evan's back was to her for the moment and she held her finger to her lips in the universal sign for shut the fuck up. She stepped into the room.

"Police! Put your gun down and raise your hands above your head." Clare watched wide-eyed as Freya barked her orders. Just as Evan turned with his gun, she kicked him square in the balls with her booted foot and he crumpled to the floor. His gun hit the hardwood and discharged. Freya collapsed, grabbing low in her abdomen. Clare got up from the chair and ran to her, praying she was alive.

She didn't care about herself—all she cared about was Freya. She knelt beside her, her hands still cuffed in the back. There was blood smeared on the floor. It was oozing between Freya's fingers as she held her hands to the wound.

"Get his gun," Freya hissed. "Hurry."

Clare awkwardly got to her feet, but it was too late. Evan had retrieved his gun and now had it pointed at her. "I guess the decision's been made about what to do with you."

"Wait! Don't do this, Evan. I'm not worth it," Clare pleaded.

He dropped his arm slightly. "It's too bad, Clare. I think we would have been good together."

A shot rang out and Clare's heart seemed to stop. She saw Evan fall to the floor. Freya was sitting up, her weapon in her hand. Her normally olive complexion was white with pain. Clare went over to Evan and picked up his gun. Then she nudged him with her foot. There was no response and she wondered if he was dead. She ran back to Freya.

"I have to get you some help. Where's your phone?"

"Jesus, this hurts."

"Where are you hit?"

"I think he broke my pelvis. I hope my lady bits are okay."

Clare laughed, despite herself. "I think you'll live, and that's all I care about."

Just as she put the gun down and pulled her phone from her jacket pocket, Ben burst into the room with several deputies right behind him, all with guns drawn. It was over. Now she could cry.

## Chapter Thirty

*Six weeks later*

Clare made her bed shortly after waking at six. Military corners, perfectly smooth sheets and blanket. There was something soothing about doing it. She was still sorting out what made her feel good or bad. Sometimes one of the other women in the sober living house would tell a story that plunged her into an anxious depression that made her want a Valium in the worst way. Triggers were everywhere, but she realized there were more good moments now. They stood out like iridescent pearls—rare but obtainable. It beat the way things had been before.

The house in Bloomington was a halfway point for many women between rehab and real life. It was an old, sprawling frame house where five original bedrooms had been turned into ten, where the living room had turned into a twelve-step meeting place, where the women in the house were meant to understand and support each other. That was the goal, anyway. She still had a hard time believing she was living there.

She watched her roommate struggle awake. Her name was Stacy and she'd moved into the house the evening before. As she threw off her covers, Clare could see she'd slept clutching her purse, not trusting it wouldn't be stolen in her sleep. Now that she'd been living in the house for two weeks, Clare left her bag in the middle of the nightstand cabinet. It was too exhausting to be paranoid and it did nothing to help her make friends.

"Good morning," she said to Stacy, who looked up at her blankly. "Breakfast is between six and nine and you make your own. If you come down with me, I'll show you how it works."

Stacy groaned and got up. She was fully clothed, her off-shoulder blouse looking defenseless against the early spring chill. She reached into her bag and pulled out a red pack of Marlboros.

"Can't do that indoors, I'm afraid." Stacy's sullen face showed a flash of irritation. Clare sighed and led the way downstairs. She'd been told that the best way to feel better about herself was to be of service to others. Stacy was making it a challenge.

At the base of the staircase was a large foyer adjacent to the living room. Lisa, the house manager, watched as they walked down the stairs. "Stacy, why don't you go into the kitchen? One of the women there will show you where everything is." Stacy went where she was pointed.

"Is everything all right?" Clare said as she joined Lisa. She saw the concerned look on her face and was fearful for the first time in a few weeks. Her life had become so simple. Get up, do her assigned chores, go to her new job at Starbucks, go to meetings. When she stayed put in the present, she had nothing to fear.

"I hope it is," Lisa said. She handed her a large envelope. "This was in the mail slot when I came down this morning. Is that the law firm you work at?"

Worked at, past tense, was more like it. She looked at the envelope and saw Nelson & Nelson on the return address. She was technically on unpaid leave from the firm. She doubted they were contacting her to reinstate her position. She opened the envelope and found a second envelope inside, from the Illinois State Bar Association. There was also a letter from Elizabeth.

"Thanks, Lisa. I'll take this up to my room to read." She climbed the creaky staircase slowly, as if to the gallows. Whatever was said in the letter would affect her future profoundly. She closed the door to her room and threw herself onto the bed. Her hands were trembling as she took out Elizabeth's letter.

*Dear Clare,*

*I hope this finds you healthy and doing well in your temporary home. I so admire how you are fighting your addiction, something I understand is very difficult. Everyone here at the firm sends you best wishes. I, especially, want only the best for you.*

*I've enclosed a letter addressed to you from the state bar. As your employer, we received a copy of their ruling on your case. You may want to take a look at it now, before continuing with this letter, but the gist of it is they've suspended your license for two years. This leaves us no choice but to terminate your employment. I'm sorry to have to do this, but you can understand how, even after the two years, we could not have a lawyer with your history on our staff. Not in a town as small as Money Creek.*

*Clare, you're a talented lawyer. I hope you find a way to continue to practice. I will feel the absence of you here.*

*Most sincerely,*
*Elizabeth*

Clare dropped the letter to the floor and put a hand over her thumping chest. How could she feel so devastated by something she completely expected to happen? She would have been much more sanguine had Nelson & Nelson sent a formal termination letter. It was Elizabeth that now made her squirm in her bed. It was the good-bye she'd been dreading.

Her shift at Starbucks started in half an hour. She scrambled to get into her uniform and make herself presentable, when all she wanted to do was throw the covers over her head. There was no room for that kind of indulgence at Horizon House. The residents were meant to stay busy and get on with things. She threw her jacket on and got out the front door without anyone seeing her.

The weather was flirting with spring, allowing the occasional warm breeze quickly followed by blasts of cold. She warmed up the Subaru and got to the coffee shop with five minutes to spare. It wasn't too far from the university, with plenty of students and professors setting up shop to study or grade papers. She was at the cash register, with her favorite co-worker making the coffee. Remo was an art student whose arms were covered in unusually beautiful tattoos. She was sharp, gregarious, and frequently flirty with Clare. She had no interest in pursuing anything with Remo, but the attention made her feel, if only for a few minutes, as if there was hope.

The morning rush seemed to go on a long time. As it began to tail off she thought of taking a break and having a cigarette. She hadn't smoked since law school, but she was seriously thinking of starting. It seemed like the only thing she could do to take the edge off that wouldn't break her sobriety or make her fat. Her mind was far away when the next customer stepped up.

"Hello, Clare."

Her eyes snapped into focus at the sound of the voice. Freya stood before her, her credit card in one hand, the other holding a cane. They had not seen or talked to each other since Freya was shot. She'd tried to visit her in the hospital, but Ben turned her back, saying Freya didn't want to see her yet. She understood. At the very least, they needed time away from each other to figure things out. Clare had still been in too much of a stupor to fight for the relationship. She didn't know anything in those first few days of sobriety, so shocking was it to not have drugs in her body. Now she looked at Freya across the counter and tried to determine whether she was happy to see her.

"Freya. What are you doing here?"

"I thought I'd buy some coffee, but then I saw you. Not sure what I'll do now."

Clare tried out a smile. "I'm about to go on break. Can I get you some coffee and talk with you a bit?"

Freya still looked uncertain. "I guess. I'll grab us a table."

Clare watched her limp across the room and fall into a seat at the farthest table. She poured a couple of cups and told Remo she was going on break. Freya still had her coat on when she reached her table. "Coffee black. That's how I remember you taking it."

Freya glanced at her before looking down at her cup. "That's right."

"Tell me how you are. It seems like so long."

"I've moved back to Bloomington, waiting to get well enough to work again." She seemed uncomfortable, almost squirming in her seat.

"You got hurt saving my life. I'll never be able to thank you properly."

Freya looked at her for a while. "I thought you might be going back to work for the Nelsons."

"No. I just heard today that my license has been suspended and they've officially fired me." That reality seemed a step or two removed. She couldn't feel it yet.

"What will you do?"

Clare took a sip of coffee and made a face. She never did like Starbucks' roast. "I have no idea. And that's a good thing. I don't know if you know this, but I'm currently living in a sober house and, as you see, working here. That's about all I can handle at the moment."

"I haven't heard a word about you other than you'd gone into rehab. Does this mean you're doing well? I mean, living in a sober house?"

"It means I'm serious about doing well. I'm not sure I'm quite there yet."

Freya was silent again. Just as Clare was going to say something else, she said, "I don't know what this means for us."

Nothing could have surprised her more. She thought Freya had written her off, angry at her deception and drug use. "You think there's some chance for us?"

Freya's eyes shimmered with tears. "You betrayed me, and I don't know if I can forgive that. Everything our relationship was based on was a lie. I don't even know who I was in a relationship with."

Her old partner, shame, took up residence in her chest. "I can't defend myself because you're right. All I can say is my actions were partly ruled by my addiction. I take full responsibility for them. I'm hoping sobriety will make me a better person."

"You're not a bad person, Clare," Freya said gently.

"Well, I was pretty messed up. I can't blame you for being wary of me."

Freya still had her coat on. "How sure can I be you'll stay clean and sober? Everything I know about drugs tells me that relapse happens all the time, that not that many make it."

Clare began to feel anxious. The talk about their relationship was unsettling. She knew almost anything was a threat to her sobriety at this stage, certainly the emotional complexities of being in love. She wanted to go home to the sober house. "I have a sponsor. Her name is Cheryl and she's been kind enough to put up with me these past weeks."

Freya looked puzzled. "Okay."

"One thing Cheryl has told me is to avoid any romantic relationships in the first year of sobriety so I can concentrate on getting better. Let's say you could handle taking a chance on me. The truth is I'm not available. I'm going to try to do what's suggested to me. I'm going to try my best to stay sober."

Freya leaned back in her chair and drank from her cup. "I'm relieved, to tell you the truth. Now is not the time for either of us to pick up where we left off."

"I wonder if there will be such a time."

"I hope so, but who knows? A lot can happen in a year."

"Yes, a lot can. If I call you in a year, will you talk with me?" Clare said. A tear leaked out and Freya handed her a napkin.

"Of course, I'll take your call. We'll see where we are."

"But you may get into a new relationship in that year." She wiped her face. "This might be it for us."

"It's possible. It doesn't seem likely right now, but it could happen. I still have feelings for you, Clare. But there've been stomped on pretty good." She finished her coffee and rose from the table using her cane. Clare was riveted to her chair. "I'll talk to you in a year." She put her hand on Clare's shoulder and walked out of the café.

How was she going to finish her shift? How many body blows could she handle in one day? She glanced at her watch and saw her fifteen minutes had long been over. The other barista on duty was giving her dirty looks. She got up and returned to work. Her sponsor had also told her if she kept doing the next right thing, everything would work out fine. That seemed impossibly naive, but what alternative did she have? She could leave work and hide in her bed all day, but she'd feel bad about that, on top of everything else.

A new customer stepped up to the counter and Clare gave her a smile. The next right thing was in front of her—do her job well and act like someone who had their act together. Maybe at some point, it would become true.

# About the Author

Anne Laughlin is the award-winning author of five previous novels published by BSB. She is the winner of four Goldie Awards and has been short-listed three times for a Lambda Literary Award. She has attended many writing residencies including Ragdale and the Vermont Studio Center. In 2008, Anne was named an emerging writer by the Lambda Literary Foundation and asked to return in 2014. Her short story, "It Only Occurred to Me Lately," was named a finalist in the Saints & Sinners short fiction contest. Anne lives in her hometown of Chicago with her wife, Linda, and their two cats.

# Books Available from Bold Strokes Books

**Bet Against Me** by Fiona Riley. In the high stakes luxury real estate market, everything has a price, and as rival Realtors Trina Lee and Kendall Yates find out, that means their hearts and souls, too. (978-1-63555-729-9)

**Broken Reign** by Sam Ledel. Together on an epic journey in search of a mysterious cure, a princess and a village outcast must overcome life-threatening challenges and their own prejudice if they want to survive. (978-1-63555-739-8)

**Just One Taste** by CJ Birch. For Lauren, it only took one taste to start trusting in love again. (978-1-63555-772-5)

**Lady of Stone** by Barbara Ann Wright. Sparks fly as a magical emergency forces a noble embarrassed by her ability to submit to a low-born teacher who resents everything about her. (978-1-63555-607-0)

**Last Resort** by Angie Williams. Katie and Rhys are about to find out what happens when you meet the girl of your dreams but you aren't looking for a happily ever after. (978-1-63555-774-9)

**Longing for You** by Jenny Frame. When Debrek housekeeper Katie Brekman is attacked amid a burgeoning vampire-witch war, Alexis Villiers must go against everything her clan believes in to save her. (978-1-63555-658-2)

**Money Creek** by Anne Laughlin. Clare Lehane is a troubled lawyer from Chicago who tries to make her way in a rural town full of secrets and deceptions. (978-1-63555-795-4)

**Passion's Sweet Surrender** by Ronica Black. Cam and Blake are unable to deny their passion for each other, but surrendering to love is a whole different matter. (978-1-63555-703-9)

**The Holiday Detour** by Jane Kolven. It will take everything going wrong to make Dana and Charlie see how right they are for each other. (978-1-63555-720-6)

**Too Hot to Ride** by Andrews & Austin. World famous cutting horse champion and industry legend Jane Barrow is knockdown sexy in the way she moves, talks, and rides, and Rae Starr is determined not to get involved with this womanizing gambler. (978-1-63555-776-3)

**A Love that Leads to Home** by Ronica Black. For Carla Sims and Janice Carpenter, home isn't about location, it's where your heart is. (978-1-63555-675-9)

**Blades of Bluegrass** by D. Jackson Leigh. A US Army occupational therapist must rehab a bitter veteran who is a ticking political time bomb the military is desperate to disarm. (978-1-63555-637-7)

**Guarding Hearts** by Jaycie Morrison. As treachery and temptation threaten the women of the Women's Army Corps, who will risk it all for love? (978-1-63555-806-7)

**Hopeless Romantic** by Georgia Beers. Can a jaded wedding planner and an optimistic divorce attorney possibly find a future together? (978-1-63555-650-6)

**Hopes and Dreams** by PJ Trebelhorn. Movie theater manager Riley Warren is forced to face her high school crush and tormentor, wealthy socialite Victoria Thayer, at their twentieth reunion. (978-1-63555-670-4)

**In the Cards** by Kimberly Cooper Griffin. Daria and Phaedra are about to discover that love finds a way, especially when powers outside their control are at play. (978-1-63555-717-6)

**Moon Fever** by Ileandra Young. SPEAR agent Danika Karson must clear her werewolf friend of multiple false charges while teaching her vampire girlfriend to resist the blood mania brought on by a full moon. (978-1-63555-603-2)

**Quake City** by St John Karp. Can Andre find his best friend Amy before the night devolves into a nightmare of broken hearts, malevolent drag queens, and spontaneous human combustion? Or has it always happened this way, every night, at Aunty Bob's Quake City Club? (978-1-63555-723-7)

**Serenity** by Jesse J. Thoma. For Kit Marsden, there are many things in life she cannot change. Serenity is in the acceptance. (978-1-63555-713-8)

**Sylver and Gold** by Michelle Larkin. Working feverishly to find a killer before he strikes again, Boston Homicide Detective Reid Sylver and rookie cop London Gold are blindsided by their chemistry and developing attraction. (978-1-63555-611-7)

**Trade Secrets** by Kathleen Knowles. In Silicon Valley, love and business are a volatile mix for clinical lab scientist Tony Leung and venture capitalist Sheila Graham. (978-1-63555-642-1)

**Death Overdue** by David S. Pederson. Did Heath turn to murder in an alcohol induced haze to solve the problem of his blackmailer, or was it someone else who brought about a death overdue? (978-1-63555-711-4)

**Entangled** by Melissa Brayden. Becca Crawford is the perfect person to head up the Jade Hotel, if only the captivating owner of the local vineyard would get on board with her plan and stop badmouthing the hotel to everyone in town. (978-1-63555-709-1)

**First Do No Harm** by Emily Smith. Pierce and Cassidy are about to discover that when it comes to love, sometimes you have to risk it all to have it all. (978-1-63555-699-5)

**Kiss Me Every Day** by Dena Blake. For Wynn Evans, wishing for a do-over with Carly Jamison was a long shot, actually getting one was a game changer. (978-1-63555-551-6)

**Olivia** by Genevieve McCluer. In this lesbian Shakespeare adaptation with vampires, Olivia is a centuries old vampire who must fight a strange figure from her past if she wants a chance at happiness. (978-1-63555-701-5)

**One Woman's Treasure** by Jean Copeland. Daphne's search for discarded antiques and treasures leads to an embarrassing misunderstanding, and ultimately, the opportunity for the romance of a lifetime with Nina. (978-1-63555-652-0)

**Silver Ravens** by Jane Fletcher. Lori has lost her girlfriend, her home, and her job. Things don't improve when she's kidnapped and taken to fairyland. (978-1-63555-631-5)

**Still Not Over You** by Jenny Frame, Carsen Taite, Ali Vali. Old flames die hard in these tales of a second chance at love with the ex you're still not over. Stories by award winning authors Jenny Frame, Carsen Taite, and Ali Vali. (978-1-63555-516-5)

**Storm Lines** by Jessica L. Webb. Devon is a psychologist who likes rules. Marley is a cop who doesn't. They don't always agree, but both fight to protect a girl immersed in a street drug ring. (978-1-63555-626-1)

**The Politics of Love** by Jen Jensen. Is it possible to love across the political divide in a hostile world? Conservative Shelley Whitmore and liberal Rand Thomas are about to find out. (978-1-63555-693-3)

**All the Paths to You** by Morgan Lee Miller. High school sweethearts Quinn Hughes and Kennedy Reed reconnect five years after they break up and realize that their chemistry is all but over. (978-1-63555-662-9)

**Arrested Pleasures** by Nanisi Barrett D'Arnuck. When charged with a crime she didn't commit, Katherine Lowe faces the question: Which is harder, going to prison or falling in love? (978-1-63555-684-1)

**Bonded Love** by Renee Roman. Carpenter Blaze Carter suffers an injury that shatters her dreams, and ER nurse Trinity Greene hopes to show her that sometimes love is worth fighting for. (978-1-63555-530-1)

**Convergence** by Jane C. Esther. With life as they know it on the line, can Aerin McLeary and Olivia Ando's love survive an otherworldly threat to humankind? (978-1-63555-488-5)

**Coyote Blues** by Karen F. Williams. Riley Dawson, psychotherapist and shape-shifter, has her world turned upside down when Fiona Bell, her one true love, returns. (978-1-63555-558-5)

**Drawn** by Carsen Taite. Will the clues lead Detective Claire Hanlon to the killer terrorizing Dallas, or will she merely lose her heart to person of interest, urban artist Riley Flynn? (978-1-63555-644-5)

**Every Summer Day** by Lee Patton. Meant to celebrate every summer day, Luke's journal instead chronicles a love affair as fast-moving and possibly as fatal as his brother's brain tumor. (978-1-63555-706-0)

**Lucky** by Kris Bryant. Was Serena Evans's luck really about winning the lottery, or is she about to get even luckier in love? (978-1-63555-510-3)

**The Last Days of Autumn** by Donna K. Ford. Autumn and Caroline question the fairness of life, the cruelty of loss, and what it means to love as they navigate the complicated minefield of relationships, grief, and life-altering illness. (978-1-63555-672-8)

**Three Alarm Response** by Erin Dutton. In the midst of tragedy, can these first responders find love and healing? Three stories of courage, bravery, and passion. (978-1-63555-592-9)

**Veterinary Partner** by Nancy Wheelton. Callie and Lauren are determined to keep their hearts safe but find that taking a chance on love is the safest option of all. (978-1-63555-666-7)

**Everyday People** by Louis Barr. When film star Diana Danning hires private eye Clint Steele to find her son, Clint turns to his former West Point barracks mate, and ex-buddy with benefits, Mars Hauser to lend his cyber espionage and digital black ops skills to the case. (978-1-63555-698-8)

**Forging a Desire Line** by Mary P. Burns. When Charley's ex-wife, Tricia, is diagnosed with inoperable cancer, the private duty nurse Tricia hires turns out to be the handsome and aloof Joanna, who ignites something inside Charley she isn't ready to face. (978-1-63555-665-0)

**Love on the Night Shift** by Radclyffe. Between ruling the night shift in the ER at the Rivers and raising her teenage daughter, Blaise Richilieu has all the drama she needs in her life, until a dashing young attending appears on the scene and relentlessly pursues her. (978-1-63555-668-1)

**Olivia's Awakening** by Ronica Black. When the daring and dangerously gorgeous Eve Monroe is hired to get Olivia Savage into shape, a fierce passion ignites, causing both to question everything they've ever known about love. (978-1-63555-613-1)

**The Duchess and the Dreamer** by Jenny Frame. Clementine Fitzroy has lost her faith and love of life. Can dreamer Evan Fox make her believe in life and dream again? (978-1-63555-601-8)

**The Road Home** by Erin Zak. Hollywood actress Gwendolyn Carter is about to discover that losing someone you love sometimes means gaining someone to fall for. (978-1-63555-633-9)

**Waiting for You** by Elle Spencer. When passionate past-life lovers meet again in the present day, one remembers it vividly and the other isn't so sure. (978-1-63555-635-3)

**While My Heart Beats** by Erin McKenzie. Can a love born amidst the horrors of the Great War survive? (978-1-63555-589-9)